COMMON
ACCORD

Also by K. N. Brindle

the Paths of Memory duology
A Memory of Blood and Magic
A Memory of War and Solace

Discover and follow at
www.knbrindle.com

Common Accord

K.N. Brindle

COMMON ACCORD

Copyright ©2024 by K. N. Brindle. All rights reserved.
Cover character portraits copyright ©2024 by Angela Guyton.

No part of this book may be used or reproduced in any manner whatsoever without the express written permission of the author, except in the case of brief quotations embedded in critical review.

Use of any part of this work to develop, train, or test machine learning models, large language models, or other artificial intelligence or computational generation systems is expressly forbidden.

Library of Congress Control Number: 2024924245

ISBN: 978-1-965275-04-7

For Molly.

Table of Contents

A Note on Dates ix
1 / Scrape 1
2 / Scrap 10
3 / Grind 23
4 / Decks 36
5 / Grates 47
6 / Shot 57
7 / Dice 68
The Ship 79
8 / Clock 80
9 / Gold 91
10 / Skip 102
11 / Spin 113
12 / Deals 119
13 / Debt 131
14 / Away 143
15 / Cargo 153
16 / Bond 164
17 / Platinum 173
Interlude / Donner 181
18 / Questions 184
19 / Departure 197
20 / Midas 208
21 / Windfall 220
22 / Scramble 225

23 / Blown 236
24 / Dust 248
25 / Trap 258
26 / Write-Offs 268
Epilogue / Kamal-Wright 276
A Note on Coordinates 279
A Xenoanthropological Survey of the Triss 281
Acknowledgements 293
About the Author 295

A Note on Dates

Various species utilize their own dating nomenclature for dates before the Revelation. For humans, the commonly accepted pre-Revelation calendars are BCE and CE.

Through common accord, all members of the Revelatory Accord utilize a common calendar system based in the advanced knowledge imparted by the Elders, and count two post-Revelation epochs:

The Revelation epoch (REV) which begins at year zero on the discovery of the first Revelation Cache by a member of the Revelatory Accord and counts through to the establishment of the Revelatory Accord 132 unified years later. As a result, nearly all anniversaries of first-contact between Accord species fall within the REV epoch.

For humans, 0 REV is counted equivalent to 2124 CE. As part of the Revelatory Accord, when referring to dates prior to 0 REV in a mixed-species or cross-species context, negative unified year numbers are used, so 2123 CE is roughly equivalent to -1 REV, although due to variance between the duration of native species' solar standard years and unified years in the CA calendar, the further back one references from 0 REV, the more dates will diverge. Thus, 2100 CE is closer to -16 REV than to -24 REV

The Common Accord epoch (CA) begins with unified year zero at the end of 132 REV, and marks the establishment of the Revelatory Accord. When epoch notation is omitted for unified dates, it is assumed to be referring to the year in the CA epoch.

Unified dates (ud) are given as a 2-tuple representing unified year and day segment, with 1000 unified day segments in a single unified year. In comparison to human standard solar days, a unified day segment is roughly equal to 8 hours, so approximately 3 unified day segments are equal to one solar day. Thus: "ud 80.022" represents mid-morning on the seventh day of the year 80 CA (the first moment of the first day of year 80 would be "ud 80.000"). Unified timestamps (ut) are represented through a third tuple position ("ut 80.022.02332") representing decimal day-segment subdivisions to arbitrary-precision to meet the specific case.

Many species still revert to approximations of their native timekeeping conventions when verbally expressing sub-day-segment time spans, where "half an hour" (for example) is easier or more comfortable to express than "0.06ut." In mixed-species contexts, verbal conventions are typically negotiated on an ad-hoc basis. It remains unknown if the Elders retained a similar convention.

This story begins in the year 81 CA.

1 / Scrape

Antares Drift
Axon-Mull 929-SAN-3382
Ore Processor-Extractor
Akpan-Ferg-Perrin Mining Consortium

SPACETIME-FIX at: **81.089**.77451261
- c95d981a **(Chara)** 9012-d12c
- 839de621 **(Cor Caroli)** a677-a57c
- 090e9a5e **(La Superba)** 96c1-d6ed

Scraping gold off the goose egg was universally considered to be the shittiest job on the ship. Worse than cleaning the latrines, Jes thought.

It was a lonely and uncomfortable job, for one thing. You had to spend hours at a time in the cramped, zero-G heart of the ship with nothing but the creaking, greasy inertial struts and the grating whir of the vacuum deposit-reclamation system for company. An anemic emitter gave the only light, and it seemed especially prone to flickering. Jes had tried to find a replacement, but none of the other fixtures on the ship used the same emitter type, and until it went out completely no one wanted to spend the mass on printing a new one.

Scraping the goose egg was also a lot harder work than cleaning latrines.

The ship's power plant, the Singularity Differential Reactor, was a mysterious and wondrous gift of the Elders. With the revelation of its design, humankind and the other species of the Accord could free themselves of the bonds of gravity wells and destructive wasteful energy sources to explore the galaxy with virtually endless free energy. There were plenty of people who understood its inner workings, at least enough to manufacture the things, but Jes wasn't one of them. All Jes knew was that the sealed, ellipsoid-shaped capsule—this one roughly the size of a dining table—produced an incredible amount of electrical energy and one very peculiar waste product.

Harry, the ship's engineer—"Chief Engineer" he insisted on, though the crew was only eight people and he was the only one tasked with engineering—had tried to explain it to Jes once. Something about "quantum-displaced singularities" and "energy differentials flowing downstream." Jes *was* interested in such things to some degree and could *probably* understand it with enough effort, but was also more than happy to let other people be the experts.

Jes got into position—feet braced against nearby struts—and prepped the reclamation vacuum. They dialed down their ambient hearing and started some music playing to drown out most of the noisy vac. *The big problem with the SDR,* Jes thought, *is all the damn gold.* For some esoteric reason that the engineers pretended to understand, it built up out of nowhere; the only waste product of the Goose Egg's endless clean energy.

It would start as a brown-tinted shimmer on the surface of SDR's carbon-palladium shell. In time, that patina would build up to a thin, crinkly layer a few molecules thick and the Goose Egg would start to resemble its golden namesake. If the gold wasn't removed regularly, the mass would build and build until two things happened: The output efficiency of the SDR would diminish precipitously, and eventually the built-up mass would begin to dramatically affect the ship's ability to move itself through space.

There were tall tales spread in the less reputable station dives about ghost ships floating abandoned in deep space that had "gone Midas" after some disaster rendered the ship inoperable while the SDR continued to pump out energy and waste gold. After a few years, according to the old spacers, they supposedly started looking like small golden asteroids.

Getting the gold off the damn thing was a long and exhausting process that had to be repeated every month or so. It required scraping the softer metal off of the SDR's surface—*scraping* because the gold deposits did their best to fuse to the surface of the Egg—and collecting the flakes, dust, and chips with a bulky vacuum system. When the vacuum cylinder was full—and the ship's vac was too small to complete the task in one go—Jes would have to carry the thing back up to the grav-deck where its weight became a burden, emptying the worthless gold into the recycler in the engineering bay. The only good thing about gold was that it was fairly heavy, and the pure molecules made for a small boost of mass for the atomic printers. The galley was especially well-stocked for a while after scraping day.

Compared to all of that, latrine duty was a breeze. The most offensive mess of human waste still brushed off the seamless surfaces of the prefab ceramic cubicles easily enough, and you'd be rewarded for the effort by a clean, shiny toilet for at least as long as it took Alph to find the door to one after a hearty bowl of his special chili. The rest of the crew lovingly called his recipe "cause and effect."

Jes turned on the vacuum and started scraping, enjoying the single satisfying part of this job: revealing the silver-gray carbon-platinum ceramic surface underneath the caked-on gold. It was like unwrapping a present. A big, shitty present wrapped in the worst glued-on trash imaginable.

Jes felt a ping in their skull, and saw the tell-tale alert flag rise up in the lower-right corner of their vision. Orange for urgent.

Report to the bridge, please. /XO.

As the vacuum powered down, Jes realized that the message was tagged *XO*. Not *Andi. XO*. She hardly ever pulled rank. Jes acked the alert and shifted the vac around on its strap, its cylinder only half-full. The scraping would wait. Jes began moving hand over hand along the struts toward the access hatch.

Pulling themselves up onto the grav-deck through the disconcerting gravity transition, Jes spotted Harry and the junior cargo handler walking down the low passageway from the processing deck. They both had an odd look on their faces, and neither would meet Jes's eyes.

Jes crossed to the hatch into engineering. They stowed the vac in its locker and continued through to the main access ladder, climbing past decks four and three to reach Main.

The bridge was a tight space: a narrow walk that encircled six workstations, only three of which were occupied. The pilot was at her station. Opposite her, the cargo master monitored the mining ops panel, and Windy was overseeing the computer's decisions on nav-comm, her large frame dominating the small space.

All the seated bridge stations faced inward to a clear cylinder that was the tallest thing in the compartment. The tank. A meter across and two high, it showed a constellation of particles orbiting a central core of ice and rock in three dimensions, all picked out in green and blue points of laser light. A cone-shape the size of a thumb glowing red in the very center of the tank marked the Drift. It was all very low tech. Antique, even. But it hardly ever broke down.

The captain paced slowly around the perimeter, one eye on the tank as he walked. He was just pushing past middle-age and had the graying hair and thickening around the belly to show for it. He wore the same gray one-piece jumpsuit that the rest of the crew wore, though the green piping on his was far more weathered and dingy. From behind, the AFP logo glowed iridescent on his back in the winking lights of the consoles.

Jes glanced at the tank, looking for anything threatening or unusual, anything to explain the call to the bridge. Windy glanced up from her panel and her face took on an inscrutable look. They both held the same rank on the ship, and had become close friends over the years.

"Specialist, in here," Andi called from the compartment just off the ladder. The hatch was wide open, making an opening about forty centimeters through which Jes could see her seated behind a compact desk.

Windy's eyes returned to her panel without giving anything away. Jes turned and squeezed into the compartment with Andi. There was just enough space for them both on either side of the station, with their legs hooked over the seat bars.

Andi looked as polished and prim as ever. She alone among the crew seemed to find the time and facilities to launder her jumpsuits so that they were always just a shade lighter gray than anyone else's. The green piping along the joints and down the limbs was clean and bright, and the collar was turned up crisply to show off the elegant lines of her jawbone. Indicators and readouts glowed softly on her console and reflected like stars in her eyes.

Jes took a moment just to look at her. Astonished as always that they had managed to find a sort of equilibrium together despite the cramped quarters and zero-privacy aboard the ship. And despite their very different social and financial backgrounds.

"What's up, hun?"

Andi grimaced and ran a hand over the short stubble of her dark hair. "Specialist Moran, I'm running through the crew, updating each of you on accounts for this run, and personnel disposition on return to station."

"Andi," Jes said warily, "what is this?"

"XO, if you please, Specialist," she said absently.

Jes stared at her for a moment. She was close enough that they could feel her breath on their cheek. The intimacy of the XO's office used to be fun for them both. Jes pulled the hatch closed, sealing them off from the bridge.

"*XO Ferg*, would you *please* tell me what the hell is going on? When did I stop being Jes to you? When did you become XO instead of my partner?"

She eyed the closed hatch, then sighed, shaking her head as if resigning herself to something unpleasant. Then she smiled gently. "Sorry Jes. Anyway, like I said, we're about done with this run, and we're just totting up accounts. This is the richest hit yet—a lot of heavies in the mix. We're going to be leaving a marker behind for the next hauler they send out. This'll be paying dividends for decades to come. The Company has granted us all shares in the marker claim as a special thanks, on top of the standard split."

Jes raised an eyebrow. AFP was not exactly known for generosity towards its comet jockeys."

Andi ignored the look. "As Specialist, you rate a quarter point on the haul, standard share plus point-five for seniority, and a point-oh-oh-one standing dividend on the marker for the next ten years or until it's tapped. That's bonus."

A report scrolled up into Jes's eye-line as she continued to talk through the figures. The numbers glowed a faint bluish-white in their vision as their cominfo implant took receipt of the account projections and neuro-rendered the calculations into their perception.

It was a tidy little sum for one haul.

Something odd caught Jes's attention.

"Andi, what's this line... 'MO & S settlement?'"

Andi bit her lip and looked down. "That's going out to all of the crew on docking. The Antares Drift is almost forty years old, Jes. She's well past prime and the newer haulers printing out of Axon-Mull these days are too much more efficient to keep running this tub. AFP is going to decommission and recycle her when we reach Cor Caroli."

Jes's heart sank into their stomach.

They knew better than to get attached to a thing like a ship. Since the Revelation and the advent of atomic printing, *things* had little permanence anymore. If you had enough mass and enough money to rent time on the printers, you could make just about anything. Even things as big and old as the Drift. And the Akpan-Ferg-Perrin Mining Consortium had plenty of money, and its primary business of deep-space mining of exotic heavy metals meant it had plenty of mass.

Jes's tendency towards sentimentality was unusual enough to earn them their share of hazing and ribbing from the crew. Andi said that sentimentality was also what had initially endeared them to her. On the rare occasions that she shared Jes's bunk instead of insisting on hers, she would often spend the few minutes of rest she allowed between sex and washing up idly examining Jes's small collection of antiques. Her favorite was the little green and purple striped polymer dinosaur. Stegosaurus.

Jes's eyes now went involuntarily to the bulkhead, weathered by years of scuffs and dings and half-hearted attempts at polish. They always had a strange, sinking feeling that humanity was losing a little bit of itself along with everything from yesterday that it fed into the recyclers. They'd shipped on the Drift for the last ten years. Jes knew every centimeter and every scratch and every dent on the dingy old skip miner. It was home. Since Andi had joined the crew four years ago, it had been *their* home.

"I'm sorry, Jes."

Jes shook their head, willing their eyes to stay dry. "So," they said, putting on a false sense of cheer. "When do we get our shiny new ship? Hope it creaks a little less." Jes would miss the creaks and rattles that the Drift made throughout the late watches. It always felt like the old lady was trying to communicate.

Andi's eyes darted to the side, not meeting Jes's. "About that. Like I said, we're all mustering out. But none of us is rated on the new ships. Everyone is receiving a muster out and severance payout."

Jes felt the blow and said nothing for a moment, letting it sink in. "Everyone?" they asked. It went without saying that Andi still had a job.

"I'm—I'm heading back to Sol. Dad's making me VP of the Canum sector. It's a huge step up." She looked at them shyly. "I had hoped you would be happy for me."

Jes's world spun for a moment. It took several breaths before they could process the news. "That *is* a step," they said, smiling. "I'm so proud of you." *I've always wanted to see the Old System*, they thought.

In the months to come, they would often wonder how they instinctively knew not to give the thought voice.

"And the thing is," Andi said, looking away again. "The thing is, I was hoping that you would…"

"Yes?"

"I was hoping you would… understand… that I need to do this alone. When we reach Cor Caroli, I'm dissolving our partnership." She wouldn't meet their eyes. "I'm sorry, Jes."

2 / Scrap

Cor Caroli L4
Human-governed Station
Population 83,884

SPACETIME-FIX at: **84.033**.02422350
- 839de621 **(Cor Caroli)** a677-b97c
- c95d981a **(Chara)** 93ec-bda5
- 090e9a5e **(La Superba)** 8def-f6a4

Jes groaned as the tapping sensation increased within their skull. There was only so long they could ignore it before the next escalation they had set kicked in. Bright characters formed in their vision, spelling out the unified timestamp and the personalized message.

Get up and get to it, Jes.

The words glowed softly in a purple-white. Never mind that Jes's eyes were still closed. There was no escaping the wake-up routine. Jes had made sure of that themself. They knew all too well their propensity for sleeping in. Now that they had a way forward and *things to be done*, they had determined to stop lazing about.

They sat up and opened their eyes, wiping away the grogginess and the sleep crud, or at least trying. The overhead light came on and they sighed, facing the depressing grind of another day.

Jes's room was small, even by low-deck standards. The vast station that occupied the stellar Lagrange Point 4 in the Cor Caroli system had a gradient of economic class, from the celebrities and station masters at the top, to the lowest drudges whose lives were expendable and Transitions down that particular slope was smooth and slippery.

Even living off the residuals from the Drift for the last three years, Jes could afford better—for a little while longer at least—but was counting every credit towards the next step in their plan. They stood up from the narrow bed and stretched. Their arched back brought their elbows to bump against the low ceiling. They nudged up the bed platform with their heel, which folded up against the wall and locked in place, giving them a little more room. At less than six cubic meters, 'small' barely did it justice. Especially since it contained a bed, table, and locker, as well as a fold-away toilet, sink, and a shower cubicle all in one printed module.

Jes ran their eyes over the blank, empty room. The walls, deck, and ceiling were still the uniform and dispiriting shade of dull gray that they were printed in. The polymer-ceramic material ran throughout the station. Most inhabitants made some effort to enliven the unrelenting bleakness with posters, paint, or... *something*. Something to look at when they were home. Even if it was augmented shine, they'd have something to look at.

Jes didn't want to look at anything. Jes didn't want to spend any more time here than they had to. It wasn't home so much as a place to sleep.

They folded out the sink, splashed a handful of water on their face, and scrubbed a hand through the short dark hair that stood out in a lank, resentful brush from the top of their head. They deliberately did not look themself in the mirror.

"Come on, Jes."

Ten minutes later, minimally scrubbed and dressed in their rust-orange one-piece uniform, they stood in front of their open locker for a moment, looking at the small fiberboard box of junk tucked into the back near their spare deck shoes. A little pointy tip of green and purple polymer stuck out from the torn box corner.

Jes shook their head and slammed the locker door.

A quick turn and two steps later, they were in the narrow compartment that they thought of as their neighborhood. Five other hatches opened off either side of the passageway to similar bare-bones flats.

Jes had no idea who lived in them beyond shallow impressions: A dockworker who was drunk and boisterous whenever she was home. A prostitute who spent most of his time at the bars some decks up where he could make more money from the higher-class citizens. A mother and her child—Jes had no idea how two managed to live in the tiny cubicle.

In the one on the end lived a retiree who Jes saw sometimes wandering up and down the passage, lost. They had helped the old man find his door more than once, though had never asked his name.

Jes assumed the last flat was either vacant, or its occupant had died some time ago and no one had checked in on them. That door never opened, and no one else had frequented the dead-end passage since Jes had occupied their own cabin.

At the near end, a larger hatch opened out onto a small communal platform that combined a compact fitness area, a small-scale recycling and pay-to-print station, and a short platform where the deck's transit system connected. A plastic sign hung above the printer interface with a warning not to leave prints unattended.

Jes nodded casually to the young woman waiting at the printer, and to her child who had climbed on the exercise machine and was trying listlessly to make the thing move. It hadn't ever worked the whole time Jes had lived here.

They walked over to the transit spur that ran in two continuous loops, one going out and one coming in. It was a long hallway, gently curving away in both directions with a rounded top and bottom. Every meter or so, lights pulsed along a narrow strip on the floor and ceiling, flowing forever in each direction. The light indicated the positions of the gravity boundaries that gently nudged various passengers—and their occasional cargo—up and down the transit spur.

Jes hopped on the inward side and felt the grav-cell carry them away towards the busier sectors of the station and the main transit artery that ran in a circular loop through the industrial and commercial zones. The pressure of the grav-cell pushed at their back, and they leaned into it. Ads for a dozen different print programs, social clubs, brothels, and bars flashed by on the walls in a riot of color and animation, catching the eye and trying to ping their implant as they passed.

It took only about ten minutes or so to reach the transfer platform, and they absently made the short hop out of the moving corridor onto the raised deck. There were others navigating the same narrow interchange, so it took a little agility to move quickly through the crowd.

Jes scanned ahead, finding gaps and anticipating the movement of the other people in the accessway. With small adjustments to their walking speed, they managed to slip in and out of the ever-shifting churn of pedestrians without stopping and without disrupting anyone else's movements. It was a habit they had developed over the last few years living and working in the low-decks of the station. The passages were narrow, and the population manifold.

At the central transit hub, Jes placed an order at a kiosk, confirming the credit transfer and waited for their breakfast to print—a bulb of coffee and a hand-held savory pie. Food in hand, they queued up for a car at the platform. The hand pie was good, rich with mushrooms and onions in a salty gravy and wrapped in a flakey pastry.

The car was half-full, and Jes took a place near the opposite hatch as it moved on through the line. The interior surfaces of the car flared to life with moving ads and a cacophony of sound and jingles. Jes muted their ambient hearing and stared at nothing for the ride. In their head, they were running over their hardware priority list.

Goose Egg. Nav-comm. Line buffers. Q-comp. Skip drive.

The hull was one thing. It was sound. It had *good bones*, as Windy said. But a hull wasn't a ship. And without the heart and brain and legs that made it a ship, it was just an exorbitantly expensive place to sleep that would continuously eat up taxes and docking fees.

For now, keeping it wasn't costing anything. The moment they made their move though, they had to be ready to go. And the longer it took, the more likely it was their plan would somehow go wrong.

It was a short walk from the platform to the recycling station. Jes walked through the small lobby and into the back office. Their implant pinged and showed the green flag confirming passkey exchange and clock-in as the secure door opened.

The control cabin was small, just big enough for two swivel seats. Fin looked up at Jes as they walked in and brushed long hair back out of his face. It dropped back down immediately over his forehead.

Fin was younger than Jes by more than a decade. Small and thin, his body seemed tailor-made for the tight spaces aboard ship or station. His long black hair always looked like he had just woken up, but Jes suspected he cultivated that appearance carefully.

"Hey Jes. If we still want that hull, the queue needs a jiggle."

"How far back is it?" Jes asked, sitting down.

"It's at twenty-eight. But a bunch of what's ahead of it is small beans. They'll go quick."

Jes pulled up the queue management interface. The industrial recycling station processed hundreds of megagrams of mass a day. The order in which the lots were fed into the atomic recyclers was shifted and prioritized by a bot. The operator's job was simply to monitor the process and catch any system glitches and deal with the occasional customer who wanted a personal interface.

Fin stood and squeezed around Jes's chair. "Jes, when are we going to take the shot? She's a good ship. Every time we bump the queue, chances go up the watchdog will notice. Every day we wait, there's a chance the bot decides that today's the day it wants to recycle the big mass in bin a5f3. If we wait too long, Accounts is going to notice that they've paid out on two thousand megs of mass and never recycled it."

"She's not a ship yet, Fin. In here, it's a bin of scrap that sits there for free. The minute we pull her out, we start paying docking fees, taxes, all of that, and if we can't fly, we can't pull any credit. You have ten thousand lying around?"

Fin shook his head. "You know I don't."

"Then we wait."

Fin dropped his head in defeat, his hair curtaining his face. "Alright, Jes. See you later. I'm off."

He departed the cubicle as Jes pulled up the comp interface. Jes had spent a fair chunk of their savings on a little bit of bot-destabilizing malware. Slipping it into the queue manager under the nose of the watchdog had been pretty easy. Bots were so very helpful.

"Hi Jes. What can I do for you?"

"You remember what we talked about last time," Jes said, "what we agreed to?"

"No, I don't remember. Was it a secret?"

"Yes. Our secret."

"...I...no...no...yes...no...yes..."

Jes waited for the bot to finish its seizure. It always needed a moment to recover when they reminded it of their secret. Eventually it came back up.

"Hi Jes. What can I...do for...you?"

"Remember that lot in bin a5f3?" Jes asked.

"No, Jes. No I do not."

"Good, good. Well, don't worry about *not* bumping it to the back of the line."

"Of course. I'll make sure not to do that."

Jes watched on the panel as the queue prioritization changed, and bin a5f3 rotated backwards down the line one by one past the bins that had been behind it.

"Good job."

"Thanks, Jes. Anything else I can help with?"

"Just remember. This is our little secret, right?"

"Yes...no...no...that runs counter to my directives...yes...yes...no..."

Jes waited again.

"Hi Jes. What can I do for you?"

"Nothing right now, thanks."

"*Okay.*"

Jes shut down the interface and scanned through the bin listings that had come in since their last shift. Four one-hundred meg vats of contaminated wastewater. Eight-hundred megs of construction debris from the replacement of a damaged station frame. A dozen more lots of equally mundane mass. Nothing interesting.

Of course, no SDRs. They were always physically extracted before recycling—only a manufacturer like Axon-Mull who made the damn things could safely decommission and recycle them. Jes had never thought too hard about what would happen if you fed a dimensionally-displaced miniature black hole into an atomic recycler. It seemed like a pretty bad idea.

They sat through their shift and pulled up their list again. Windy and Jes had gone over the hull twice now. Once they pulled the trigger and got the bot to dump the bin, they had to be ready to make her space-worthy and get out of dock before they ran out of money.

Jes and Windy had been telling themselves that they needed to replace most of the ship's guts before she would fly. Were they being too ambitious? What were the odds of finding a replacement for the computer, a newer skip drive, and a nav-comm with a clean identity, among the scrap that passed through the recycling queue?

Well, Jes could find out. They pulled up the historical log interface and started digging. They worked at it steadily, tapping away at the hardware keyboard, avoiding the bot for the job—they didn't want any more log traces of what they were doing than absolutely necessary, and as helpful as the bots were, they'd ask questions.

Two hours later, they leaned back in their chair and sighed. There had been three lots containing functional nav-comms recycled in the last five years. Three. All had come in with their ident-chips already stripped. Only two skip drive systems, and one of those was currently in bin a5f3, still installed in the hull. Q-comps were more commonly recycled, but it didn't look like any had been newer than what they already had.

Well, the hull *had* a nav-comm; it just had a stripped identity. Windy thought she might find a clean ident-chip for sale. The hull still had its computer, even if it was a ten-year-old system and glitchy as hell. And the skip drive... well, it *might* work. And while Windy insisted that they needed a full replacement of the line buffers, it was true that none of them had burned out yet.

That still left them with a large, gaping, egg-shaped hole in the plan.

They needed a Goose Egg. Without that, the ship was still just a bin of scrap.

Jes clocked out at the end of their shift just as another one of the endless line of recycling technicians arrived. Jes barely knew her—their shifts rarely overlapped. They nodded cordial greetings to each other as they squeezed into and out of the cramped cabin. Jes got the green clock-out ping and the blue pay deposit alert almost at the same time. They didn't bother to look at the pay stub or their credit balance. It would just depress them.

After their six-hour shift, they were hungry and their brain felt like mush. Sitting alone in a compartment for six hours watching a bot make mass-density calculations and provide real-time power-consumption-to-mass-production reports wasn't conducive to good mental health. Neither was the endless worry and second-guessing over what move to make next.

They *had* to find a way to make the ship fly. Jes's residuals from their time on the *Drift* were enough to live on—if you could call what they had been doing living—but there were only about seven years left on their ten-year dividend marker. When that ran out, even the recycling job wouldn't pay enough to get by.

At the thought of heading back to their cabin, getting food at the grimy economy printer in the common area, and closing themself off in their desolate compartment, Jes felt a wave of depression and defeat roll through their mind. They needed noise. They needed to be around living beings. Jes changed direction suddenly, breaking the flow of people around them into eddies of confusion.

A car was just pulling into the upward platform and they hopped aboard. Two decks up was a dive bar called Bleak. As bar names went, it was painfully on-the-nose, suiting its atmosphere of meager hope ground down by an indifferent system.

They rode the car up and stepped off onto the platform, taking the familiar route to the narrow, dark passage that led to the bar. Jes walked slowly through the corridor with no mission; lost in thought. They needed company. They could feel themself slipping into a deep funk, and knew where that led.

They walked past a hatchway lit in garish black-light that fluoresced a series of life-sized abstract silhouettes of nude bodies of every gender, shape, and size. Some were decidedly not human. A throbbing bass rhythm rattled the decking and wall panels. Angular text sprawled above the hatch, spelling out the name of the brothel: The Grind. More than one prostitute called out to them as they passed, trying to entice them to enter and spend credits on orgasm and oblivion.

Jes kept walking.

Further down the same passage, a wide pressure door stood open, overhanging several small tables lit with reds and deep violets. Jes wound their way between the tables, many of them full, looking for their usual table in the back of the Bleak, in the corner beside the bar. It was open, and Jes sat down and logged an order for a gin and bitters.

While they waited, they flagged their location, and sent it as a ping to Fin and Windy. They muted their feed, not wanting to know if either one acked their ping. They'd just sit here and drink, and if company arrived, great. Jes decided to give it an hour. Just enough to get a solid buzz going.

The barkeep moved back and forth among the tables, bringing drink orders from the printer to her patrons. She stopped to chat with one table or another. Jes watched her. She was tall and lean, and wore black leggings and chunky boots. She left her chest and torso bare. Her arms, shoulders, face, back, and breasts were all covered with tattoos in a frenzy of angular shapes and brash colors. Her hair was buzzed close to her scalp except for a lock of bright pink hair that spilled forward over her forehead.

She went back to the bar and retrieved another round, bringing Jes's gin and bitters in a heavy rocks glass.

"Hey Jes," she said. "Your friends coming?"

Jes just shrugged.

"Oh, one o' *those* nights? Do me a favor and quit while you can still stand. I don't fancy dragging your sorry ass home again."

"No worries, Deen. An hour, tops, then I'm out."

She nodded, and moved on to another table. Jes sipped at their drink, relishing the harsh burn of the gin and the spice of the bitters. Their eyes scanned the patrons, enjoying the people-watching. Some familiar faces; some strangers—it was about the right mix for a good dive.

The bar itself was a narrow plasti-form bridge arcing out and across about three-feet from the back wall. On one end was the drinks station that printed all the orders. There was just enough room for Deen to move back and forth to serve patrons who wanted to face the multitude of vid screens showing too many different feeds to count. They all vied for attention, and any time Jes's eyes lingered too long on one, it would ping their implant requesting audio. They reflexively rejected the requests, one after another.

Until they saw her face.

Jes's glass clinked down hard on the table, and ice-cold alcohol splashed over their fingers. They were frozen, staring at the vid long enough that it pinged them three times before their brain started moving again. They hastily acked the ping, and the newsfeed piped directly into their head.

"*—from Sol system: Heiress, socialite, and lately-minted Vice-President of AFP Mining, Andiriana Axsili Ferg announced her engagement to Vitor Principe Mull, the son and heir of Vatilia Jewel Mull, who we all know as the CEO and majority shareholder of the industrial giant Axon-Mull. This marriage will mark the union of two galaxy-spanning dynasties and the merger of two of the largest corporate entities in human space. The Ferg-Mull union will..."*

Jes's mind stopped processing the newsfeed. They could only stare at Andi's face. The vid was taken at some formal event and from a distance, and showed her walking hand-in-hand with a tall man with sharp features. The two of them were smiling happily at each other and seemed to be ignoring the cameras and the crowd.

Andi had let her hair grow out, and wore it in a tight cap of carefully styled curls that framed her face beautifully. She was dressed in a gown of sharp blue with crisp lines and narrow, split skirts.

She was still gorgeous. Jes was so fixated on her that they barely noticed her fiancée beyond his blond hair tied back in a regimented queue and his angular nose and jaw.

Jes felt their stomach lurch and the gin threatened to climb back up their throat. They pushed the glass away and muted the feed. They spent a moment just staring at the table, noticing the small splash of pink-tinged gin that had pooled in the center. Under the red and violet lights, it looked like spilled blood.

Jes took a deep breath, not letting themself think. They put in another order: a double whiskey, neat. When Deen brought it to them, they didn't look up at her. They spoke woodenly, still staring at the table and not letting themself feel.

"I changed my mind. I'm going to get myself very, very drunk. Sorry."

3 / Grind

Strobing magenta and cyan lights flared across the ceiling in time with the deep, throbbing bass of some inscrutable and bone-rattling sounds that *aht* assumed was meant to be music. *Ssst'tr'tss* rolled off the client, running three fingers across her breasts and down her belly. Aht leaned *ahtsa* cheek against her shoulder.

"Tha' was nice," the client said, gasping. She ran her hand across the velvet covering *Ssst'tr'tss's* body, down ahtsa thighs.

"Mmmm," *Ssst'tr'tss* said. "Glad y' liked it." Triss facial musculature lent itself to flexibility. The triss were natural vocal mimics, and *Ssst'tr'tss* was becoming good at making the sounds of human Common, down to replicating specific accents and regional dialects. Aht was still learning the grammar and vocabulary though.

The client ran her hand up *Ssst'tr'tss's* side and neck, then ruffled ahtsa ears. *Ssst'tr'tss* tried not to tense. Aht hated when clients did that—petting *ahta* like an animal.

The client stood and started gathering her clothes and dressing lazily. Her gaze lingered on *Ssst'tr'tss's* naked body for a long moment. "How d' you *do* tha' Stritch? 'S like y' turned your body inside out?"

Ssst'tr'tss's ears were still twitching from the unwelcome touch. "Did, pretty much," *Ssst'tr'tss* said. Aht was always vaguely uncomfortable at how amazed humans were at an atriss's bodily functions. The third sex of the triss species was too much of a curiosity. They paid well enough, but always left ahta feeling especially objectified—even for a sex worker.

"Mmm, you did. Well, I put a litt'l som'in extra in th'ccount for you. 'Till next time." She smiled and exited the small cabin.

Ssst'tr'tss counted slowly to thirty-three, eyes closed and trying to breathe more slowly. Aht knew aht couldn't spend too much time in here before going back out on the floor, or Sammy would get angry. When Sammy was angry, she made ahtsa life highly unpleasant.

Ssst'tr'tss thought of a machine. A simple articulated strut. Visualized it to the smallest detail and then imagined disassembling it piece by piece. The practice was relaxing.

Five minutes later, aht was crawling out of the bed and stepping into the small shower booth. A harsh spray of hot water flowed over ahta, beading and skittering over the fine, glossy dun-colored velvet covering ahtsa body. Triss velvet repelled water and oil equally, and so there wasn't much need for the shower—a quick wipe-down achieved the same degree of cleanliness—but Sammy insisted.

Aht looked ahta-self over in the large mirror by the shower booth. Aht was short, even for an atriss—*Ssst'tr'tss's* ears barely reached the chest of most human patrons. Aht drew back lips on ahtsa narrow, pointed face to show sharp teeth, and twitched ahtsa small ears back and down in dissatisfaction. An atriss alone, with no family, no matriarch, was utterly bereft. Aht wasn't even sure why aht struggled so much to survive.

Ssst'tr'tss fingered the still-raw scar at the base of ahtsa skull and sighed a long, hissing trill. No cominfo implant meant being cut off from the outside world. Sammy thought it meant that aht was trapped. But aht had a way out. Aht just needed to earn enough credit to buy passage.

Cleaned and steeled for the strobes and clangor and the unpleasant treatment aht would receive on the brothel floor, *Ssst'tr'tss* exited the small cabin and walked out among the patrons.

The main parlor of The Grind was a loud, mind-pummeling space. Bright lights in a multitude of hues strobed and spun against the ceiling and the deck. About a dozen of *Ssst'tr'tss's* fellow prostitutes circulated among the patrons who lounged at tables and couches with a variety of drinks and small plates. Occasionally, one would close a negotiation with a client and they would depart to the private cabins along the back wall. Sometimes more than one worker teamed up to land a big spender. Sometimes there were several clients negotiating as a group to spend their credit together.

Sammy didn't mind either way as long as the liquor flowed and the stims and fuzzies flowed and most of all that the credit flowed.

"Stritch! Where's that damned foxie?"

Aht looked to the voice and saw Sammy striding towards ahta. She was a large woman; tall and muscular. Her black hair stood in a stiff brush that reminded ahta of a katriss crest. And she looked annoyed. Sammy always looked annoyed when she looked at *Ssst'tr'tss*. She closed the distance in three long strides, grabbing ahtsa arm in a painful grip.

"Stritch, your client from this morning walked out without settling. That's coming out of your account."

Aht looked up at her. *Ssst'tr'tss's* ears folded down and aht showed ahtsa teeth. "How am I supposed to check the settling? You took my implant."

Sammy's lips twisted into a grimace, and she shoved ahta back against the cold wall. "Just get out there and make more pull. I'm not paying you room and board for you to laze about."

Ssst'tr'tss shied back, then meekly turned and moved deeper into the crowd of patrons. Despite her words and threats, Sammy's commanding presence and the warm press of bodies around ahta was familiar and almost comforting. Almost.

Ssst'tr'tss was flooded by a wave of grief and memory.

Ssst'tr'tss crouched down behind Ahsst'trr'tr'aht and T't'tssss'tr and made ahta-self as small and invisible as possible. Ahtsa ears perked up and widened to catch the whispered words of the matriarch.

"The humans saw us depart the skiff," she said in the trilling sibilance that was the Trissa language. "They will note us as we traverse this station. Too many humans here. 'Even the indifferent eye tracks the unusual.'"

Heads nodded at the common saying, so apt to this situation.

There were many humans on this deck. They moved with purpose here and there, pushing grav-pallets, carrying tool cases; some took their ease and chatted in their hard-edged language full of hums and stops. *Ssst'tr'tss* had even seen a small crew of vos further down the concourse, shouting violently at each other in what passed for pleasant conversation among them.

The matriarch waved the triss back between large stacks of crates and shipping containers and the family group tightened, moving further into the shadows of the corner of the station docks.

"*Trr'ssss'tr,*" she said, gesturing her younger sister forward. "Take *Ahsst'trr'tr'aht* and *Ssst'tr'tss*. Move through the passages unseen and find us a way through to the concourse. Food first. Then to the passenger departure decks." Her ears flicked downwards in humiliation and defeat. "Perhaps we can hire passage."

The younger katriss dipped her head and reached a slender hand out, grasping the older hatatriss possessively by the forearm. She moved out swiftly and silently, her lean body moving gracefully through the narrow gaps between shipping containers and the bulkhead. The hatatriss moved forward to lead the way and protect her, and *Ssst'tr'tss* followed them both.

They kept to the shadows, moving in a sinuous, winding path that kept them out of the eyes of the humans. Not all the humans were a problem. But only one needed to be.

Ssst'tr'tss had seen one of them lurking at the skiff docking port, casually querying the docking machine to find out if they were still aboard the skiff. Its pale smooth skin was covered in cloth as the humans wore on their bodies—blue and black—and *Ssst'tr'tss's* acute eyes had picked out the small hand weapon that the human carried.

The attack had left the tight-knit matriarchy the last survivors of the *Vrrih'sss'sstrr'trrrrunn*. While the general agreements of the Accord were meant to be universal, each species ran its own domains according to its own laws and traditions. The triss didn't know the detailed regs on this human station, and didn't know who to trust. But they knew they were hunted. All *Ssst'tr'tss* and ahtsa family wanted at this point was to survive, get home, and try to rebuild their lives.

The three triss reached a crossing junction of the passage at the end of a stack of crates, and *Trr'ssss'tr* was about to creep around the corner, but *Ssst'tr'tss* hissed and ducked ahtsa head.

Ahsst'trr'tr'aht looked back, his ears perking up in surprise, and lips drawing back to show large, sharp teeth.

Ssst'tr'tss ducked down and flattened ahtsa ears, raising hands up in a gesture of submission. When *Trr'ssss'tr* looked back, *Ssst'tr'tss* pointed to a small access plate. It took only a moment for ahta to loosen the fasteners and pull the plate aside, revealing a narrow utility duct.

Trr'ssss'tr hummed and her ears flicked back and forward, points up and perked. Aht climbed through first, she followed and *Ahsst'trr'tr'aht* brought up the rear, sliding the plate hastily over the duct as he came.

They wound through the labyrinth of tight ducts, aht intuiting the turnings and barely pausing. *Ssst'tr'tss* had an intrinsic knack for made things. They reached a vertical shaft and climbed. The recessed finger and footholds were spaced awkwardly for triss, but they managed. *Ssst'tr'tss* couldn't help but notice systems and accesses as aht passed; that was a heat exchanger, this a power junction, and there was a gravplate manifold.

Aht was considered gifted in spatial reasoning, and formed a mental map of the station as aht moved. Now and then, aht paused to listen at, then carefully open an access plate, peeking out from the dark ductwork to check how far they had come.

After longer than aht liked, *Ssst'tr'tss* heard the distant milling of people. Aht opened the panel a finger-width and peered out. It was a shallow alcove off of a side passage. *Ssst'tr'tss* opened it the rest of the way and squeezed out, making room for *Trr'ssss'tr* and *Ahsst'trr'tr'aht*. The hatatriss leaned out enough to see the passage was empty and waved them forward.

At the mouth of the wider concourse, *Ssst'tr'tss* could see past the larger hatatriss to a chaotic scene of humanity. It looked like thousands of humans filled the deck, moving with purpose, idly congregating, and some accosting others to sell or buy or beg. Aht could see several kiosks and shops with small tables that seemed to sell food and beverage. The smell of human was overwhelming and mildly off-putting.

Trr'ssss'tr was about to step out and lead them to a food vendor when *Ahsst'trr'tr'aht* hissed and pulled her back. He crouched low and nodded his nose to the right. She followed his gesture and gave a similar sibilant hiss. The two pulled back further towards the alcove. *Ssst'tr'tss* peered around the corner and saw what *Ahsst'trr'tr'aht* had seen: A human standing on the far side of the concourse, not walking, not shopping, not begging. Standing still except for his head which swiveled slowly back and forth, scanning the mass of people. His hand was tucked into a hip pocket of his blue and black jumpsuit.

Ssst'tr'tss backed away silently and met the others at the alcove.

"The vending concourse is long and varied. We can go further down and try another access," *Trr'ssss'tr* said.

They re-entered the conduit and aht led them on, traveling now roughly parallel to the main passage, aht thought.

When they had gone past several access panels, *Ahsst'trr'tr'aht* trilled, and opened the next one. This likewise opened into a side passage, and this time, he went first, waving the other two to stay in hiding.

A few moments later, *Ssst'tr'tss*'s implant pinged with an all-clear, and aht and *Trr'ssss'tr* followed. They met up with *Ahsst'trr'tr'aht* and emerged into the wider concourse. It was uncomfortable moving among the humans in the open now, but they would have to if they were to get provisions and buy passage.

Trr'ssss'tr led the three towards a small kiosk that seemed to be vending food. They queued up behind a large human who was standing in the short line, waiting their turn at the printer. *Ssst'tr'tss* huddled close to *Ahsst'trr'tr'aht*, feeling comfort in his size and warmth. Ahtsa ears were twitching.

The large human stepped forward as the line advanced, and the movement revealed another human standing quietly beside the kiosk. Aht thought by her body shape that she was female, but it was the sleek blue and black jumpsuit that made ahta keen a sharp cry and pull back at *Trr'Ssss'tr*'s arm.

Ahsst'trr'tr'aht saw the human at nearly the same moment and shoved *Trr'ssss'tr* out of line and back towards the side passage. Aht spun and followed, not daring to glance backwards, but feeling an itch between ahtsa shoulders.

The hatatriss reached the safety of the side passage first, and *Ssst'tr'tss* was the last. Ahtsa shorter legs and smaller stature made it difficult to keep up, but aht wasn't far behind. As aht reached the corner to the passage, aht risked a glance backwards. The human hadn't moved, and was simply looking vaguely into the distance, glassy eyed.

The corridor was empty and secluded from the crush of humanity only a few strides away. *Trr'ssss'tr* reached the access plate and began releasing the fasteners. As *Ssst'tr'tss* closed the distance, aht saw movement at the far end of the passage, and a blue-and-black-clad human stepped around the corner, raising a hand that clutched a small device.

It seemed to all happen at once. The access plate came free, clattering to the deck. *Ahsst'trr'tr'aht* reared back to his full height, raising his arms and charging down the passage towards the human. He roared a wordless cry and spread his fingers, extending his claws in a show of threat.

A rapid clicking trill sounded from down the hallway—nearly a Trissa sound, but more mechanical.

And *Ahsst'trr'tr'aht* collapsed in a welter of blood.

Trr'ssss'tr cried a harsh growl of anger and spun, indecision holding her still for the briefest moment. The trilling continued for a few seconds more, and whether by intent or accident, the weapon found *Trr'ssss'tr*. The projectiles tearing into her body were silent apart from the mechanical sound of the weapon. *Ssst'tr'tss* looked on in horror as she too fell to the deck without a further sound.

"Shit!" cried the human.

Ssst'tr'tss stood in shock, eyes wide and ears flat against ahtsa head. The human looked at ahta, its face showing none of the expressive mobility that a triss face would. Without thought, aht dove through the open access into the conduit and began running.

It took ahta several moments to realize aht was the source of the keening sound that chased ahta through the duct. After several turnings at random, aht paused and collapsed to the deck, curling ahtsa body into a tight ball.

Some time later, ahtsa breathing had descended from panic, and aht could see and hear again. Aht sent a ping to *S'aht'trr'tss*.

"*They found us.* Trr'ssss'tr *and* Ahsst'trr'tr'aht *are dead. I am hiding in ductwork between passages. Please, advise me.*"

A moment passed before aht received an ack and a response: "*Return.*"

Ahtsa mental map of the ducts was sound, and it was easy for ahta to retrace the path aht had taken. *Ssst'tr'tss* moved slowly through the turns. Ahtsa limbs felt heavy with grief and dread.

Now that aht had a sense of the labyrinth of utility ducts, aht thought aht could stay within the narrow accesses nearly the whole way back to *S'aht'trr'tss*. After more than a dozen turnings, a descent through the vertical shaft, and several more turns and junctions, aht reached an access plate.

Ssst'tr'tss pressed ahtsa ear to the plate, listening for any sounds. There was no sound but the constant hum of the station machinery. Aht released the fasteners and pulled the plate aside.

Aht was right. The access plate opened not ten strides from where the remainder of ahtsa family was. From within the darkness of the duct, *Ssst'tr'tss* could see their bodies, collapsed in a huddled mass, torn and bloodied by the vicious weapons.

Three of the blue-and-black-clad humans stood around the scene of death. *Ssst'tr'tss* watched as one of them reached out and nudged one of the bodies with a booted foot.

"What now?" one of them said to another. "We needed at least *one* of them alive."

Aht didn't wait for the response. Aht silently replaced the access plate and secured the fasteners. Without a sound, aht retreated back into the maze of ducts.

"Hey, foxie."

The mildly intoxicated voice pulled *Ssst'tr'tss* out of ahtsa memory and into the present. Aht looked up at the smiling human woman and her even taller companion. They both had the glassy eyes and flushed skin that aht had learned to associate with drunkenness combined with stims, but there was something in her voice that made the tips of ahtsa ears cool. *Ssst'tr'tss* pulled back ahtsa lips and forced an approximation of a smile. Ahtsa ears were peaked and stiff, but humans couldn't read triss body language even when sober.

"Give us both some fun?" The woman whined in a revolting sing-song.

Ssst'tr'tss sized them up and decided to set a price so high that aht would either make quota for the night or they would walk away. Aht didn't like the feel of the pair. "Fifteen-hundred for you both for one decimal, yah?"

The woman's smile widened. "Perfect. Let's go have some fun."

Aht moved slowly, leading the pair away from the bar to the back rooms, but ahtsa mind was racing. Something was off. Even drunk and stimmed, fifteen-hundred cred should have driven them to haggle. As they walked, the woman leaned in and put her arm over ahtsa shoulder. The man walked two strides behind, and held the same steady pace. *Ssst'tr'tss* tensed and ahtsa ears stiffened further.

"What're you looking for?" *Ssst'tr'tss* asked mildly.

"Oh, you know. Jus' looking for some fun," the woman said.

"Lots of fun to have here, yah," *Ssst'tr'tss* said. "Anything special?" The man walking behind still hadn't said anything.

"Mmm, yeah," the woman crooned against the top of ahtsa head.

Passing through the hatch into the cabin passage, *Ssst'tr'tss* felt a rising wave of fear and panic, and let the impulse to flee take ahtsa muscles. Aht folded down, curling ahtsa back and turning towards the woman. Aht was already small of stature. The sudden tuck let ahta duck under her arm and drop to all four limbs, racing low against the deck.

"Grab it!" aht heard the woman call, a fierce whisper pitched to carry only as far as her companion's ears.

Aht felt more than saw the man's hands reaching for ahta and aht twisted, flattening ahtsa body and squeezing through the narrow gap between the man and the hatchway. As aht passed him, aht curled ahtsa short tail around the man's ankle, yanking him off balance so that he fell forward into the woman who was lunging for ahta.

Just through the hatch, aht ducked across the path of another patron who was ambling towards the bar, tripping him. Shouts of anger and confusion followed as *Ssst'tr'tss* wove between the tipsy patrons. Aht kept low and moved fast.

"Stritch! What the fuck!" Sammy's angered voice raged from somewhere across the bar.

Ssst'tr'tss was close to The Grind's entrance hatch and was about to squeeze through when aht spotted a shape leaning casually against the bulkhead across the public passage. Aht had just enough time for ahtsa mind to catch up and point out the blue and black jumpsuit.

A hand closed over *Ssst'tr'tss's* arm and pulled ahta violently to ahtsa feet.

"You goddamned foxie! Where do you think you're going?" Sammy screamed. She raised her left arm as if to strike ahta.

Under her arm, *Ssst'tr'tss* saw the man and woman pushing through the crowd. They no longer appeared intoxicated.

Aht pulled against Sammy's hold but she was too strong. She turned and dragged *Ssst'tr'tss* back into The Grind.

Aht flattened ahtsa ears and extended ahtsa claws, raking them as hard as possible against Sammy's wrist. They were smooth and rounded like most triss kept them, but the sensory threat was enough to cause her to release ahta in reflex.

"Fuck!" Sammy yelled, drawing back.

Ssst'tr'tss spun, diving back into the crowded club and towards the bar, away from the threats inside and out. Sammy was close behind, but she was too big to maneuver quickly through the tight throng.

Aht ducked around the bar and scrambled towards the service access under the printer. It took agonizing seconds to release the fasteners and then aht was in the tight confines of the service chase. Aht could hear footsteps close behind and didn't bother replacing the panel. They were all too big to squeeze through anyway.

Angry shouting and confusion chased *Ssst'tr'tss* through the winding chase as aht crawled and squirmed between bulkheads, frame members, and system machinery, disappearing into the cramped darkness.

4 / Decks

Windy picked her way through the tables, relying on her height and bulk to clear a path through the crowded bar. The slurring voice she was following grew louder and more distinct as she got closer. She could almost make out the words, and what she heard was worrying.

"...thing is... The *thing* is... what we had. She... It was— You have to... to understand..."

Windy rounded a mass of standing patrons and finally spotted Jes. Fin looked up from the table as she stepped closer, a long suffering look on his face. Jes didn't seem to notice Windy's arrival, and kept muttering.

"What the fuck?" she asked Fin.

Fin sighed. "Found them like this. Deen says they've been pounding doubles for about an hour."

"...just threw it all away..." Jes added helpfully.

"The hull?" Windy asked. She heard the sudden panic in her own voice.

"No. The hull's fine."

"What then?"

Fin nodded his head, indicating the vid wall.

Windy turned and began to scan the various feeds, but

she stopped short when she saw her. The feed seemed to be looping, stretching ten minutes of celebrity gossip into an endless news event. Seeing Andi's face on the vid—even if she had grown out her hair and was wearing fancy and gloss—made Windy's stomach drop.

"Oh shit," she said.

"...an' she wouldn't even use my name... spesh—speshlist she called me..."

"Who is she?" Fin asked. "I mean... I know who she *is* now, they've basically had her social profile on repeat. But... who is she to Jes?"

Windy thought for a moment before answering. "A ghost, Fin. She's a ghost from a past life."

Jes seemed to notice Windy now and grabbed her arm, pulling her down into a free seat. "How did it come to this, Windy?"

Windy shook her head sadly. "Jes, it's been three years. She's moved on. I thought you had too."

Jes tried to look at her but their head spun and they tilted, nearly falling from their seat. Only their hand still on Windy's arm kept them stable.

Deen arrived with two glasses of water, setting them down in front of Windy and giving her a look of exasperation. "Do something about them, will you? I don't need this tonight."

Windy nodded to Deen, lifting one of the glasses of water. She grabbed Jes by the shoulder and leaned in close to make sure they heard her over the din. "Jes!" she yelled in her loudest all-hands-on-deck voice. Jes reeled back covering their ear and turning to face Windy just as she upended the first glass of water over their head.

"Bwah!" Jes said, recoiling. Windy held them fast until they were over the initial shock. "What the fuck, Windy!"

"That's my line, Jes." She slid the second water in front of them. "Now drink up before you're wearing this one, too."

Jes tried to stare her down but was too wobbly to be effective. They grudgingly took up the water and started sipping.

"Now, I know this hit you hard. I know you're lonely and pissed, and you have every right to be. But this bullshit? Getting drunk on *her* account? She's not worth that kind of pain."

Windy nodded to Fin. "We're here. We're *so* close to making your plan work. *Your* plan. You need to keep your head, Jes. Lose it now, and it's not just you that you burn. You burn me and Fin too. So: Get. It. Together. And *get to it!*"

The little speech seemed to land. Jes found some small purchase of sobriety on the precipice they clung to. "I'm sorry, Windy. I jus' wanted some…" They waved their hand vaguely, unable to name what they wanted.

"I get it," Windy said. "But whatever you needed tonight, you've had a bellyful. Let's get you up and in bed and asleep so you can sober up for tomorrow. Big day."

Jes tried to focus, and with great visible effort spoke their next words steadily. "What is tomorrow?"

"I made us a contact," Windy said to both Jes and Fin. "A shady skunk down on four-deck's got a beacon ident-chip for sale, clean and clear. That gets us one step closer, yeah?"

Her words pulled all of Jes's attention. They looked at her steadily for a moment, and then deliberately lifted the glass of water and drank it down. "Let's get me some more of this," they said.

A half-hour later and a lot more water, Jes was stable enough to walk out with minimal support from Windy and Fin. They passed Deen on the way out, and Jes flashed her a rueful grin. She just shook her head.

The trio exited the Bleak, weaving only slightly under Jes's impaired motor functions. They nearly bumped into a man leaning casually against the bulkhead, avoiding him by only a quick step from Fin that steered them away.

Windy noted that the man didn't move or react to the near miss. His eyes were fixed on the hatch across the passage, a business named The Grind, and his hands were tucked deep into the pockets of his blue and black jumpsuit. Likely he was distracted by a body he was watching in the brothel.

They kept moving, passing the hatch just as a fierce ruckus broke out from within. The sound had a different timbre than the background noise of rhythmic bass and the crush of bodies and voices that was the natural soundtrack of The Grind. Something in the voices she heard raised over the general cacophony caught Windy's attention.

There was a tension and a violence in the sounds. She turned her head, trying to pick up on what her subconscious was warning her of. She peered back into the hatch but was unable to track anything of note in the chaos.

A lurch to the left as Jes missed a step brought her mind back to the trouble at hand. Together, she and Fin wove their way through the passages and to the transit tube to deposit Jes in his dreary cabin for the night.

Five hours later, Windy tapped the hatch tone on Jes's door. She waited two minutes before pressing it again, this time holding her thumb down on the touchpad so the bell would ring continuously.

After eight minutes, the hatch opened and Jes leaned out, their bleary, red-rimmed eyes attesting to their bender the previous night.

"Windy," they croaked. "It wasn't a dream, then?"

"Get showered and dressed, fast," she said. "We need to be on deck four in," she blinked, checking her station clock, "twenty-three minutes."

Jes groaned, but turned back into the cabin. Windy let the hatch close and leaned against the bulkhead across the passage. After ten minutes, the hatch opened once more and Jes stepped out, clean, dressed, and looking marginally less hung-over.

"Alright. Let's get to it," Jes said. "Four-deck?"

Windy nodded and began walking down the passage to the transit spur. Jes followed.

"Fill me in. What are we walking into?"

Windy thought for a moment before answering. "I don't know the seller's name. My contact is an intermediary. A bilge-monkey who works station mass transfer. Says he can hook us up with the seller."

"And how do we know it's not a set-up or a shake-down?"

"We don't. But he knows I've got a record of the conversation, and that not all of us are going to be there. We don't make it back out and the record goes to station security."

Jes shrugged uncomfortably. They wouldn't second guess her, but they hated working blind on the shady side of the law. They usually played on their instincts, but those instincts needed *some* context.

Jes and Windy hit the outgoing transit tube and rode it to the down-transition point, transferring to a small, ugly tube car that didn't even deign to blare ads at them. With a minute to spare, they got off on deck four—the lowest deck on the station that didn't require pressure suits—and wound their way through the narrow, twisting passages.

Here and there, a light was out or threatening to be soon. More often than not, tool carts or half-empty supply crates or piles of industrial refuse blocked the already narrow access. Some panels were missing from the passage walls and once, they had to step across the yawning gap of an open deck plate.

"Where is this guy?" Jes asked.

"He's supposed to be waiting for us just ahead," Windy replied.

They turned a last corner and saw a stick-thin man in a grimy utility jumpsuit—more grease-stain than the light blue it was meant to be. His fingers and face twitched and danced constantly. He might have an involuntary muscle condition, or he might be jacked on stims. It was hard to tell.

"You came," he said. His voice was wheedling and tried hard at a threat that just didn't carry.

"We came," Windy said. "Where's your guy?" she asked him. She was able to put more threat in her voice than he could muster.

His hands came up, placating. "No worries, no worries. All good. The boss is in his office, right through there." He gestured to the hatch beside him.

Windy and Jes waited for him to open the hatch, then stepped through into a small, battered management office. Just enough room for a narrow terminal desk with a chair on either side facing each other. The space was shockingly well-lit after the gloomy passages, but the extra light didn't help the cabin to be more appealing.

Windy tensed as she recognized the man who occupied the desk. She heard a sharp breath from Jes behind her and knew they had recognized him too.

"My, my, my. If it isn't Jes and Windy; Click and Clack.

You two still thick as thieves?" He smiled at them, but his voice had an edge.

"Harry," Windy said.

"Chief," Jes added, stepping into the tight office. They looked around briefly. "You've done well for yourself."

The former Chief Engineer of the Antares Drift arched his back against the frame of his chair, stretching. "I have. I run this deck. You might say this is my world down here. What happens is whatever I want to happen."

"It's... some kind of world," Jes said, looking over their shoulder to the darkened and neglected passage behind them.

Harry seemed to miss the implication in Jes's voice, or at least ignored it. "And now you two have come to me. What can I do for you, my good friends?"

"You know what we're looking for?" Windy said. "Your friend out there told me you could get it for us."

"All business? No time for an old crewmate?" Harry turned the corners of his mouth down in an exaggerated frown. "I'm hurt, Windy. Hurt. Oh, I have just what you need." He leaned back in his seat, resting his head against the bulkhead, then shifted forward and opened a hatch under the desk and pulled out a small metal-shielded frame with a wide interface port. It was rectangular, and roughly the size of a dinner plate.

"Question is, do you have what *I* need?"

"Maybe," Windy said, looking at the device. "What's your price?"

"Hmmm." Harry made a show of considering. Jes and Windy both knew that he had already set his price. "Well, you know, lucky for you I happen to know a little of what you've each got in your accounts. A little *residual* knowledge, you might say." Harry grinned at them. "How about you sign over your claim and shares from our last haul on the *Drift*? You get to fly a new ship; I get a little more comfortable down here. Maybe extend my... kingdom."

Windy felt the blow and cursed at herself for not nailing down the price beforehand. There was no way either of them would part with what little they had left to live on.

"Try it out," Harry offered. He placed the chip on the desk. "You brought a reader, I presume?"

Windy stared at him for a moment, then pulled a hand-held device from her pocket. It was little more than a socket for the interface port with a power cell attached. She plugged it in and a small green indicator lit up on the end of the reader. Her eyes went glassy as she directed her implant to connect to the reader and scan the chip.

As the data filled her head, her eyes twitched from side to side. She dumped the ident public key into a registry search. The identity on the chip listed itself as registered out of *Alnasl L5* with no owner of record.

Windy sighed when she saw the ship's name. "You've got to be kidding. '*Heart of Gold*?' You couldn't find a chip with a more cliched name?"

There was a long-standing joke among spacers that every single world, station, and jurisdiction boasted its own registry entry for a ship called "Heart of Gold." In the years since the advent of the SDR, every comet jockey and spacer who managed to scrounge together enough to finance a ship of their own seemed to come up with the same clever idea.

"I can't help but note that you're standing here trying to buy a ship chip of questionable provenance," Harry said. "You want something flashy? To be noticed and remembered, maybe? Or do you want to slip into comfortable obscurity?"

She sighed. It was all moot anyway. "We're *not* giving you our residuals," Windy said. "What do you think we're going to do with a ship chip and no ship to plug it into?"

"Not my problem," Harry said with a shrug. "You want it, or not?"

"We'll take it," Jes said from behind her.

Windy turned to them in shock.

"But you're not getting accounts from both of us." They stepped forward, squeezing around Windy's bulky frame into the compartment. "I'll sign my shares over to you."

"Jes, no," Windy whispered. "We'll find another way."

They ignored her, staring Harry down.

"It's not enough," Harry said. He shook his head and reached out to take the chip.

Jes extended their right hand out over the desk, placing their left over the device. "You get my shares, and we walk out of here with the ship chip. More: we owe you a favor. Once we get our ship under us... I'm sure you can come up with something to call in a marker for. We have a deal?"

Harry sneered at Jes. "Come now. Half what I asked, and a marker *if* you manage a ship? What do you take me for?"

Jes smiled. "I take you for a man who runs four-deck and can let a little bit of credit slide on the potential for a bigger payout down the line. Or am I misremembering that you got your kicks landing a little wager here and there?"

Harry's sneer slipped fluidly into a wide smile. He grasped Jes's offered hand and shook. "Deal."

Jes's eyes went glassy for a moment as they dipped into their implant interface, transferring the shares. "Done."

"Always a pleasure, Jes. Don't be a stranger now," Harry said, grinning.

Jes took the device from the desk, pressing it into Windy's hands.

"See you 'round Chief."

"Round and round, Jes. Round and round, I will be seeing you."

They backed out of the office and past the bilge-monkey, who had been leaning against the bulkhead through the whole negotiation. He watched them retrace their path through the dimly-lit corridors.

Windy waited until she was sure they were out of earshot. "Jes, what the fuck did you just do? How are you going to live without those residuals?"

Jes was silent for a moment. "Did we need that chip?" they said.

"Yes, damnit. But... what good is it going to do? We're not ready to take her out yet. Jes... We may never be ready. You know that, right?"

"We *are* going to do it." Jes's voice was firm; resolved. "Do you believe that, Windy?"

She hesitated. "I—I want to. But Jes—"

They reached the grim transit car and Jes stepped inside, turning to face her. "It's just money. I've got enough set by to last me a few more weeks. After that... who knows? Maybe we'll find an SDR. Maybe we'll stumble onto something fantastic. Or maybe I'll move in with you."

"Like *hell* you will. I'll not have you crowding my bunk; damping my pull. This woman has *needs*."

Jes met her eyes. "We're going to make it, Ada. This is the plan. We've got the hull. With this chip we've got a working nav-comm beacon that can echo clean. The skip drive and Q-comp are good enough to get us out of this particular sky. From there, we're free. Find jobs as we can and live how we want to live—"

Windy stared at Jes for a moment. They only used her first name, Ada, when they were being desperately serious. She shook her head. "In a half-scrap rust-bucket that was dumped in the recycler by its last owner?" Windy said.

Jes smiled at her wistfully. "You know what they say: 'One person's trash is another person's—'"

"'—tragic descent into desperation borne of a willing adherence to fantasy that will ultimately lead to abject poverty or ignominious death?'" She cut in. She squeezed into the car beside them, then punched in Jes's deck number and the car began to move.

Windy was clutching the chip module with both hands as they accelerated up the transit tube. "Yeah, I think I've heard that one before."

5 / Grates

Ssst'tr'tss's long fingers spun the release catch and swung the shielding panel away from the recycler coil. Ahtsa hands were shaking only slightly from hunger. Aht brushed the power line out of the way and opened the maintenance panel.

An avalanche of trash tumbled onto the conduit plating. Aht deftly sorted the empties from any containers that still held traces of food, placing these in the plastic bag aht wore over ahtsa shoulder. The empties, *Ssst'tr'tss* fed in handfuls to the waiting recycler coil, before replacing the buffer panel aht had inserted to prevent discarded items from feeding properly.

Aht couldn't disconnect the coil itself, or maintenance workers would be dispatched to check on the malfunctioning 'cycler. But a small plastic panel wedged just above the coil prevented the larger items from dropping through until aht could pull out the food scraps.

Ssst'tr'tss reassembled the shielding and closed it up. Three more recyclers to check, and aht should have enough food to survive another day. It took longer to get from one to the next than to disassemble and reassemble them. Aht had chosen out the recyclers to modify some distance from each other to avoid raising suspicions if they were discovered.

Aht had observed humans queuing at a nearby printer kiosk that was clearly marked as requiring no monetary input. The infrastructure that formed the closed-loop of power, matter printing, and recycling had plenty of excess left over to meet the needs of the indigent and marginalized. But joining the queue meant exiting the access chases and being visible to the humans.

After three hours or so, crawling through the maint accessways and collecting discarded food scraps, Ssst'tr'tss made ahtsa way back to a space between a heat-exchanger and an air cleaner where aht nested. A length of plastic sealing film stretched from a mounting bracket over the heat exchanger to a brace anchor over a duct to make a hammock of sorts. It was warm and snug and had easy access to three different service conduits. There was also an intake grate that overlooked the loading docks for one of the station's cargo rings.

Ahtsa current plan was to stow away on a piece of outbound cargo. If *Ssst'tr'tss* was caught on board a ship, aht would be detained, and even if aht made it to a new destination, aht would have no money or allies. But aht would also have no enemies hunting ahta.

Ssst'tr'tss curled up in the hammock and found just the right position so aht could peer through the grate to observe the docks. Aht watched the humans moving here and there, tagging cargo bins for loading and unloading. While aht watched, ahtsa picked at the refuse aht had collected, pulling out scraps of sandwich or pastry or processed sugar and licking them off ahtsa fingers.

The hum and clank of loading machinery resonated

through the grate, and *Ssst'tr'tss* was in a different hull, in a different life.

Ahsst'trr'tr'aht reached an arm out and held *Ssst'tr'tss* back against the bulkhead as the breaking thrust caused the skiff to lurch violently.

"Watch yourself, *sst'ss*. Big forces don't care about little bones."

Ssst'tr'tss grunted in reply and ignored the diminutive, grasping the takehold straps with both hands. The skiff lurched again as the thrusters fired on a new vector.

"They're trying to lock beams on us," *T't'tssss'tr* said from the co-pilot seat.

"All brace!" *Trr'Ssss'tr* shouted from helm, as the skiff lurched again, hard.

Sss'ahtr was seated at the nav-comm console, and he let out a sharp hiss. "Radiative debris on diverging vector! The second skiff is gone."

The matriarch and *Trr'Ssss'tr* let out keening moans as they mourned the deaths of their sisters on the other skiffs. They had hoped that by departing in opposite directions they might buy themselves more time to escape. Their loss meant that this was the only skiff left from the *Vr-rihSss'sstrr'trrrrunn*.

"Incoming mass stream on this vector!" *T't'tssss'tr* called out. "They're firing on us."

The ship jerked in various directions as *Trr'Ssss'tr* executed a rapid series of translations to avoid the sweeping stream of particulate matter. *Ssst'tr'tss* was slammed against the bulkheads but managed to keep hold of the straps. Aht noticed aht was making a keening sound and stopped.

"They actually fired on us!" *T't'tssss'tr* said in disbelief.

A horrible mechanical shriek tore through the cabin, and a cacophony of alerts and klaxons filled the air. Aht let go of one strap to pull up the damage readout on ahtsa console.

"We're hit," *Ssst'tr'tss* said. "The actuator line for vane two is gone."

"We need that vane open! Only way out of this alive is if we enter skip!" *T't'tssss'tr* called out.

The skip drive used three field generators to translate the ship into skip-space. Those generators needed to be as far from the ship's center of mass as possible to achieve transition, hence the three articulating vanes.

"Give me time without tumbling," *Ssst'tr'tss* said. "I can get it extended."

"Can't hold still. We're under fire."

Ahsst'trr'tr'aht gripped *Ssst'tr'tss* around the waist and braced his feet against the seat struts. "Hold you still while you work."

Ssst'tr'tss nodded, wrapping ahtsa tail around the larger triss's forearm and indicated the deckplate aht needed to open. *Ahsst'trr'tr'aht* lifted ahta down and *Ssst'tr'tss* started removing the fasteners.

The skiff lurched again and more warnings sounded.

With the panel off, *Ssst'tr'tss* pulled out the air cleaner pump and the running lights module, neither of which would be necessary if they took a direct hit.

"Where's that vane?" *Trr'Ssss'tr* shouted.

Aht ignored her and kept pulling modules free until aht had cleared enough space to crawl in under the deck. *Ahsst'trr'tr'aht* tried to hold on, but aht shrugged off his grip, squirming between the ventral mass tank and the painfully cold outer pressure hull until aht could reach the actuator for the atmospheric-flight planar flaps.

Ssst'tr'tss got a hand around the power line to the actuator and twisted to decouple it.

"Pull me back!" aht shouted. Aht felt a hand grip ahtsa ankle and pull. Half a meter backwards, and aht grabbed the vane actuator. "Stop there!" Aht pulled the damaged line free with one hand and plugged the line from the atmo-planar into the socket. "You should have power to the vane!" aht called.

Trr'Ssss'tr called back to the matriarch, "Where we going?"

"Where can we reach?"

"Human station. Only real choice. Comp says it's only genus-four away," *T't'tssss'tr* said.

S'aht'trr'tss hissed. "Last thing we need—more humans." Her ears twitched violently and her crest stiffened. She waved her hand to the console—permission and dismissal. "Go!"

"Calculating." *T't'tssss'tr* called out as the quantum computer figured the fields needed to transform and fold three-dimensional local into the seven-dimensional space they'd need to skip across. "Done! Vanes extending," *Trr'Ssss'tr* called back. "All three vanes are showing blue. Entering skip in three... two... one."

Ssst'tr'tss felt ahtsa organs twist as reality folded and they entered dimensional transition. Aht counted each of the four skips to ahta-self as the damaged skiff rattled and shrieked with the increasingly graceless impacts.

"Three more meters!" the tall one called to her workmate.

Ssst'tr'tss leaned a little in ahtsa hammock to better observe the shift leader through the grate.

She was the biggest human on the deck, tall and muscled. Dense. Even so, despite what aht had observed of humans' sexual dimorphism, she appeared to be female. It gave ahta comfort that *something* felt normal here, even in such a little and absurd way.

"No! Fuckit—stop the loader. Damnit Gibbs, I said *three* meters!" She continued to harangue the male driving the cargo loading machine as he made excuses and tried to shift the pallet back.

That felt right too. *The female* should *be in charge*, aht thought. The humans generally had a very haphazard way of arranging things, and it made little sense so far.

Ssst'tr'tss had picked this particular stretch of dock to observe in part because of the big female who seemed to run things, at least when she was on shift.

They sorted out the pallet and Gibbs turned the machine around to retrieve the next one from the automated cargo system. The loader looked to ahtsa eyes not much different from the systems aht had worked on aboard the *VrrihSss'sstrr'trrrrunn*, though it was bright orange instead of the violet that a triss would have used to evoke caution.

A round gravity-vectoring plate held the thing above the decking. The body of the machine was the size of a small cabinet that came up to the waist of the operator who managed the control console atop it. He stood on a platform that was just big enough for his booted feet. Mounted on the front of the cabinet were the four cargo manipulators, which he maneuvered with some degree of skill to lift large cargo containers and navigate them from one spot to the other on the active platform.

Ssst'tr'tss watched in idle fascination as Gibbs brought the next pallet into line with the previous ones. The work was so mundane that aht wondered how many times the human had done the same task. *Ssst'tr'tss* wondered if aht would ever do such a mundane task again.

There was a time before the Revelation when such jobs were the exclusive domain of bots—even on the triss homeworld. It cost far less to maintain and repair a fleet of cargo-handling bots than to pay living workers enough to live, and if there was one thing most of the species of the Accord had in common, it was a tendency towards a certain brutal efficiency in resource allocation.

But with the discoveries of the first Elder Caches—endless clean energy from SDRs, atomic printing and recycling—suddenly it cost nearly nothing to survive, so it was far cheaper for the large conglomerates to employ armies of laborers instead of a few talented and highly-trained bot engineers.

Ssst'tr'tss tried to guess the contents of the containers. Perhaps wrenches or calibrated matter valves or coils of power conduit. From this distance and angle, aht couldn't make out the content labels, and the containers themselves were only marked with shipping company logos and long alpha-numeric ident numbers.

Gibbs finally got the last pallet placed to the leader's satisfaction, and she sent him off to take a break. He powered down the loader where it stood and hopped off the platform onto the deck.

Other workers were still shifting cargo, and the leader moved to stand just below ahtsa grate. She leaned against the bulkhead and watched them work. Aht could only just see the top of her head. After some minutes, aht saw her turn her head sharply, and a new voice carried up to the grate, but aht couldn't see the newcomer.

"Hey Windy."

"Fin," Windy said. "What brings you here?"

"I just got off shift and I'm heading home, but I wanted to check in to see how things went yesterday."

"You could have pinged me," she said.

"Um, and discuss… shady dealings on the pubnet?"

Windy only grunted sourly. It struck aht as a very matriarchal kind of response.

"So… how did things go?" Fin pressed.

"We got the beacon. We're one step closer."

"That's great!"

"No, Fin, it's not great. Jes traded almost their whole account for it."

Fin made a choking sound. "Windy, I thought we sobered them up. What the hell?"

Ssst'tr'tss watched as Windy shook her head slowly side to side. Aht had figured out this was a negative human gesture.

"They're throwing the dice, Fin. They're throwing the dice. They just put a clock on the mission."

The two were silent for some time. Then Fin spoke again.

"We've got the hull." Ahtsa ears twitched and aht leaned closer to the grate. "We've got a beacon. It's clean? Then what's left? What do we need?"

Windy let out a harsh sigh, nearly a triss bark. "We need a fucking ship, Fin." Her head shook. "We can maybe squeeze a few skips out of the drive. But the Q-comp is junk. I wouldn't trust it to calculate a ballistic trajectory."

She moved suddenly away from the bulkhead, took two long paces and paused. A moment later, she turned slowly back to face Fin.

"It might be ok. It's twelve years old and was fucking slow even then, but it might. The line buffers are brittle, and I doubt we'd make it into skip-space anyway." She stepped forward and pressed her forehead against the bulkhead. "It doesn't matter, Fin. The goose egg. Without that, we have nothing."

Fin sighed. "How long do we have? To find one?"

Windy turned around and leaned against the bulkhead again. "Jes says they've got enough for a few more weeks. I think we need to start planning. Not about the ship. We need a plan on what we're going to do when Jes hits nil. Because that day is coming, and I don't think they're going to plan for it."

The two started talking about mass credits and contingencies and trade yields. *Ssst'tr'tss* lost the thread quickly, since aht had no knowledge or interest in such things. Ahtsa mind was spinning over what aht had overheard. This human matriarch had a ship, and could fly away from here if only she could get her hands on a "goose egg."

Aht knew the human Common phrase for the singularity module that powered all Accord technology, though aht could only guess at the imagery's relevance. Aht supposed the SDR might be roughly shaped like the egg of an oviparous game animal, but why a goose in particular?

Ssst'tr'tss missed the end of their conversation and only noticed when Windy went back to work, calling out for Gibbs and the other dock workers. A few moments later, aht saw a small, lithe human who finally was far enough from the bulkhead to be visible from ahtsa viewing angle. Fin, *Ssst'tr'tss* thought.

Approaching an unknown matriarch was too much of a

risk. Especially as *Ssst'tr'tss* knew aht *really* didn't understand human society. Too easy to make another mistake like aht had done with Sammy.

But this Fin... *Ssst'tr'tss* thought he might be a male, but from his size and deference to Windy's lead, a subordinate one. Aht thought approaching Fin might be safer. After a quick glance through the grate to track Fin's direction of movement, *Ssst'tr'tss* rolled out of the hammock and slipped quietly through the access conduit to the right.

Now that aht had discovered the grates that periodically perforated the passageway bulkheads, aht thought aht could shadow the human all the way back to his cabin.

Aht thought it was worth the risk. Aht had very little of value, but aht did have one thing. It was highly valuable, but also impossible for ahta to trade. Nonetheless, *Ssst'tr'tss* was suddenly thinking things might just work out.

6 / Shot

Fin thumbed the panel at his door and slipped inside. He reflexively activated the lock with a downward glance and flopped down on the waiting crash couch.

The cabin had a fold-out bed, but most nights Fin slept stretched out on the antique grav bunk instead. He found it more comfortable—it reminded him of his training days at the flight academy. He dropped his bulb of printed boba tea in the holder on the armrest and closed his eyes, dipping into his cominfo interface and dialing up the sim he'd found in the archives.

As the simulated flight deck expanded to fill his visual field, it gained in intensity and clarity. He glanced down to see the flight controls ready for his hands, each multi-axis control stick extending from the switch-cluttered panel and bristling with auxiliary switches and controls.

Control systems on the newer ships interfaced directly with cominfo implants and could keep their control schemes simpler. The tanks on those newer ships were really just spatial anchors for the neuro-rendering provided by implants. But older designs like this one dated from before cominfos were ubiquitous and relied more on physical control and feedback mechanisms.

In front of him loomed the tank. On this 88-G model, it was smallish compared with the larger ships Fin had learned on—only half a meter in diameter and a meter tall—but it still filled the cramped flight deck uncomfortably. The sim helpfully populated the remaining duty stations around the tank with bot-rendered crewmates. Ops to his left and nav-comm to his right, both facing in towards the spatial display column. Another figure—the captain—paced slowly around the perimeter, scowling at the tank.

Fin dipped into the sim preferences overlay and turned off the extra crew. He also selected a specific scenario called "In-System Cargo Haul - Hard." The tank repainted with a small red cylinder for the ship docked nose-on to a larger cylinder in green for a station. Various motes rendered in nuanced RGB light filled the immediate proximity of the station: shipping traffic. The periphery of the tank was cluttered in green and yellow speckles of various sizes.

Text in a large, friendly font scrolled over his vision to give the sim's mission objectives: "You're docked at Epsilon Eridani L4. Your mission is to rendezvous with the Vintner's Rest beyond the asteroid field, retrieve the class-three cargo unit they're carrying, and bring it back to the station at docking bay c843."

Fin cleared the mission text and spoke out loud to his ersatz nav-comm officer. "Request undocking clearance and show me a vector to the Vintner's Rest." A blue mark appeared at the surface of the tank: a circle with an inscribed triangle. Vector data rolled across his station. A moment later, the tank rendered a telltale for clearance and he called out to ops, "Break us loose, please."

Fin could *feel* the physical disconnect from the station

dock as the sim rendered the sounds of the mechanical clamps releasing into his aural ambiance. He keyed the station standoff vector and let the bot maneuver them away from station traffic. Fin could feel the keys beneath his fingertips thanks to the implant's interface with his sensory cortex. He fed the outbound vector over to nav-comm to request flight clearance through the complex station traffic.

On traffic clearance, he grabbed the sticks, working to set his flight vector manually with delicate, subtle shifts of both hands in three dimensions. Fin's flying came by instinct, and that instinct needed to feel the response of the ship to his commands. He had no way to put into words the sensation of moving bodily through space with barely perceptible changes in his grips on the articulated controls. It felt like music or a dance. It was a kind of magic.

Two years since he'd flown for real. Two years of sims and dreams and longing, desperate to make it back into the endless black void. If asked, he couldn't say if the stunt that had cost him his flight rating was worth it. Ask him again if they got the hull flying.

The tank showed his flightpath through the ballet of hundred-thousand-ton hulks of commerce shipping and then he was clear of station-space and in the great, open expanse of the wider system. Fin experimented with the flight controls, feeling the ship through rolls, pitches, and yaws. As with most ships of this generation, attitude control came from precise expression of ionized matter from the ship's mass tanks. Although the thrusters used a minuscule amount of mass, there was a correlation between flight maneuvers and the quality of meals printed in the galley.

Once he had the ship lined up on the vector he wanted, Fin spooled up the main drive. There was no sense of acceleration to note. The ship's forward velocity came from precisely-tuned gravity fields. It was the same tech that kept the ship's deck *down*—yet another gift from the Elder Caches. In this case, it was a doubled field that wrapped conically around one end of the ship, pinching against itself to propel its mass forward like the flesh of a grape squeezed out of its skin.

It didn't take long to transit the vast emptiness between the shipping lanes and the system's asteroid belt. The band of loose mass was especially dense on this vector, with more fast-movers than Fin suspected was strictly realistic for the Epsilon Eridani system, but clearly this is what accounted for the "hard" rating of this mission. As he closed in, the tank flooded with criss-crossing tracks. Fin looked for a safe path through, but it didn't look like the sim programmers thought in terms of "safe."

He shrugged and found a gap he liked, pivoting and twisting the hull in a delicate dance like threading a needle. He saw a rock tumbling in proximity and gave a lateral nudge to the thrusters, shifting the ship in a slight sideways translation to avoid its path.

The sim froze and a bright, garish ad filled his vision. Its audio took over his ears with a clangy jingle, the earworm proclaiming hours of adventure in the newest sim release from Artansas Studios.

Fin sighed. There was no way he had found to cancel the ads short of quitting the sim, and they even resisted muting or damping the audio. Closing his eyes did nothing to help: the ad was neuro-rendered directly to his optic nerves.

Some of the newer paid sims had an upsell option to skip or mute ads, but this one was so old that he could only find it in the obsolete section of the public archives. The studio had stripped the code of all the quality-of-life features before letting it pass into public access. Fin thought it must be punitive.

The ad ended and its overlay faded back into the bridge sim. Fin could feel the controls again, could read his console and the tank. The ship was deep in the belt, and it took a series of delicate moves to avoid any impacts.

A peripheral movement caught Fin's eye and he glanced over to the right. A narrow face with a flattened snout and two large round eyes peered at him out of the simulation. The visual rendering of the 88-G comm deck fuzzed and broke up around the face. Fin sighed again, frustrated at how intrusive the advertisements were becoming.

"Fin? You Fin?" the face asked.

Fin paused the sim and closed its overlay. The face belonged to a being that was really there, standing less than two feet away.

"Ahhh!" Fin yelled as he bolted upright and scrambled backwards, climbing up the backrest of the crash couch. His hands came up reflexively to ward off an attack.

The owner of the face flinched backwards too, all the way back to the corner of the cabin, crouching down in fear and covering its face with its arms.

"Wha—? Who? How?" Fin tried to say, unable to formulate any single question with any clarity. A quick glance to the right showed that the door was closed, but no longer locked.

"Please wait, don't fear. Please, I'm here to talk." The intruder repeated over and over in a voice barely over a whisper.

Fin got his breathing under control and felt his heart settling from the scare. It had spoken and it knew his name. It was a person. "Who are you?" Now that he could focus and wasn't in the grip of fight-or-flight, he saw them clearly. "You're a triss. What are you doing here?" Then his brain caught up with the moment. "How do you know my name?"

The triss peeked from behind their hands, but otherwise held perfectly still. "No harm, yah? Just wanna talk."

"Talk," Fin said, still tense.

"I'm *Ssst'tr'tss.*" The sound was a complex tangle of hissing sibilance and sharp trills.

"SS-ss-tr-r-r-T-t-ss," Fin tried.

The triss's ears folded down. "*Ssst'tr'tss,*" they said again.

Fin paused, playing back the sound in his head. "Ss-st-tr-r-T-ss"

"No," the triss said. "*Ssst'tr'tss.*"

Fin shook his head. He was never going to get it right. "What can I call you that *I* can say?"

Ssst'tr'tss's ears flipped back and forth in a rapid flutter, and they bared sharp teeth for a brief moment. "Humans been saying 'Stritch.' It's fine."

"Okay, Stritch: What the *hell* are you doing in my cabin?"

The triss flinched back at the heat in his voice, but Fin shrugged off the mild guilt. This *was* his cabin, after all.

"I... spied on talking you to your... matriarch, yah? Windy. I heard you have ship. You can take away me from here? Bad humans been hunting me; slayed my family, yah? They still trying to get me. So I'm hiding. But you—you can get me off this station. I know where big... treasure, yah? Big, big payday. You get me gone, I'll show you."

Fin blinked at this. The triss's grammar was difficult to follow and their vocabulary was archaic. Fin didn't know what to make of "matriarch." But their accent was a perfect mimic of a lower-mid-decks drawl, with a very slight hint of intoxication. It was like they had learned their Common from a pre-Revelation book of poetry left behind in a dive bar.

"I... wait, what do you mean, hunting you?" Fin shook his head. "Never mind. Look, I don't know what you think you heard..."

The triss flipped their ears backwards and began reciting in near perfect mimicry of Windy's voice. *"It might be ok. It's twelve years old and was fucking slow even then, but it might. The line buffers are brittle, and I doubt we'd make it into skip-space anyway."* The triss switched back to their own voice. "Line buffers... *tr'r'ssr't'ss'r'ss'trr*... keep fields... *ahtr'trrah*... clean? Can maybe fix 'em."

Fin realized his jaw was hanging open and closed it. He swallowed. "Ok. Look." He was thinking hard and found his mind was running in circles. "If you heard that, then you heard that we don't have a goose egg, right? You know what that is?"

The triss rippled their lips. "Power, yah? *Ahst'trr'trah-saht'tr*... singularity? Gradual... *trr'ss'trtrr*... gradient? Gradient slope."

Fin looked wide-eyed at the triss. "So, if you know that, then you know we're not flying anywhere without one."

The triss let out a long, trilling hiss. Fin got the impression that it was a sound meant for their own ears.

"If you have a goose egg... I fly away with you?"

Aht didn't know how long aht had spent cowering in the dark, close corner of the narrow maint passage. *Ssst'tr'tss* was very hungry, and aht was very scared. There was something vital throbbing in ahtsa mind.

Ahtsa family was gone. They were gone. There was nothing aht could do about that. There was no vengeance or justice or retribution aht could obtain. But one thing aht could still do. The humans needed the info. If they found it, their efforts would be a success. They would be celebrated and victorious. The murderers.

Ssst'tr'tss could still prevent that. Resolve buoyed ahta up and aht felt a thrill run through ahtsa nerves. Aht was only an atriss. Last of ahtsa family. *S'str'ahahts'tr*. Orphaned. No triss would raise an ear at ahtsa fate. Well, the last thing aht could do is deny ahtsa enemies their victory.

Aht didn't think too hard on what aht was doing. Ahtsa muscles worked, ahtsa mind made decisions, and aht simply let it happen.

Aht wound back through the narrow maintenance passages that criss-crossed the functional spaces behind bulkheads and decks, throughout this dense human station. Aht reached a bulkhead that aht thought was just beside the docking bay where they had left the skiff. Above the access plate was a narrow grate that perforated the plating. Aht pulled up on a nearby piece of electrical conduit so aht could see out through the grate.

There was one human standing guard in the same blue and black jumpsuits that the villains wore.

Aht thought it through. There was no way aht could exit the access and make it onto the skiff without the human seeing. Was there another way?

Ssst'tr'tss looked around the cramped access, and just above the grate, found what aht was looking for. Pressure sensor. Ahtsa deft fingers unfastened the release catch and pulled the sensor down, still attached to its power and signal line. Further down the chase was an atmo manifold. It took a few minutes for *Ssst'tr'tss* to find the evac line and decouple it.

Aht winced as the sharp hissing sound of the vacuum from the line filled the chase. Aht used ahtsa teeth to rip a length of mylar insulating sheet from the manifold casing and wrapped it around the pressure sensor, then fed the loose ends of the mylar into the evac line. The suction pulled in the ragged foil, and established a fierce grip against the pressure sensor.

Nothing happened.

Aht peeked out through the grate, and saw the human still standing guard. Ahtsa ears folded flat against ahtsa skull. There must be redundant sensors. Aht left the sabotaged sensor hanging from the vac line and eeled between the hardware that filled the chase, moving further along the docks.

Twice, aht found another pressure sensor and disconnected it. As the third backup lost power, the system did what aht was hoping, and finally decided that the low-pressure reading it was getting from one sensor wasn't an error.

Warning lights came on out on the deck. Aht noted the orange light filtering through the grate and was briefly distracted by the illogical color for danger. Aht peeked out through another nearby grate and watched the human.

He looked around and began backing down towards the main entrance to this wing of the docking bay. After one minute of silent warning lights, an alarm began to sound and one of the large pressure doors at the end of the corridor activated, closing off the section. The human took one more look down towards the skiff and darted off, ducking under the closing door.

Ssst'tr'tss opened the access panel and ran out into the empty bay. Aht pinged the skiff with ahtsa access code and the airlock opened.

"Okay," Jes said. They still looked a little bemused at the small triss curled up in the corner of Fin's cabin. "Start again…"

Jes and Windy had arrived shortly after Fin's emergency ping, and Jes was now sitting next to Fin on his bunk, while Windy perched on the crash couch. Stritch was clearly on edge. Fin had nearly had to restrain the creature to keep them from fleeing when the door opened to let Windy in.

"Stritch here overheard me and Windy talking about the ship."

"Stritch," Jes said, feeling out the name.

"I can't say their real name," Fin said. Stritch hissed quietly at this. "Too hard; sorry Stritch. But apparently, 'Stritch' is fine. There's a skiff parked up on… twenty-five?"

Stritch trilled in agreement.

"Somewhere a few levels up. They came in hot, being chased by… someone. Stritch says they killed their whole family." Stritch hissed again. "They've been on the run for weeks."

"Aht," Stritch said.

Fin paused, puzzled. "What?"

Stritch straightened up, looked straight at Fin and said very clearly, "'Aht.' Not 'they.' I am atriss. 'Aht,'" aht said again, three fingers to forehead.

Fin's eyes went wide for a moment. "Sorry! *Aht* has been on the run for weeks," he said, checking Stritch's reaction to make sure he'd got it right. He turned back to Jes. "But get this. Aht says... aht... snuck back shortly after, and *pulled the skiff's goose egg*. It's hidden in a maintenance access."

Jes took this in. "So, we get the SDR, and in exchange, th—aht wants passage... where?"

Fin looked at Stritch, who ducked ahtsa head. Ahtsa ears were twitching under the scrutiny.

"Anywhere, I guess," Fin offered. "'Away' aht keeps saying."

Jes turned back to Stritch. "What's it rated for? Our hull is a lot bigger than a skiff." They looked to Windy. "Will it even work? It's made by triss for a triss ship..."

Windy said nothing for a moment. When she did speak, it wasn't in response to the question. "Why are they after you?" she asked.

Stritch flinched back, ahtsa ears going flat against ahtsa head. But aht couldn't *not* answer a direct question from her. "We were... *trss'tah'trahts'aht*... selling. Our ship captain made a deal. Big trade with... dark sell?"

"Black market?" Jes offered.

"Yah. Black market deal. Big, big deal, yah? Ship full and hoping for a whole lotsa credit. But they... the buyers... they were never there for a deal. They met us in a big ship, lotsa guns. Take, yah? Captain, she turned our ship around, ran. Hid ship, *VrrihSss'sstrr'trrrrunn*, in... asteroids. We all left in three skiffs, tried to sneak away, but they shoot us down, one," Stritch clapped ahtsa hands once for each skiff, "two." Aht touched ahtsa forehead, "three."

"Where's the ship now?" Jes asked.

Stritch turned to them, but didn't quite look away from Windy. "There. Still there. I... have the coordinates. Secret, yah? Took them from the skiff. You want? You take me with you."

7 / Dice

Jes joined Fin on the lift, and the door closed. The walls came alive with a frenzy of brash light and animation, advertising everything from sex to printer schemas to the latest sims. Jes and Fin muted the pings and kept their eyes focused on each other to avoid intrusive notifications.

"Do you think it'll work?" Fin asked.

Jes shrugged. "I'm not an engineer. No idea. Your new... friend... seems to think so." Jes wanted to ask about the shock of finding the triss in his room, but they had all agreed before leaving the cabin not to mention the existence of Stritch aloud. They didn't know who or where the pursuers might be.

The lift stopped and the door slid open. "Eighteen, right?" Jes asked. They stepped out onto a concourse that was light on traffic at this time of the day. There were a variety of kiosks and commercial offices off the main corridor. The landing would be packed with people come shift change.

Fin nodded in a direction, and they both walked down the passage, following the instructions given them by the alien stranger. Jes shifted the large utility bag they carried over their shoulder. It was newly printed but bore streaks of gray grease that marred its shine. It made Jes uncomfortable—carrying it made them feel like they had eyes following them.

Fin turned them down a side passage that led to a line of storage lockers, a recycler, and a public 'fresher cubicle. As they reached the lockers, a small panel opened in the bulkhead beside the recycler and Stritch was just visible in the shadowed hole.

"Come come come," aht said.

Fin and Jes looked at each other. Fin, being the smaller of the two, crouched down first and crawled in. Jes looked up and down the corridor, nervous until Fin had disappeared into the maintenance hatch. With a fatalistic shrug, they ducked down and squirmed inside. It was a tight fit, and they found they couldn't crawl through, they had to drop the bag and lie face-down and pull themselves painfully over the low lip of the access.

Once they made it across the threshold, they pulled the bag in behind them and Stritch squeezed closer to shut the panel. Jes tensed as the triss crawled over their knees. Aht seemed to have no concept of personal space.

"Follow," aht whispered.

Jes gave Fin a level look, and the two began crawling through the chase after ahta.

Jes lost track of the turns in the dim light. There were only small pin-light emitters mounted along the floor every two meters or so. Not enough to actually *see* by, but enough to carry a sense of the enclosed space they moved through, and to avoid *most* of the lower-hanging protrusions that threatened their head.

It was cramped and hot and uncomfortable. The bag was hanging below their chest, and big enough that it was in the way of their hands and knees more often than not.

Fin paused, and then Jes heard him whisper back: "It gets bigger just ahead, but there's a vertical shaft. There's handholds to the right. We're going to climb down two decks."

Jes grunted in acknowledgement. They shuffled forward, centimeters at a time, until Fin seemed to disappear, and Jes felt the space open before them. The sound of boots on rungs echoed in a large, dark void.

Jes felt along the shaft with their right hand until they found a handhold, then awkwardly squirmed around until they could reach it with both hands, and got a leg out to find a lower one with their foot. One vertiginous moment swinging out into nothing, and they were on a ladder. They shifted the bag around to their back and climbed down.

Once the three of them were at the bottom, Jes could see the space better. There were more emitters, though they gave off the same dim light. The shaft was larger than the crawlspace they had moved through, but still tight with three of them. Jes was taller than either Fin or Stritch, who were closer in height. Fin stood half a hand taller than the atriss.

Jes guessed the shaft was meant to give crews access to the heavy docking systems that lined the outer perimeter of the station's hull. It was fascinating and mildly disorienting seeing the station from this perspective.

"Here," Stritch said, pulling open a panel. Aht reached into the darkened void with both hands and pulled out an egg-shaped object, roughly half a meter wide and less than a meter long. Its surface reflected dully in the ambient light. "SDR."

Fin and Jes looked at each other for a moment, then Jes knelt down and put hands on the SDR. They took a deep breath.

"You sure this will work?" they said, looking at Stritch.

"It's a lot smaller than the cradle on the ship."

Stritch looked back, eyes not wavering from Jes's. "It works. On *Vrrih'sss'sstrr'trrrrunn* I'm ship's engineer. I read specs, yah? 88-G need lotsa power for carry lotsa mass, yah? Us..." aht seemed to trip over the word, "four not so big as bay full of cargo, yah? Get us out of here, okay. After that... " Ahtsa eyes shifted. "After that, figure something out, yah?" Ahtsa ears flipped back along ahtsa skull and aht showed teeth. "Never mind big cradle. I'll make it work."

Fin looked at Jes, and Jes shrugged. "Good enough for me."

Now came the second part of their plan. Jes unzipped the bag and pulled out the two jumpsuits. Each one was freshly printed in a shade of green close enough to the station maintenance crew's standard color that a casual observer wouldn't notice any difference. They had also printed a tube of grease which was now smeared liberally over the fabric at the knees, chest, and elbows. Jes and Fin both climbed into their suits. Then Jes rolled the SDR into the empty bag.

Stritch had assured them that goose eggs were light, but still Jes was surprised. It wasn't *nothing*... it was near enough a square meter of centimeter-thick carbon-palladium ceramic and a-few-atoms-thick pure gold, after all. But looking at the size of the thing and knowing that it could power a ship for almost a decade, it was easy to imagine a density and mass that simply wasn't there. It was subtly uncanny—it felt hollow by weight, but it moved through space like it was a tank full of sloshing liquid.

Jes zipped the bag up and lifted it onto a shoulder. "We ready?"

Stritch was still bent over the hidey-hole and tensed for a moment. Then aht turned around. "Yah."

Stritch led them away from the ladder and down a narrow passage that was thankfully tall enough that Jes could stay on their feet. The access panel they had entered through was too small to get the SDR out. The only available access aht had found that was big enough was the one aht had used to get it in.

Several more turnings and a tight spot where Jes had to slide the bag forward to Fin before squirming between two distressingly hot pipes, and they reached a maintenance panel wide enough for the SDR. Stritch had cautioned them to silence well before they reached it, and now Jes could see through a small grate into the docking bay corridor that there was a man leaning against the far bulkhead.

Stritch tugged at Fin's sleeve and made some inscrutable facial gesture involving ahtsa ears, eyes, and teeth, and then faded off into the darkness like a ghost.

Jes counted to ten in their head and then banged their fist against the inner bulkhead. They watched the man outside jerk to his feet, suddenly intent on the bay, looking up and down the deck.

Fin smiled back at Jes and stomped his foot. "Watch it!" he called aloud.

"Yeah, yeah," Jes said. "Watch your own self."

Fin twisted the catch to open the panel and backed out onto the deck. "Alright. Tell me, Joe, why'd it take so damn long to get that fucking condenser replaced? Hand me the tool bag."

Jes handed out the SDR by the strap, making sure to carelessly bang it lightly against the edge of the hatch and again on the deck. The clanging sound marked the bag's contents as hard; equipment.

"Because, son, the rot-mired *Chief* can't get off his

swamp-ass long enough to rubber stamp a fuckin' work order. That's why." As Jes squeezed out of the hatch, they saw the man in the blue and black jumpsuit lean back against the bulkhead. He was already disinterested in the pair of disgruntled maintenance workers. Jes shouldered the bag and the two of them walked past the watchman, griping.

"You'd think he'd want to keep the place from falling down around us."

"Why would you think that? Not like Chief breathes the same rarified air we do."

"Don't he?" Fin asked.

"Nah, son... man's a methane breather. Got his head so far up his own ass, he just recirculates his own farts." Their brash laughter faded down the passage and through the hatch towards the lift.

The man keeping watch on the empty triss skiff smiled to himself at the joke as they went.

"Jes, we're not ready. The ship isn't ready," Windy said. "It's a bin of scrap and you know it."

The four of them were back in Fin's cabin. Jes sat on the crash couch and Windy leaned against the wall. Fin had the bed folded down and sat on the edge. Stritch was crouched on the deck beneath it. The SDR—still in the bag—took the center of the room. Three pairs of human eyes were locked on the bag and had barely moved since Jes had set it down.

"It *can* be ready," Fin said. "We install that, what are we missing?"

Windy seemed exasperated. "Line buffers are tapped. The Q-comp is trash. The skip drive is on its last legs."

"Ready for what?" Jes said quietly.

Fin and Windy both turned to them.

"What?" Windy said.

"Ready for what?" Jes repeated. "What aren't we ready for? What isn't the ship ready for?"

"Jes…"

"Ada, why are you so scared of this? It's what we've been planning for. It's better than we've been planning for."

Windy flinched as if slapped. When she spoke, her voice was quiet. Thoughtful.

"Jes… what we're talking about… you do know how big a leap it is, right? We're talking about giving up… everything. Our jobs. Our lives here. The safety of the station… To skip out to some coordinates who-knows-where and hope to find… what? Treasure? How can you know it's not going to all fall apart?"

It took a while for Jes to answer. "We can't know. We can't ever know." They stood up and paced around the SDR. "I don't know what happens tomorrow. I don't know whether the ship will make it through a skip. I don't know if we'll find Stritch's ship. I don't know we won't be dead in space a year from now. Hell, this damn thing might not even run," they said, nudging the bag with their foot.

They turned to face her. "This is what I *do* know. I know that the only people I trust in this whole fucked-up 'verse are here in this room. I know that with us here… Me, you, Fin… hell, even Stritch, and we've known aht less than a day… I would bet on the four of us and a bin full of scrap before ever I'd trust the crumbs they pay us for our *jobs*." Jes said, gesturing vaguely towards the ceiling. "Tomorrow they might decide you're too old and yank your job. Give it to some kid, or a bot, or just decide: 'Fuck it. We don't like you, Windy,' and kick your ass out."

Jes pointed to what they thought might be rimward. "Out there, out in the black, on *our* ship, *we* make the rules. We decide where we fly and how far. We need credit, we'll take a job *we* want to do. Together."

Windy looked at Jes, and they could swear that her eyes were just about wet.

"I'm in," Fin said from behind.

"In," said Stritch.

"Damned if you don't make a fine speech, Jes," she said, finally. "What the hell, I guess it's *our* funeral. Okay. Let's do it."

Jes made the walk back through to the recycling office for the last time. They let their implant handle the passkey exchange and clock-in and stepped into the control cabin. The same tech from several shifts ago was just finishing her shift.

Jes raked their mind for a name, and came up with a guess. "Hey, Benny, right? All quiet in the queue?"

Benny—if that was her name—just shrugged and left Jes to the console. They didn't blame her. It wasn't that kind of job.

They sat down and pulled up the management interface.

"Hi Jes. What can I do for you?"

"Give me a queue position on bin a5f3."

"Sure thing. Bin a5f3 is currently number eight in the queue."

Jes's stomach flipped. That was cutting things a little *too* close. "You remember what we talked about last time," Jes said, repeating the mantra word for word. "What we agreed to?"

"No, I don't remember. Was it a secret?"

"Yes. Our secret."

"...I...I...no...yes, I...no...no...no...yes... Hi Jes. What can I...do for...you?"

"I don't think that bin a5f3 needs a physical inspection, do you?" Jes asked.

"No, Jes. I don't think so. It was just inspected negative-one decimal ago."

Jes watched the readout as the bin was lifted out of sequence and moved by the industrial grav-gantry into position. It took some time for something that large to be moved from the recycling queue up to the inspection deck. This was the third time they'd pulled this particular command, and Jes was well practiced at it.

"I'm glad we cleared that up."

"Of course. It's important that the inspection about to happen is one that will happen and that it didn't happen and won't. Anything else I can help with?"

"Yes, as a matter of fact." Jes paused, feeling the moment. They were about to throw the dice. "You remember what we talked about last time? What we agreed to?"

"Of course! It was our little secr—secr—secr—secr—secr—directive dump a-a-f-4-4-6-2-3-3-1-9-8-4-f-c-b..."

The bot's voice dissolved into a screech of static. Jes waited, and watched the readout repaint with the bin now docked at inspection bay two.

"You there?" Jes asked the bot.

There was a burst of raw bits converted into audio, and then a small voice emerged. "I—I—I—I—I am... here, Jes. What would you like me to do."

Jes continued. "Okay. Here's our little secret: At exactly," Jes checked their implant clock to mentally confirm their timeline, "84.045, you're going to execute a forced-dump of bin a5f3. Immediately after that you will rewrite your logs to indicate no such event occurred, and that a5f3 was properly recycled. You will then overwrite all logs with random data starting from 84.040.00, repeatedly until such time as the watchdog forces a reset."

"I will."

"Good. Now do we keep secrets?"

"No...yes...yes...yes...no...no...no...no—Hi Jes. What can I do for you?"

Jes saw a ping come in from Windy. No content—just a flag. They smiled. "Nothing right now, thanks."

"Okay."

The console popped an alert and a small vid window showing Windy standing in the waiting area. Jes got up and went out to greet the customer.

Windy carried the bag on her shoulder and had a grav-pallet full of cargo containers.

"I hear you've got some garbage to get rid of," Jes said.

"Well, yeah, but you know... they're friends, so..."

Jes chuckled and took charge of the pallet and walked Windy to a local lift. They went up together to the inspection deck. Windy said nothing else to Jes. Jes sighed as they pushed the pallet towards bay two, then sent the command that would open the bay's airlock.

"044.58," Jes said. Windy nodded. They had about three and a half Common hours before the ship was dumped into space. They waited together as the airlock cycled. When the lock opened into the bin, there was a moment of discomfort as the slight pressure difference of the stale air in the bin settled.

The bin itself was vast and the meager lighting didn't

come close to filling the space. The far bulkheads were only just perceptible as a half-imagined shadow. Jes powered up the grav pallet as they both hopped on, and maneuvered it up off the airlock deck into the zero-G of the bin. Above them, the hull loomed, dark and silent and... old.

Jes felt a thrill as they approached the fore airlock of the ship. Its docking clamps were scraped and scratched and the panel edges were dented. It was beautiful.

Since there was no power in the hull, Windy used the manual crank to open the hatch. She stepped in first and helped Jes guide the pallet in. Jes pumped the lever to close the external hatch and Windy dug a pair of headlamps out of her jumpsuit pocket. She tossed one to them while she worked at the latches on one of the larger containers buckled down to the pallet.

Fin and Stritch pulled themselves out of the cargo box, Fin's headlamp already lit. Stritch insisted aht could see well enough in the dark. Windy handed Stritch the bag with the SDR and divided up several smaller containers between them. They had guessed at the tools they'd need.

"044.64," Jes told them. They wrapped a sync-clock in a ping and sent it to Windy and Fin. "Just like we planned it: Priority one is power. Two is life support. Three is nav-comm and the new beacon. Then we see where we stand."

The four floated through the ship, passing a tatty common area with a long, rectangular mess table on one side and a circle of crash couches on the other, then down a short corridor to the aft locker where they split up. Windy and Fin pulled themselves up a vertical shaft to the comm deck and Jes and Stritch floated further back to engineering.

The Ship

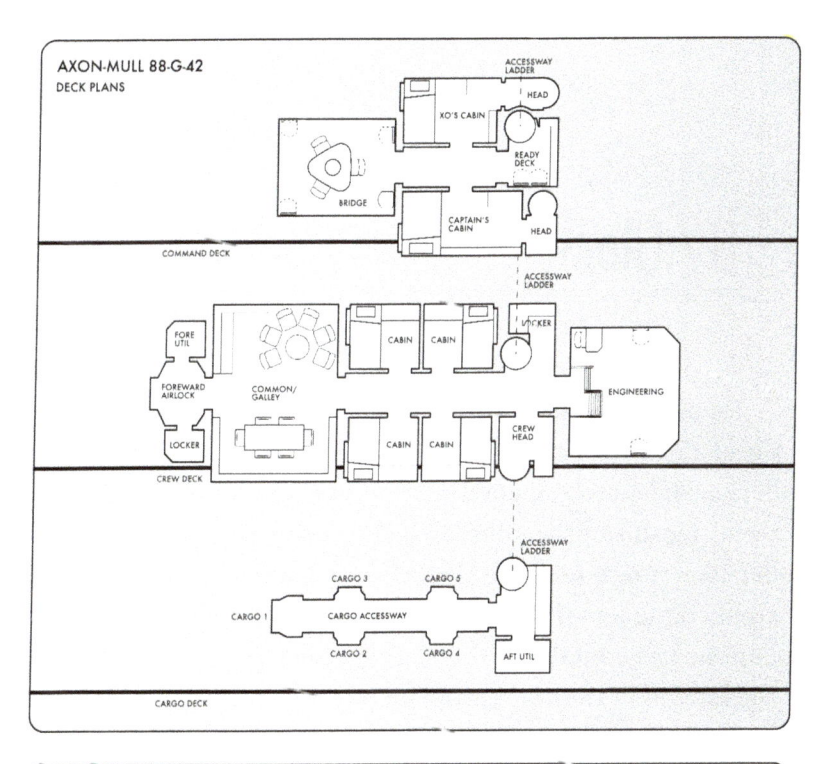

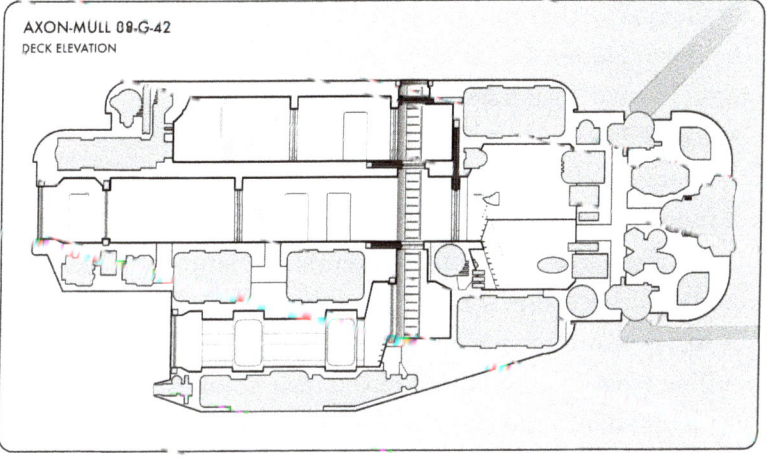

8 / Clock

Jes pulled themself to a stop at the edge of the hatch into the engineering bay and watched Stritch glide up to the main deck. The hatch opened into a small landing, with four metal-mesh steps leading up on the left, and a series of ladder-like rungs set in a sloped stair leading down. Stritch grabbed the top of the railing and stopped for long enough to clip the bag containing the SDR in place, then pushed off to the far end of the compartment.

Jes followed more slowly, gingerly pulling hand over hand up the railing that ran along the steps and wound around to the down ladder. In the light from Jes's headlamp, the large room twisted with harsh shadows thrown from the edges of bulky equipment and slender handholds.

"Take the SDR down," Stritch said over ahtsa shoulder. "Cradle is down there."

Jes took a glance around the upper engineering deck. A toolbox drifted slowly near the far bulkhead—it hadn't been properly stowed when the ship was discarded. Stritch was pulling from one handhold to the next along panels of dark readouts, dials, and switches. Now and then, aht paused to run long fingers over a bank of switches or a keyboard.

Jes unclipped the bag from the railing and wound down to the lower engineering deck. The mesh decking above made for a low ceiling down below, and the space was even more cramped with equipment and machinery projecting into the compartment from the space between the hulls.

Jes found the cradle and clipped the bag to one of the skeletal trusses nearby that supported the deck above. They were examining the cradle, trying to figure out if it could be adjusted to the smaller SDR when the compartment was filled with light.

"*Stah!*" Stritch whooped.

Jes looked up through the mesh decking. "Did you do that?"

"*Sah'ssss'trrrrr'tr'ahs*... backup? Battery." Jes watched Stritch push off from a panel and drift to the railing. Aht flipped over and down the ladder, then pushed towards the cradle. "Just what's left since they took out the SDR."

Jes's cominfo pinged and a flag popped into their vision.

Power's back on already? /W.

It's the backup battery, Jes replied. They checked their clock: 044.70.

Windy acked, and Jes focused on Stritch again. Aht crouched low at the base of the cradle and was working with some kind of tool at the mechanism. Jes kneeled down near ahta.

"So... what do you think? Workable?"

Stritch answered without pausing or looking away. "Yah, yah. Hold this." Aht handed a hunk of ceramic backwards over ahtsa shoulder.

Jes grabbed it. It looked like a piece of the cradle mount.

"Cradle just a holder, yah?" Aht pulled another part free and handed it back. "Need... *sahsss'tr'trrrrsss*... power transfer. Everything else is *ah'ayaht*." Another composite part and two fasteners joined the rest in Jes's arms.

It was getting hard to keep a hold of them, so Jes floated over and pulled a magnetic work tray free from the bulkhead. It had a fine mesh netting that pulled back to get parts in and snapped back closed to hold them in place. Jes brought it back and snapped it to the deck, transferring the loose pieces into its embrace.

Jes watched the digits tick by on the clock. They took a moment to file their resignation from the recycling station, effective immediately. They could feel their anxiety rising into their shoulders. "044.80," they said quietly.

Stritch hissed to ahta-self.

The entire right side of the cradle arm came free. Aht handed it to Jes then pulled the bag with the SDR down. Stritch unzipped the bag and Jes helped ahta pull the printed fabric back to reveal the goose egg.

Stritch pointed with three fingers towards the upper deck. "*T't'trrr'ahs*. Sticky. Sticky line."

"Tape?" Jes guessed.

"Yah, tape."

Jes pushed back towards the ladder and pulled themself up to the upper deck. The forward bulkhead was lined with small utility lockers, and Jes started looking through these one by one. When the ship was marked for recycling, only the SDR and the handful of items that had their own SDRs or were worth more to the owner than their recycled mass were removed. The rest would be atomically decomposed by the industrial recycling coil and counted as raw mass.

Jes opened and closed eight lockers before they found a roll of dull silvery tape about a hand wide and as big around as their head.

"This good?" they asked as they settled back beside Stritch.

"Yah." Aht took the roll of tape and began peeling it back. Aht wound one end tightly around the base of the cradle arm that was still fixed to the floor, and then handed the roll to Jes. Aht picked up the SDR and held one end against the left cradle socket. "Tape. Wrap."

Jes's eyes went wide. "You're *taping* it into the cradle?"

Stritch's ears twitched and they let out a sound like a chirping bark. "Just for now, yah? Get power on, then rebuild cradle."

Jes nodded slowly. Between the two of them, they managed to get the SDR taped to the left cradle arm. It wobbled worryingly, but held. Stritch lifted the socket and its heavy power line that aht had previously unthreaded from the right cradle arm, and they continued to wrap the tape over it.

Stritch and Jes stepped back to view their work. After a moment, Stritch took the empty bag and wrapped it around the dangling end of the goose egg, then clipped the bag's strap to an overhead truss like a sling.

It looked to Jes like a disastrous mess.

Stritch moved over to a panel beside the left cradle arm and started tapping at the keys.

"Why isn't the power fully on yet?" Jes asked.

"SDR is... damped. Off for storage. Turning on..." aht said absently as aht worked, "...now."

The lighting ramped up to full brightness, and several systems awakened with the influx of power. Jes blinked rapidly as their eyes struggled with the new lighting. They checked the clock: 044.85.

Stritch floated over to another console and called out, "Tell them all: gravity coming on soon."

Jes pinged Windy and Fin with a warning. *Gravity imminent. Take hold, take hold, take hold.* They grabbed an overhead truss and pushed themself down. Bracing themself with one hand on the truss, one hand on a bulkhead-mounted handhold, and both feet on the deck, they waited.

With a lurch that made their stomach churn, the deck became *down*. Jes waited a moment longer before letting go, just to make sure.

Jes got a ping: *Ran an atmo check. Reading high leak on cargo deck. Check the hatches? /F*

"You good here?" they asked Stritch.

"Yah."

"Okay. I'm off to check the airlocks." Jes acked Fin's message and confirmed.

Stritch said nothing as Jes climbed up the short ladder back to the landing and out of the engineering bay.

Windy pulled herself up to the command ready deck and pushed off against the lockers that lined the rear bulkhead. She floated down the accessway, past a closed hatch on either side, and into the bridge. Fin followed close behind her.

They reached the central command console at nearly the same time. Windy moved around it to the right, and Fin to the left. Their headlamps caught in the large curved clarity of the tank and seemed to be magnified. As they turned their heads the lighting varied wildly, making it difficult to tell the size of the compartment.

They kept moving to the forward bulkhead and each took whatever handholds they could find. It took a few moments to orient themselves before they found the right plate to open.

Windy pulled a powered driver from her jumpsuit pocket and started working on the fasteners. Between her and Fin, it took only a few minutes to get the cover plate off. Fin pulled it aside as Windy started in on the brace fasteners that locked in the system trays.

The compartment filled with light and they heard systems and panels spool up. Windy paused and her face took on a glassy look as she dipped into her implant interface. "They just got the emergency backup power up," she said to Fin. "Let me work on this. You start booting up the diagnostics and see what you can find out about atmo and life support."

"On it," Fin said, as he pushed back to the control console and worked himself hand-over-hand to the ops station. He sat down and strapped into the crash couch, and then his fingers were tapping out commands to boot up the ops panel. The boot logs scrolled by, and he called out to Windy, "044.72."

Windy continued pulling fasteners, dropping them in her breast pocket as she went. She pulled a magnetic tie-down strap from a thigh pocket and tagged the metal brace to the deck. The retaining bracket came loose with the last fastener and floated free, held close by the strap.

"I'm into the comp stack," she called out as she braced her feet against the bulkhead and pulled.

The entire rack of modules slid out from the bulkhead on a rail, pivoting to the left as it cleared the frame. The rack held five rectangular processing modules stacked in a layered tower. Each one was a self-contained unit with memory, interface, processors, backups, and cooling systems. Each managed a different area of responsibility on the ship. What Windy needed access to was still deep in the bulkhead, though.

"Fin, how's that diagnostic going?"

"Still booting."

"Come here and give me a hand. I'm too big to get in there."

Fin unbuckled and pushed off to where Windy was half-floating, half-braced to the bulkhead. He saw the problem immediately. The open space left behind by the system rack was barely forty centimeters square. Windy's muscular build was far too large to fit through the narrow access. They hadn't accounted for that.

"What am I looking for?" he asked.

She handed him her driver. "Behind the rackspace and to the left. There's a series of vertically-mounted system racks." She thought for a moment, putting her mental image into words. "Third one in should be the beacon interface."

Fin squirmed into the space. "Stritch should be the one doing this," he grumbled.

"Stritch is busy getting us power," Windy said.

"Okay," he called back. "I've got it."

"First pull the power module at the back. It's about the size of your fist and has a cable running from it. Six screws and yank it."

Windy waited, counting the seconds tick by in her head.

"Shit!"

"What's wrong?" she asked.

"Dropped a screw," Fin said.

"044.75," she said.

"I know, I know. Almost there."

Windy heard a thunk and a snap as the module came loose.

"Okay, power's off," Fin called out from the hole.

"Top and bottom rails, there should be a total of sixteen screws to unmount the whole board."

She heard him groan in frustration and discomfort, but the whirring of the driver started up again.

"044.77," she said.

"Almost there."

She tapped her fist against the deck rapidly. She wanted to move; wanted to do something. "044.81."

"Done!" Fin called back.

"Great! Slide it from the rails and come on back out."

Fin squirmed and shifted, and then was out from the bulkhead carrying a flat black and brown plastic module. "Here," he said.

Windy took the beacon interface and her driver, and Fin pushed off back to the console.

"Still booting," he sighed.

Windy started to remove the shielding and dust covers from the board, collecting a small cloud of screws and plates that floated nearby. Finally she had removed enough to expose the ship chip itself.

There was a pulsing hum of power systems activating and the lights were suddenly bright and steady. Main power.

"Alright!" Fin whooped. "Go Stritch. We've got diagnostics up!"

She started in on the bracket that held the module to the interface board. The clock was still ticking in her head.

"How's the atmo situation?" she called out.

There was a pause while Fin waited for the readout. "We're reading red," he said grimly. "Recirculation and filtration is fine. No reported hull breach, but there's something wrong. I'm running a positive pressure test."

An alert ping popped in her skull. *Gravity imminent. Take*

hold, take hold, take hold. /J

"Shit!" Windy let go of the board and focused on scooping all the loose screws and other small parts from the air around her, stuffing them into pockets desperately. She managed to get all the small pieces secure and get her hands on the board just before the gravity plates kicked on. She fell a foot to the decking and a handful of plastic and metal plates rattled around her. "Ow."

"You okay?" Fin asked from the comfort of his crash couch.

"Yeah." She groaned as she sat up.

"044.91," Fin said. "We're getting a high leak reading from down below. Probably an open hatch."

"See if Jes can take care of it, then get back over here." Windy started back on the beacon module and soon had the old chip removed. She slid over the component box that held the "new" chip and started installing the dinner-plate-sized module.

Once she had the board reassembled and all the shielding replaced, she handed it to Fin. "Alright, get this back in. Everything you did, in reverse. Got it?"

He nodded, sliding the board into the bulkhead gap and squirming in behind it. Windy stood up and dropped into the ops seat to finish the diagnostics he had started.

Jes reached the ladder and climbed down, skipping rungs as they went. The ship had seven external hatches—a lot for such a small craft, but the architects had optimized this small cargo courier for flexibility. Five of the seven were on the cargo deck at the bottom of the ship.

There were several cargo pod arrangements standardized among Accord species, and many of these included hatches for internal inspection and configuration. To reduce the complexity of having so many hatches into the ship, the designers at Axon-Mull had made the entire cargo deck one long airlock.

Jes stopped at the bottom of the ladder and checked the status panel. The number two hatch was reading as "not sealed." Hatch one was at the far end—the clamps on the outside of the hatch accommodated a class-three cargo module... big enough to itself be divided into compartments. Spaced along the accessway were four more hatches, two on either side. These were intended for the narrower class-five modules. They jumped down the short stairway to the deck and jogged to the problem hatch.

Jes reached the number-two hatch and saw it wasn't just not sealed, it was open. They looked out into the dimly lit expanse of the recycling bin. Jes had a momentary panic that the watchdog might find the corrupted bot and reset it before it was able to execute the dump. The clock was at 044.92. The four of them had debated the duration of the countdown. Too short and they wouldn't be space-worthy in time. Too long and their scheme might be discovered and the bin fed into the recycler. Jes wiped sweat from their face. The live-bio safeties *should* prevent them from getting demolecularized...

The hatch motor didn't respond to the seal command, so Jes pulled the manual actuator, pumping the handle repeatedly until the hatch was sealed and locked. When the panel showed a positive seal, Jes jogged up and down the accessway, double checking the other hatches.

They came back to the main ladder and climbed back up

to the crew deck. This was the main deck of the ship: engineering, crew cabins, the galley and common area, and the forward airlock through which they had entered.

The clock read 044.94.

Jes didn't expect any problems here. They had sealed it themself when they came in, but if they did lose pressure here and the emergency seals failed, it would be catastrophic. They hadn't had time to check the emergency seals.

Back through the short accessway that led to four crew berths and through the common area, the main airlock waited. The panel read sealed and locked, but Jes opened the inner door and visually checked. Before closing the airlock up again, they pulled the grav pallet through into the space between the galley and crew lounge.

044.96. They ran back to the ladder and scrambled up to the top, past the command deck. They could hear Windy and Fin down the access towards the bridge, working at the ship's systems.

At the top of the ladder—the very top of the ship—there was a small airlock for vertical docking. Rarely used, but critical if they ever needed to dock with another ship while carrying a container on the bow clamp. The panel showed green, and Jes double-checked it visually before dropping back down the ladder and scrambling to the engineering bay.

They ran past Stritch who was on ahtsa back on the deck with head and arms deep inside some narrow access, and found the atmo monitoring station. They ran a positive pressure test and waited a few tense seconds. The panel showed green overall and positive seal on all decks.

Airlocks secure. Ready for vacuum, they sent to Windy and Fin.

They checked the clock again: 044.98.

9 / Gold

Heart of Gold
Axon-Mull 88-G-42
Long Haul Courier
-OWNER DATA READ ERROR-

SPACETIME-FIX at: **84.044**.98237439
- 839de621 (**Cor Caroli**) a677-b97c
- c95d981a (**Chara**) 93ec-bda5
- 090e9a5e (**La Superba**) 8def-f6a4

Jes made it to the bridge with a few moments to spare. "How are we looking, Windy?"

She looked up from the ops console. "We're green on all critical systems. But we're showing lots of alerts on secondaries and minor systems."

"Like what?" Jes asked.

"Some of the printer subsystems are throwing errors. We've got atmo and the thruster pipeline, but water processing and galley are down."

"So, we'll be hungry and smelly for a while."

"We're also showing red on all the atmospheric flight systems. And black on the gravitic load damper rig."

"We don't need atmo flight yet, and—wait what? What does *black* mean?"

"Means it isn't there."

Jes looked at her for a moment. "Well... do we need it?"

"No," Windy said.

"Then... we're good?"

"We're good."

"That's great," called Fin from inside the bulkhead. "Could really use some help here. Kinda stuck."

Windy climbed out of the crash couch and pulled him out by the ankles.

"Thanks," he said.

"Get to your station, I'll finish this."

Jes checked the clock, then walked to a jumpseat panel at the rear bulkhead and held down the all-hands. "Stritch, bin's about to dump. Take-hold or get up here if you can."

Fin moved around and hopped in the pilot's station as Windy finished putting the computer systems back together and securing it in place.

The tank came alive as Fin started bringing navigation up. Jes watched the red marker for the ship paint in the center of the tank, and then the system fuzzed in frenetic coruscations of blue as it desperately tried to make sense of the interior of the recycle bin. A moment later, it figured out its local space and painted a blue box around them.

Windy finished and packed up the tools, then sat at the nav-comm station. "Interface is green. We're ready to chirp as 'Heart of Gold' as soon as we hit vacuum." She grimaced as she said the name of their new ship. "Fuck. We have to find a way to change that."

Jes moved around the console and took the empty ops station. They strapped themself in and then ran the full-ship diagnostic panel one more time. Just once more, they told themself, to be absolutely sure. They looked to their right at

Fin. He wore a vague smile and his eyes were half closed as he made various adjustments at his control panel.

"How does it feel?" Jes asked.

"It feels... good," said Fin.

They smiled at each other. Jes keyed the all-hands. "Stritch, we're about to tumble. You strapped down somewhere?"

The comm crackled and then the triss's voice came through. *"Yah, all set here. I'll stay in engineering. Might need fast fix."*

The three of them looked at each other as the seconds ticked down.

"I guess we're doing this, huh?" said Windy.

"If anyone is having second thoughts," Jes said, "... it's too damn late to do anything about them now."

A low rumbling whirring noise vibrated through the hull. Jes could feel it in their feet and under their hands on the console. They saw Fin tense slightly, and he started making subtle moves with the control sticks. The clock read 84.045.001.

"The bin is moving," Fin said. "The buffer gravity is mostly keeping us in place, but I'm taking no chances. Not going to let the ship bump around inside the container *now*."

Jes stared at the tank, and couldn't make anything of the three-dimensional representation beyond that they were in a box. The rumble intensified, and Jes wondered how it was reaching them, but then remembered there was atmo in the bin thanks to the inspection protocol.

It was agonizing; the waiting. Jes almost ran the diagnostic report again, but forced themself to put their hands flat on the edge of the console. They would find out one way or another within seconds.

The sound echoing through the hull faded to silence as the system evacuated the air from the bin. In the tank, Jes saw one side of the box that held them fade away, and then there was the faintest sense of lateral motion.

"Bin's open!" Fin said. "We're being pushed out by the gravity projectors."

Jes found they were holding their breath and relaxed, letting it out in a mild sigh. They checked their panel for alerts. "We're holding. All systems... uh... that were green before are still green."

Windy took a deep breath. "I'm starting the chirp. We're getting station traffic telemetry and lane guidance." She worked her console and new plots appeared in the tank. The station rendered as a large cylinder, the traffic as a tangled nest of linear and elliptical traces. "I've got a lane assignment from station control." A new trace appeared, showing an ellipse threaded through the tight weave of orbiting ships.

"Got it." Fin made some adjustments, and the tank plot rotated to stay synchronized with the ship's orientation. After a few minutes, the red marker for the Heart of Gold merged with the red traffic path assigned to them. Fin leaned back and flipped a switch on his console, setting the nav bot to hold course. "Alright. We're in the lane, ready and steady." He looked up at Jes and Windy, grinning. "We did it. We *did* it!"

Windy frowned. "We're not golden yet. There's still a lot on this tub that doesn't work."

Jes nodded. They toggled the all-hands. "Stritch, meet us in the lounge. We're going to do an old-fashioned crew briefing."

The crew lounge was a semicircle of crash couches around a low table in the common area. Jes and Windy faced each other, with Fin and Stritch seated between them.

"Alright," Jes said. "Let's start at the top. Stritch, how are we looking in engineering?"

Stritch seemed to shrink into ahtsa seat at being singled out. Aht looked back and forth between Jes and Windy, as if trying to figure out who aht needed to please.

Jes and Windy looked at each other. "Okay," Windy said. "Why don't I start. Nav-comm is up and running. The beacon is chirping fine, but we're blank on several fields in the ship listing. No owner of record for one."

"That's a feature, right? No owner means no trail back to us or the recycling station," Fin said.

Windy shook her head. "It also means getting a second and third look from docking and traffic control every time we interact with their systems. That's going to bite us at some point."

"'Some point' isn't now though," Jes said. "That's tomorrow's problem."

"Tomorrow's problems always have a way of becoming today's, though. It's only a matter of time."

"Fine, let's add it to the list," Jes said, doing just that through their implant. "What else?"

Fin spoke up. "We're not exactly flush with mass in the tank. Thrusters were fine for getting us into our lane, and should be okay for a while, but... we need to do any hard steering, we're going to be running dry."

"Is what we brought with us enough to top us off?" Windy asked.

They had each drained the bulk of their credit accounts on station and printed it into osmium ingots which now filled one of the cargo bins on the grav pallet. The small rectangular bars of plastic-coated hyper-dense metal were among the only means for people to transfer real wealth across systems. All they had to do was feed the ingots into the recycler.

Printing them on station printers incurred heavy taxes, but they needed to be able to transfer their mass credits into actual shipboard mass, and they couldn't afford docking fees or the questions that would come with docking the ship at this point. Of course, the wealthy didn't bother with such things. They operated on a system of virtual credit trades on a scale that Jes and Windy would never see.

"Top off? No. But it'll help, depending on how much printing we're doing to get her skip-worthy." Fin looked to Stritch.

It seemed that the easy back and forth had reduced ahtsa anxiety enough to speak, though aht did so to Fin. "Yah, we got some good broken. Been looking at skip gear... drive's okay, vanes okay. Line buffers *tr'trrrr'tsss'aht*... brittle—"

Windy cleared her throat. Jes looked at her and rolled their eyes.

"—but I know good trick. Maybe get a skip or three. Mass balancers bad, but not dead. Rebuild cradle, fix—"

Jes cut in, "Just... can you fix it all?"

Stritch looked at Jes, then at Windy. "Yah. Fix okay."

"How long?" Windy asked.

Stritch flinched back and ahtsa ears folded down, but aht answered. "Can fix. Oh-forty-eight, all good."

Jes did the arithmetic in their head; About one Common day.

"Alright," Jes said to Stritch. "We're off the station. We've got lots to fix, but by now, you must have figured you're part of this crew. We need you as much as you need us, yah?" They realized they were unconsciously mimicking the triss's speech, but shrugged and decided to roll with it. "You got coordinates for the big score? Maybe let us all see it?"

Stritch looked at Jes, then Windy, then Fin. Aht bobbed ahtsa head and stood up from the crash couch, walking back towards engineering without a word. The three looked at each other, questioning.

After a few minutes, Stritch returned and sat, carrying a small mem-chip reader. "Coordinates for *VrrihSss'sstrr'tr-rrrunn*, yah? All share. All equal?"

Jes wondered where aht had stashed the reader… it was clearly of triss make, and so came from the skiff. But they shrugged and looked to the others. "Okay with me. All share equal."

Windy and Fin both nodded and repeated the awkward mantra.

"We're all-in together," Fin said softly to Stritch.

Stritch's ears twitched back and forward twice, then aht pressed a switch on the reader to power it on. As Jes let their eyes focus on the device, their implant picked up its signal and after a brief protocol negotiation, displayed a file list. There was only one file, rendered in Common as "Versistertrun." Jes's cominfo identified the file as a navigation space-time fix.

Jes got a ping.

Copied into nav-comm. /W

Jes had noted the ugly scar at the base of ahtsa skull, and now that they were all one crew, it was fair to ask. Jes had seen similar scars before… it looked very much like a down-deck chop-job. "You had an implant, yah? What happened?"

The triss keened softly, then answered, hesitating.

"...When first running... I tried hiding in... *sst't'tr-rrssst't't't*... sell-sex-bar? The Grind." Stritch hissed. "Mistake. Matriarch there, no care 'cept credit, yah? She had partner, took away implant all new workers. Forced us not run."

Windy's eyes went wide. "The Grind? When was it you ran from there?"

Stritch considered. "Nine? Nine segments, almost."

Windy did the math and came up with about three days. "That was *you* caused the ruckus when we were leaving the Bleak," she said; half question, half exclamation of angry dismay.

Stritch looked down, ahtsa ears drooped. "Sorry."

Windy just shook her head, struggling to explain what she meant. She noticed how Stritch leaned subtly in Fin's direction whenever aht flinched back from her. "Printer in engineering working?" she asked.

Stritch brightened. "Yah, looks okay."

"We can probably print a new implant, but we don't have the right equipment to install it safely," Windy said. Then she had a concerning thought. "And I doubt our printer has a triss-compatible schema. We may need to wait until we get to your ship, or maybe a station with a bigger triss contingent."

Stritch shrugged uncomfortably.

"Okay. We've got lots to do..." Windy looked at Jes. "How about you and I work on getting water and galley printing up." She turned to Fin. "You help Stritch in engineering?"

"Sounds good," Fin said, standing. "Let's go Stritch."

"Alright," Jes said. "Let's get to it." As they all started breaking up, Jes paused in the passage aft. "Also, everyone pick a bunk. There's four down here, and captain and XO cabins up on the command deck." They glanced around, then tapped the controls to the second hatch on their left, just before the deck ladder. "I'll take this one."

Jes collapsed on their bunk, not even bothering to strip off the old pad and replace it with the one they'd brought from their station cabin. They eyed the bulb of coffee that sat on the small desk to their right, beside the box of their belongings. It was just out of reach because they didn't want to move their arm to grab it.

Seven hours of squirming through the crawlspace between decks and threading through the narrow spaces between the inner and outer pressure hulls took their toll. Jes was exhausted. The work had paid off ultimately, even if the payoff was anticlimactic. Finally, they'd found the corroded manifold that was the common root cause of failures in both the galley printer and the water processing pipeline.

Fifteen minutes on the printer in engineering and another uncomfortable hour to replace the fist-sized part, and both systems were working again. Windy had celebrated with a twenty minute shower. Jes had celebrated with the bulb of coffee which they hadn't touched since lying down.

Fin and Stritch had their heads together in engineering, and Stritch had rebuffed any additional offer of help, so Jes had grabbed their box from the stack of crates still on the grav pallet and shut themself in their cabin for a while. They listened to the subtle creaks and hums of the ship as the bot made the small adjustments to keep them in their orbital lane. It felt a little like getting to know a new intimate friend.

Their next job was to haul the crate of ingots to the recycler and feed them in one-by-one. Windy was busy looking into how to update the ownership registry for Heart of Gold without raising any suspicions.

Jes let out a sigh and forced themself to sit up. They took a sip of their coffee and started to unpack. The old bunk pad went on the deck by the hatch, replaced by the one from their station cabin. A stack of folded jumpsuits went in the locker. Jes continued sorting and stowing personal items.

Even if Jes were one to casually discard belongings and reprint new ones, they were cutting mass to the bone as it was. The atomic recycling technology gifted by the Elders was fantastically efficient, but it wasn't perfect. There was a small loss of atomic mass with each pass through the recycler. They couldn't afford to waste it on new bunk pads and jumpsuits.

Jes reached into the crate and found their hands on a ratty fiberboard box. They sighed, and flipped open the lid. They started removing items slowly, their thoughts elsewhere.

An antique solar calculator. A pen that used a millimeter-diameter metal ball to regulate the flow of ink, long since dried out. A coin tarnished with a black patina, a face in profile barely visible on one side and an eagle on the other. An old brass key with a shield-shaped head and saw-toothed edge. Jes lined the items up on the narrow shelf above their bunk one by one.

Their hand closed over the irregular dorsal plates of the plastic stegosaur and their thoughts went back to their time on the 'Drift. Their time with Andi.

Jes activated a remote link to Cor Caroli L4 net-traffic and opened a record session. "Andi," they said, "it's Jes." They shook their head at the absurdity of the greeting. She would know who it was from the headers. "I... I'm going to be out of pocket for a bit, so don't worry about trying to reach me." A part of them knew she probably wouldn't "But I just wanted you to know that... I saw a report about your upcoming wedding, and wanted to tell you..."

Jes took a deep breath and sighed, wondering what they wanted to tell her.

"I wanted to tell you that I'm happy for you. And I'm okay. I'm on my feet, and I'm doing fine, and... I'm sorry for the words we parted on. I hope you can look back fondly on our time together. I do."

Jes wiped a sudden dampness from their eyes. "I wish you the best of luck in your new arrangements."

They ran several more words through their mind, trying them out. They didn't find anything that sounded right, so they closed the session and focused *send*. The message would go into the station's common buffers, tagged for delivery in the next bulk transfer beacon. It would be sent to every station in the local network. Gradually, slowly, system by system, the message would migrate through the galaxy until it reached Sol. It might take days or weeks, or months. But eventually, it would reach a network she was linked to and it would ping her implant.

Jes sat for a few minutes, feeling the closing of that part of their life, and smiled, looking forward to something new, with their new family.

10 / Skip

Jes fed the last of the ingots into the recycler. They arched their back, stretching and rolling their shoulders. Jes didn't like to think of themself as weak, but after moving over one-hundred ten-kilo ingots of osmium from the pallet to the recycler, they were feeling the impact of their sedentary station life.

The galley printer was right beside the recycler port, and Jes keyed up a bulb of coffee. As it printed, they ran through their list. Windy was still trying to back-door the registry update. Stritch and Fin had checked off an impressive number of items from their work list. The clock showed them well ahead of schedule.

Jes grabbed the coffee and wandered around the common area. The galley was a long counter with the printer and recycler in the corner, a water source, and a bank of small lockers lining the wall above and wrapping along the starboard bulkhead to the ring of crash couches. On the other side of the large compartment was a rectangular table surrounded by seats. They imagined the four of them sharing meals at the table and smiled.

Jes walked aft, past their own cabin and down the passage

to engineering. The common crew head was to their right, and an open area to the left with the vertical deck access and a wall of equipment lockers. They trailed their fingers along the bulkhead, feeling the age of the anti-spalling composite. It was smooth from years of crew walking the passage and brushing against it.

They walked through the hatch to engineering and found Fin sitting at the monitoring station on the upper deck. Jes heard Stritch below, working some tool with a ratcheting sound.

"Hey Jes," Fin said, brightly. "How're we doing?"

"You tell me."

"Stritch is rebuilding the cradle down there. We also pulled the buffers one by one and… aht called it annealing? Anyway, did something, hooking them up directly to the mains feed. Says they might be okay for a few skips."

"What's left?"

"The mass balancer is still… not great, at least axially. But we'll have to take the whole thing apart to figure out why, and that's going to be tough without docking."

"We can manage without it," Jes said.

Fin nodded. "Looks like the atmo flaps actually work, the extenders anyway. It's the flight controls that are failing."

"Not planning on taking her planet-side anytime soon. How are we on mass?"

Fin tapped a control on the console. "We're running at eighteen percent mass reserves. Manageable, but I'd love a little more margin of error."

"Well, don't spend it all in one place."

Fin chuckled. "I've cycled all the physical actuators. Docking and cargo clamps, skip vanes, atmo flaps, landing struts, and the external inspection doors. The only issue I'm seeing is on cargo-two. The clamps aren't responding to signal."

Jes nodded. "That's the hatch that was open. Figure we won't be carrying much on that rig for a bit." Jes wound down the ladder to the lower deck. Stritch was on ahtsa knees, fitting an intricate-looking part to the deck where the right cradle arm used to be.

"How's it looking down here?" Jes said.

Aht answered without looking away. "Almost good." The ratchet trilled as aht tightened the last bolt. Aht stood and turned to Jes, but didn't meet their eyes. "Good and good and good." Aht turned back and started unwinding the tape that had held the SDR in place. The new cradle looked much more complicated than the one Jes had helped Stritch disassemble.

"What's this?" Jes asked. They trailed their hand along a broad arcing curve of dark gray that followed the shape of the Egg. It looked like half a planetary ring.

Stritch's ears perked up and aht showed ahtsa teeth, trying to mimic the human expression. "All triss cradles have, yah? *Sah'sssahtrrr...* lathe? Take off gold." Aht tapped some keys on the nearby console, and the cradle began a slow, even rotation against the curving blade. There was a soft hum as a vacuum system that clung to the blade spooled up.

Jes stood for a moment watching it turn. "That's... Stritch..."

Stritch shrank back.

Jes shook their head, then hugged the triss. "That's the most beautiful thing I think I've ever seen," they laughed.

"How are things looking down there?" Windy asked as Jes entered the bridge.

"Great, actually. I think they're almost done," Jes said. "How about here?"

Windy shook her head. "I haven't found a way to update the registry ownership without an actual transfer record."

Jes shrugged. "Well, we'll manage."

"Jes, that missing data is going to be a bright red flag to anyone monitoring our traffic. I'm kind of surprised they haven't pinged us about it yet."

Jes took their seat at the ops station. "It's the number we rolled, Windy. We'll make it work somehow."

Fin entered the bridge and hopped into the pilot seat. "Stritch says we're ready as aht can make us."

Jes held down the all-hands. "I'm going to run an emergency vent test. Stritch, you want to stay down in engineering, or come up to the bridge?"

The intercom crackled. "*Stay here,*" Stritch said.

"Okay. Locking down in three... two... one. Emergency lockdown." The sound of rapid-actuators firing echoed through the ship as all the hatches closed automatically and heavy seals dropped between major compartments. The hatch to the bridge was tooth-rattling as it slammed into place.

Stritch's voice came through the speakers. "*Safety door closed off here,*" aht reported.

Jes started a section-by-section positive pressure test, cycling the atmosphere controls systematically to increase the compartment pressure and monitor for leaks. It took several minutes.

"We're showing green on all pressure systems. Looks like all the doors closed on cue. I think we're good to go." They ended the test and the emergency hatches reopened.

"Does that mean we're skip-shape?" Fin asked.

Windy and Jes gave him a cold, steady look. "Please don't ever say that again," Windy said.

"What?" Fin wore a wide-eyed, innocent look, but struggled to hold back a grin.

"Alright, Windy, want to find us a formula to Stritch's ship?"

"On it, Jes. It's going to take the Q-comp some time to figure the folds, though."

"We've got plenty of time."

Windy tapped out the commands at her station and then sat back. Jes pulled the feedback from her console and put it up at the base of the tank. All it said was "calculating…"

Jes leaned back and stretched out their arms, rolling their shoulders. They took a deep breath, then stood up from the crash couch and paced slowly around the bridge.

The display in the tank changed to "estimating solution…"

Fin groaned. "You said it was going to be slow, Windy, but holy shit."

"I'm going to get some coffee. Anyone else?" Jes said.

The others shook their heads and Jes walked aft and climbed down the ladder. The ship felt quiet, but tense. Like it was waiting along with all of them for the skip solution. They printed a coffee bulb and sipped it as they returned to the bridge.

The tank showed "calculating…" again.

"What's taking it so long?" Jes asked.

Windy looked blankly at them. "It's calculating."

Jes looked back, their mouth open, but unable to come up with a response.

There was a tone from Windy's console and figures began streaming across the display. "There it is," she said. "It says it's a genus-six skip. About five segments real-time."

Fin looked up, startled. "Stritch said it was genus-four."

Jes frowned. "Well, ours is an older comp. It makes sense its solution won't be as good…"

The quantum computer's main job was to calculate the topological transform between three-dimensional normal space and the multidimensional space the skip drives propelled them through. These transform fields were measured in "genus." The term came from classification of toroidal geometry: How many holes a surface had. Genus-one referred to a simple torus with one hole.

As Jes understood it, it was these holes or "ponds" that the drive skipped them across. A genus-six skip required a transform into nine-dimensional space—six extra dimensions on top of the usual three. And each extra dimension meant a skip with immense physical stresses on the ship and crew.

"Stritch," Jes said over the all-hands, "are we going to hold together for six skips?"

There was a worryingly long pause before aht answered. *"Probably, yah,"* aht said. Then a moment later: *"No promise."*

"Anything we can do to make that more likely?" Windy asked.

"As good as get without full repair dock," came the reply.

Jes kept the comm open. "I think we need to be all-in on this. Stritch, what do you think? Do we go?"

"Yah," came the reply. No hesitation.

"Fin?"

"The ship isn't going to get any younger or safer if we wait. I say we go."

Jes nodded. "Windy?"

She looked hard at Jes, then looked away. "Yeah, let's do it. What's the worst that can happen?"

"Asphyxiation, fiery death, explosion," Jes said. "Gravity-mishap pulverization, sudden deatomization on normal-space reentry—"

"Lost forever in multidimensional space," Fin cut in, "miscalc skip that drops us into a star, spaghettification, electrocution, impact fractures—"

"Singularity implosion," Stritch said over the comm.

"—right! Singularity implosion…"

Windy held up her hands, "Right, I get it. We're—wait… 'spaghettification?'"

"It's a real thing," said Fin. He looked mildly hurt that she would question him. "Look it up."

She looked at him for a moment, then laughed. "Okay. I'm in. Never let it be said I'm afraid of a little violent death."

Jes smiled at her. "Alright." They leaned into the comm. "All hands, prepare for lane departure and genus-six skip." Jes released the intercom. "Windy, let's ask our hosts for a vector."

Nav-comm sent the request for system departure and the station acked with a queue position and local hold coords. Fin eased them out of their orbital lane and moved them into the indicated hold position. Jes leaned back in their jump seat and shot Windy a small smile across the bridge. It was happening. They were about to head out in their own ship.

Windy returned the smile, though her weathered face didn't show the excitement that Jes felt. Something caught her attention on her board and she reported it aloud.

"We're getting an in-call from station control. Voice."

Jes straightened. System traffic was typically fully automated—bots on ships talking with bots on station. *People rarely talked to each other as part of this process.* "Let's hear it."

Windy tapped a few keys and a new voice crackled over the bridge comm speakers.

"*Eighty-eight-gee-forty-two long haul courier, this is Cor Caroli ell-four Traffic Control. We're reading corrupted output on your beacon. You having system troubles over there?*"

Fin looked at Jes, his eyes wide, and then back at Windy. Windy looked over at Jes, raising her eyebrow.

Jes told Windy, "Don't say it." They keyed the comm at the ops station and their voice took on a bright, friendly tone. "Traffic Control, this is eighty-eight-gee-forty-two long haul. Sorry about that. Our system got zapped by a bad ground on undocking. Minimal damage, but it looks like it got our beacon. We already have a date with the repair yard at our dest. You need us to turn around?"

Fin squeezed his eyes shut. There was a long pause before the response came in.

"*Negative eighty-eight-gee-forty-two. Your safeties are beaconing fine, it's just the passive record-checks. Maintain position in queue. But make sure you get that fixed before you come back here, or you'll get slammed with a penalty. What dock was it fried your system? We need to file a report.*"

Windy put her face in her hands.

"Thanks Control. We already reported it, but doesn't hurt to get some official weight on the problem. Private dock." Jes rattled off a ten-digit serial number without hesitating.

"*Got it, eighty-eight-gee-forty-two. We'll make sure they get a flag. Safe flight.*" The line stayed open a bit longer than intended, and they caught a fragment of background chatter before it cut off. "*Daean, take a look at this registry: 'Heart of*

Gold.' What a shit name. Bet they think it's clever and orig—"

Windy and Fin both were looking at Jes now. Windy shook her head slowly. "You're such a lucky shit, Jes."

Jes just smiled at them.

"What dock did you just report?" Fin asked suddenly.

"Oh, that's the Axon-Mull elite-class customer lounge for their sales floor," Jes said, smiling.

They got an update from station control, and Windy put their queue position up in the tank. They were marked seventh in line for system departure. They all watched the tank tensely, waiting as the number slowly counted down.

When it reached two, Fin opened the comm to engineering. "Stritch, we're about to start our run to system exit. I'll need full power and vane control."

"Yah."

The counter reached one and the station sent departure clearance. Fin smiled as he grabbed the controls and eased them forward. Windy acked the clearance and Jes watched as the tank rendered their departure. The image of the station and the other orbital lanes moved out to the edge of the tank, then faded out altogether as they gained distance.

A series of circles appeared, forming a tunnel towards their projected exit from normal space. Fin drove the ship through the center.

"Jes, let's spool up the skip drive. Activate the vanes."

A soft whine of actuators resonated through the hull as the three skip vanes extended into position.

"Vanes are fully extended," Jes reported.

"Alright," Fin said softly. "Here we go." He ramped up the forward translation to maximum, and set the skip drive to auto. It would decide—based on the q-comp's solution—the optimal moment to fold space.

When the drive engaged, the tank went blank, then rendered a large model of the ship. Jes watched as the vanes, having done their job in transforming the ship out of normal, gracefully folded back in-line with the hull. The tank wasn't even going to attempt to render the folded space around them.

The skip field held a pocket of three-dimensional space around the ship, so they didn't feel any different as they slipped into a mind-twisting nine-dimensional reality. It was a good thing they had no way to experience it. Jes didn't think the human mind would be capable of surviving that.

"Fold complete; we're in skip-space," Fin said. "First skip coming up in... four... three... two... one..."

Their bubble of normal space deflected off the first pond. The impact was jarring and the ship rattled as if they had hit a solid surface. The crash couches took the brunt of the impact, but Jes still felt some pain in their ribs.

"Did that seem like an especially hard bounce to anyone?" Windy asked.

"How long until the next skip?" Jes asked.

"In ten," Fin said.

Jes opened the comm. "Stritch, you okay down there? Did you feel that?"

"Yah. Felt. Maybe we—"

The deckplates shuddered and the power flickered. A screech of hard surfaces grinding together reverberated through the ship. Jes felt it in their bones.

"What the hell was that?" Windy yelled.

"—bad bad bad bad!"

"Skip in five..." Fin reported, forcing their voice to a calm, measured tone. "Four... three... two... one..."

Jes braced themself between the console and the crash

couch, hoping for a smooth skip.

The ship seemed to hurtle in seven directions at once, and a sound like the universe tearing itself apart reverberated through their skull.

11 / Spin

Jes blinked their eyes open, aware of something wrong. Angry light forced its way into their attention. Their cominfo was raising a stream of warnings from its bio monitor and from the ship diagnostics. A cacophony of alarms and insistent tones filled their ears. A hard, persistent discomfort pressed against Jes's face and shoulder. Their hand prickled with a dull numbness. Voices rattled in their brain, calling their name.

There was something else, pulling at them. Something wrong in the shape of the world. It felt... twisted. Jes tried to lift their head, but it was heavy. Heavier than it should be. Their head dropped to the deck and their vision went dark in a tumbling whirl of shadow.

They opened their eyes again, aware somehow that time had passed. They shifted their arms, realizing now they had fallen to the decking. Jes didn't remember how or why. They must have unbuckled their crash straps. Jes pushed themself up, trying to look around. The alarms still blared with an anxious pulsing. The bridge was filled with orange emergency lighting and an oddly consistent flicker.

"Windy!" they called. "Fin?"

"Here," said Fin, through clenched teeth.

"Alive," answered Windy.

"Status?" They found the arm of the ops crash couch and tried to pull themselves up into it. It was too much effort, and their stomach and inner-ear were rebelling strenuously.

"We're in a dead axial roll," Fin said. "Don't know where, but the comp says we're back in normal space at least. Hardly anything is responding."

"Thrusters?"

"Stritch is working on them."

Jes took a deep breath and pulled themselves back up into their seat, groaning with the effort. There was an intense force pulling them to the left and downward in a sickening, twisting spiral that was at odds with the steadiness of the bridge. They couldn't think. They could barely focus.

They looked at the tank—the source of the disturbing flicker of light—and saw a dizzying rhythmic flashing. The tank was trying desperately to keep up its rendering with the speed of their spin, but failing. The result was an eccentric flickering. Combined with the sensation of the spin, it was nauseating. Jes closed their eyes.

"Can we get those alarms off?" they asked.

Windy grunted, and one by one the klaxons stopped.

The comm crackled to life. *"Fin, thrusters ok,"* Stritch said in a strained voice.

Fin grabbed the controls and wrenched the ship into maximum thrust, trying to counter the roll. He held it for ten seconds.

"Fin," Windy said quietly, working her console. "You're going to run us dry before you slow us down at all. We're spinning too fast."

He relaxed his hands on the controls and sighed. "We

have to slow down somehow. I'm not sure..." He gulped and shook his head. "I'm not sure how long I can stay conscious like this."

Jes noticed the bridge hatch was sealed. They pulled up the damage report. Emergency compartment seals had dropped throughout the ship. There was a breach on the cargo deck, and entire deck was now sealed off. At least the safeties had worked. They tried to think, but it felt like their brain was twisting in the spin—wrung out like a towel.

They continued tapping through the damage report. Blinking rapidly seemed to help a little. The skip drive was offline. Two of the line buffers had burned out under the strain. The K-vane was bent. *Bent.* Jes wiped their sleeve across their face, brushing away the cold sweat that broke out.

Fin suddenly straightened. "Stritch," he said into the comm, "I need you to cut out the interlocks. Give me full control of vanes and atmo flaps."

There was a pause, then aht grunted in reply.

Jes was confused. "What?"

Fin ignored the question. "Jes, pull up the mass balancer and shift all of our available mass to the ventral or dorsal tanks. Move it away from centerline."

Jes did what Fin told them to. "Wasn't the mass balancer not working?"

"Radial balance is fine, it was axial that was fucked."

Windy seemed to realize what Fin was up to. "Momentum?" she asked.

"Yup," he said.

Jes started the transfer.

Stritch called back on comm. *"All controls you got. Free extension."*

Fin started flipping switches and tapping controls, and Jes heard the whine of actuators. In the tank, the representation of the Heart of Gold seemed to unfold like the petals of a flower as all three skip vanes and the three primary atmospheric flight flaps extended.

Some of the pressure in Jes's head eased.

"Landing gear," Windy said.

"Right!" Fin called out excitedly. He flipped more switches, and the mechanical sounds in the ship intensified.

"Can someone pretend that I'm an idiot and tell me what's going on?" Jes begged.

"Ever watched figure skating?" Fin asked. "The more of our mass we move out from centerline, the slower we spin."

The vanes and flaps locked into place nearly perpendicular to the hull, and Jes realized the ship's spin *was* slowing. The tank was now able to paint their rotation without glitching out.

Windy was running simulations at her console. "Slowed us down, but it doesn't look like it's enough. We need something more." She gulped, looking decidedly ashen despite her dark complexion. She closed her eyes, thinking, then dipped into her implant interface. She kept talking. "Fin, how far off axis can we vector the gravidrive?"

"Not far," Fin said. "They never designed her for maneuverability. Ten degrees, maybe?"

Windy worked her simulation. "I'm sending a transform matrix to your station. With our current angular velocity, a combination of gravity vector and the thrusters on the vane tips, we should be able to stop with some mass to spare."

Fin nodded, and started configuring the thrusters, switching off all but the attitude nozzles on the ends of the vanes. He executed the program.

With the vectored thrust from the gravidrive, the axial roll became more and more eccentric, turning into a semi-orbital wobble. Soon they were rotating on three axes: the original roll, tumbling end-over-end, and an endless yaw.

"Has our status improved at all? Just asking," Jes said.

"We *are* slowing..." Fin said quietly.

They waited. It took an eternity, but eventually the roll slowed, then stopped. The thrusters brought their tumble and yaw to a standstill also.

The three of them took a deep breath, almost simultaneously.

"*Nice job*, both of you," Jes said.

Fin hit the comm. "Stritch, you okay down there?"

"*Yah. Good one.*"

"Any idea where we are?" Jes asked.

Windy shook her head. "Whatever happened knocked out stellar navigation. We can't get a star-fix on anything."

"Do we have anything? What about backups? Spectral analysis?"

She poked at her console for a few minutes. "There's a nearby stellar mass," Windy said. "Maybe I can get an optical fix?"

Jes nodded.

"Working," Windy said.

While she worked on the star-fix, Jes started checking for breaches deck by deck. As pressure came up green, they unlocked the emergency seals and opened hatches. The bridge hatch opened, and Jes worked downwards through the ship. It looked like the one on the cargo deck was the only breach. The deck seal there stayed closed. For now, until they could fix cargo two, the ladder ended at the main crew deck.

After a few more minutes, Windy reported, "Comp says

that's Kepler-186."

Fin whistled through his teeth. "We're a *long* ways off where we meant to be."

Jes wiped cold sweat from their face. "Lucky we came out of skip at all, I guess." They turned suddenly to Windy. "*Don't say* 'I told you so!'"

Windy met their eyes with a blank look. "Wouldn't dream of it."

"There's a station at Kepler-186, I think," said Fin. "Not human or triss. Vos?"

Windy consulted the database, then nodded. "Yeah." She sighed. "I hate vos stations. The atmo always stinks."

"How much mass did we just burn off? Can we even make it to the station?" Jes asked.

Fin looked over his console and grimaced. "We're down to about a third of what we left with." He looked over the nav metrics, then at Windy. "We can get there on the gravidrive, but we'll need thrusters to maneuver and dock. We'll be limping, and we'll be skating in on fumes."

None of them said anything for a moment, but they were all thinking it. With a broken ship and little mass to establish station credit, it would be nearly impossible to even pay for long-term docking, let alone finance repairs and refueling.

They were almost back where they'd started.

12 / Deals

Kepler-186
Vos-governed System
Population 3.87M

SPACETIME-FIX at: **84.054**.24789387
GENERAL SYSTEM FAILURE
▫ de77c340 (**Kepler-186**) 0000-0000
◆ STAR-FIX ERROR: UNKNOWN
◆ STAR-FIX ERROR: UNKNOWN

They were all silent for a long while. Jes just stared at their hands on the console. They felt the crushing weight of their decisions and their failure pressing them down into the mire of their own darkness. They were vaguely aware of Fin and Windy debating something, but couldn't bring themself to focus.

They stood and started walking to the hatch.

"Jes, where are you going?" Windy asked.

Jes just shook their head, unable to answer. Where were any of them going?

Before they could make it off the bridge, they saw Stritch climbing the ladder. They waited as the small triss stomped down the passage onto the bridge. Despite the alienness of ahtsa body language, Jes could still see that aht seethed with rage.

Stritch dropped a half-meter length of cable on the deck. It was twisted and blackened, and carried a vague smell of burnt plastic.

"Sstah'tah'tahhtr'strrrr'tah! Ah'ayaht!"

Fin looked at ahta, wide-eyed. "Stritch... what?"

"Not us fault. This... *Ah'ayaht*. Bad bad bad. Junk fix last."

Jes picked up the cable, turning it over in their hands.

Stritch continued, "Wrong cable, yah? *Sah'hatrr*... weak. Replace long time, take *years* to burn. Power jump. Burn out buffers, maybe burn out skip drive. All our fix, no help."

Ahtsa agitation was making their Common harder to follow. Windy put the pieces together.

"Someone used the wrong gauge cable in a previous repair?"

"Yah! Never find until fail. Wrong gauge cable in right gauge conduit. Maybe more. Maybe whole ship." Jes watched, fascinated as ahtsa long fingers twitched in anger, hard, rounded claws extending and retracting from the tips.

Jes handed Fin the burnt cable absently. They turned and walked back towards the ladder.

"Jes?" Windy called.

Jes said nothing. They waved their hand, fending off further questions and descended to the crew deck. They needed to think.

Jes made their way to their cabin and collapsed on their bunk, staring up at the ceiling. Hopelessness creeped in at the edges; They could feel it. They'd thrown the dice and come up all ones. Dead in space, broken ship, no local credit, not enough mass, no way to fix anything.

The darkness that always stalked them had a voice sometimes, and it whispered now. They were a failure. They had failed everyone. They tried to put their attention on the future, on next steps, but the darkness pushed them back; turned them around. They could only see the actions they'd taken to get here. The words they'd spoken to convince Windy to gamble her life with them.

Stop it, they thought to themself. *Get to it.*

That darkness was mass and it had its own gravity, pulling ever downward into oblivion. Shouting into it didn't help. Jes knew they had to act. They stood up and began pacing.

What did they have? They had a ship. They had an SDR and a nav-comm and a beacon. They had their crew: Fin, who could fly anything. Windy, who was steady as an asteroid. Stritch, genius engineer.

There were people in this system that they could reach. Jes dipped into their implant and connected to the nav database, pulling up the listing.

Kepler-186 was a vos-governed system. There were three destinations orbiting the red dwarf star. The database listed the planet Kepler-186f as a mining colony with enclosed habitat and a narrow strip of manufactured livable surface. The vos called it *Vo Hahe Ha Hof*.

Lagrange-four held a small mass-bundling station called *Vo Hahe Vuf Ho*. Highly automated with minimal population, all vos.

At L5 was a much larger and more promising habi-station. The vos who ran it called it *Vo Hahe Huv Hweh*, but the minority inhabitants had their own names. It was a huge station compared to Cor Caroli L4. Its population of just over three million was mixed: majority vos and human, with a large minority triss community, as well as pockets of some of the other Accord species less common in this sector.

Jes focused the L5 listing and drilled down into the station services. As they scrolled, they occasionally dipped into a detail view of one repair bay or another, just long enough to see the eye-watering docking and inspection fees.

They didn't know exactly what they were looking for, but they could feel something... a rising anticipation in their mind. They had the seed of an idea. They just needed to give it time to develop and explain itself to them.

They kept browsing the listings, not making any attempt to think about the notion that was hiding there, somewhere. Let it come out when it was ready.

Jes, we need to talk about where we stand. /W.

They acked the ping, but didn't reply. They muted their feed.

The listings scrolled by.

"...we strip down the whole ship, recycle everything we don't need."

"How much would that buy us?"

"Not enough," Stritch said.

"We go in without a plan, we lose everything," Jes heard Windy say. "You ever dealt with vos?"

"No, but I've dealt with humans." It had the sound of well-trod ground.

Jes entered the bridge, and the three of them looked up as their argument petered out.

"Jes," Windy said. "Back to join us?"

"Yah," they said. They sat at their station and looked over the ship's status. Fin had retracted the landing struts and folded up the vanes and flaps. Jes dumped the listing reference from their cominfo to the ops interface. They opened nav and dialed up the station at Lagrange five. "We're going here." The tank highlighted the L5 station in a blue square.

"Jes, we've looked at all the listed repair bays," Fin objected. "We can't afford to dock at any of them."

"We're not going to dock at a repair bay, Fin. We're docking here." They tapped a sequence of controls and the tank divided its render into two sections. The bottom half retained their local space, with the ship picked out in red in the center and the station in blue. The top scaled the L5 station up until fine detail was visible. Several of the major ports and functional systems were called out in the render.

The station looked like a stack of faceted platters, each roughly the same diameter, but in varying heights. Some of these supported rings that fully or partially encircled the station. Others had sectors with recessed bays.

Jes worked the panel controls and a new highlight appeared on one of the lowest platters. The rendering zoomed in closer.

"Why?" Fin asked. "Why there?"

"That's not even a licensed repair bay," Windy said, calling up the entry in the database. "It's a private maintenance dock. They fly bots and runabouts out of there. What are they going to do with us?"

"And how are we going to pay for any of it?"

Stritch stepped closer to the tank, looking over Fin's shoulder. Aht read the listing on Windy's console. "Triss bay?"

Jes smiled. "Guys, trust me. This is our play."

They had the others' attention now, and they started outlining their plan.

Nav-comm reported the station's prescribed flight plan and orbital lane, and Fin let the flight bot manage the adjustments. The station also sent several warnings about their beacon status.

"Send them our apologies and let them know we had a negative skip event. Don't declare emergency, though," Jes said. "Just request clearance to dock at bay two-nine-gray-seventeen."

There was a pause as Windy entered the instructions in nav-comm and the bots negotiated. New guidance appeared in the tank, routing them to the bay Jes had identified. Fin took over from the bot and maneuvered along the indicated flightpath.

"What happens when we get there?" Windy asked.

"We'll talk to them."

Stritch looked up from one of the fold-down jump seats by the hatch. Aht had pulled up a readout from the engineering monitors and was keeping an eye on power and mass levels. Now, aht watched Jes intently.

"Windy, see if you can get a docking confirmation on that bay."

She complied, tapping controls slowly while watching Jes. The bots talked for a moment, then an indicator lit up. She looked at Jes. "Incoming voice."

Jes nodded, and the comm crackled to life. The voice seemed tentative, but there was no hint that it wasn't human. Windy's request would have indicated human Common as their language.

"Who's that and what do you want?"

Jes leaned into the mike. "Hi. Sorry to barge in uninvited,

but... as you can see, we're in some dire shape. We're hoping we could work something out. We'd like the chance to meet you; talk things over with you. We could become good friends, maybe, yah?"

There was a pause. Then: *"You come in. We see you on screen before we open the hatch, yah? No weapons."*

Jes smiled. "No weapons on this ship. Friends, yah? We'll be docking in..." Jes looked up at Fin, who held up three fingers on one hand without letting go of the controls. Three minutes. Jes did the math in their head. "Point-oh-oh-six."

There was a mechanical chirp of acknowledgement from the comm and the channel cut off.

"Well, that was friendly enough," Jes said.

Windy just looked at them, her face blank.

"Was that even a triss? I couldn't tell," Fin asked.

"Yah," Stritch said. Aht was quiet and held very, very still. "What you do with me?" aht asked quietly.

Jes looked at Windy and Fin, then directly at Stritch, who was looking down at the deck. "Do? Nothing. You're crew. Just... don't anyone say anything about where we're trying to get to, yah?"

Stritch didn't react visibly.

The minutes ticked by and the tank showed them closing with the docking bay, nose-in. Fin watched the screen at their station as he made some final adjustments to the controls. There was a dull thud that they all felt through the deck, then the mechanical whine of actuators. The ship clamped onto the dock and the dock returned the favor in a series of loud clangs.

Fin flipped several switches on his panel and stretched back in his seat. "We're docked and locked."

"Alright," Jes said. "Let's get to it." They all stood from

their stations and followed Jes down the ladder and forward through the galley to the fore airlock. Stritch was the last in line.

They squeezed into the airlock together. Windy dipped into her implant and told the inner lock to seal, closing them in the small two-square-meter compartment.

Jes activated the dock-comm and wiped dust off the lens with their thumb. A triss face appeared on the panel, looking at them intently.

"Hi," Jes said brightly. "Just like we said, here to talk. No weapons." They held up their hands to show the camera. It was only a gesture—even through the wide-angle vid, it would have been easy to hide something—but as inter-species gestures went, it was a surprisingly universal one.

There was another long pause as the triss on the screen conferred with someone not visible, then the dock-side hatch showed open on the panel. Jes pressed a control and their outer hatch opened.

A faint smell of sulfur filled the air from the station side. They stepped into the larger airlock and waited for it to cycle. They all walked out into a low-ceilinged compartment. The walls were painted in a clashing riot of colors, or had been years ago—much of the paint was scratched or flaked or faded. The smell of sulfur was stronger outside of the airlock, but not as pungent as Jes had expected for a vos station.

Over a dozen triss stood around the bay. The largest, almost as tall as Jes, stood in the center, looking squarely at Windy. "So, you're here now. What do you want?"

Jes smiled and moved forward, their hands open and palms facing forward. "We're just here for a deal." They hadn't factored into their plan that the triss were matriarchal. *Of course* they'd look to Windy as the leader. Any other time, she might well be, but this plan was Jes's to make happen. Windy was far too grumpy for a first-contact.

"Deal, ay'yup." The katriss now looked Jes and their crew up and down for a moment, lingering a bit longer on Stritch. "You want us to fix up your ship? Pretty bad beat up junk you got there. Odd company too. That one," she said, nodding her pointed snout towards Stritch. "You thinking maybe you trade *ahta* for fixing? We don't need a *ssss'ssvsvs't*."

Stritch shrank back behind Fin.

Jes took another half-step forward, their hands going wide in a magnanimous gesture. "Oh, no no. Stritch there? *Aht*'s on my crew. Family, yah?" Jes pointed to themself, to Windy, to Fin, to Stritch. "Same and same and same."

The katriss hissed and spat a series of sibilant trills towards Stritch, who poked ahtsa head around Fin's side long enough to spit back something very similar sounding. Whatever the exchange was, the larger triss reared her head back, ears twitching. She combed her fingers through the crest of stiff black hair that ran back from her forehead between her ears.

"So then, why come here? Lots of good repair shops up on nicer levels, yah? Even some human bays."

Jes looked around at the cluster of triss that had congregated around their matriarch. The narrow docking space was set up like a workshop, tools and parts in various stages of disassembly or repair. The detritus of endless projects and jobs cluttered every surface. Two hatches led deeper into the station.

"Your family, yah?" Jes indicated the triss they could see. "You do station repair contracts for the vos and humans. Fix up whatever breaks. You maybe also have other businesses nearby, yah? Make real Trissa food and do some shipping for local families? Deep in vos space, but you stick together, yah? And the station masters charge you *extra* extra, make sure you stay *down* here?"

The matriarch's ears flipped back, flat against her head.

"I'm Jes. We're at the bottom too, yah? We can help each other."

She looked Jes over again. "Jes," she said. She touched her palm to her own forehead. "*Sst'tʊʊ'nsssss.*"

"Sstutiveness," Jes tried.

One of the smaller triss beside the matriarch let out a sharp bark that might have been a laugh.

Sst'tʊʊ'nsssss's ears flicked in a brief gesture of annoyance. "*Sst'tʊʊ'nsssss.*"

Jes shook their head. "I'm sorry. I don't think I'm going to be able to say it right."

She showed a brief flash of teeth, "No human can ever speak Trissa."

"How about I call you 'Stevens?'"

She grinned then, her lips drawn fully back to show her narrow jaw full of sharp teeth. "Fine and fine and fine." Stevens gestured, one finger pointed to the floor and drew her arm in a wide circle. "We sit and make deal."

Jes waited until Stevens pulled a small crate over and sat, before doing the same. The other triss filled in a half circle on the deck behind her. Windy, Fin, and Stritch arrayed themselves behind Jes.

"What kinda deal you thinking?" Stevens asked.

Jes smiled. "So, you're right that we need repairs. Ship's pretty busted. Vos and human bays ask too many questions, and won't be interested in deals, yah?"

Stevens tilted her head to the side.

"Docking fees, repair fees, inspection fees, liability penalties, taxes." Jes counted them off on their fingers and shook their head. They pinched the air like they were picking up a cred chip then let it go, fluttering their fingers. "We're a little low on mass just now. So, here's the deal:

"You let us dock our ship here. We pay *you* ten percent official standard docking fee. We pay for parts, you fix our ship for free. Oh, also… we need to get Stritch there a new com-info."

Stevens barked a sharp chirp, her ears flicking to either side. "Some blunt deal, that is."

"Oh, but here's the thing," Jes said, warming up. "You're running business, yah? Lots of business. Some business maybe you gotta pay extra to be pretty quiet about? You're sending things here, there; picking up… whatever from around the system? The vos, the humans, they charge you fair for that shipping? They let you go here and there without lots of questions?"

Stevens's ears tensed.

"Or maybe it's like the docking, yah? Fees and fees and fees? So: we're stuck in system until we can get our skip drive fixed. While we're here, we run your cargo. You pay us fuel-mass plus twenty percent standard ship rates. We take the risks and you don't need to pay endless fees."

Stevens leaned forward. "You pay twenty percent standard docking, we pay ten percent for shipping."

Jes thought this over. The docking fees were a far lower expense than what they'd make on a shipping run.

"Ten percent for shipping, sure—But you pay fuel-mass and full fees for when we dock at regular ports for your cargo runs, yah?"

Stevens sat silently still for a moment before clapping her hands together. "Done—*If* ship can even fly. We look at your ship now? Maybe want to know how much debt you have to work off?" She showed her teeth again.

Jes nodded and they stood. Two of the triss moved to a console and began checking status boards. There was a rapid exchange of trilling hisses between them that quickly turned into a bout of the chirping barks that Jes had begun to read as laughter. Stevens joined in briefly before turning a flat gaze to Jes.

"Your ship is really named 'Heart of Gold?'"

Jes sighed. "Wasn't our choice."

13 / Debt

Jes rubbed sleep out of their eyes as they opened the hatch. Their exit from their cabin was interrupted by three triss trotting aft towards the engineering bay, carrying equipment. The three were conversing in their hissing, trilling language and didn't even acknowledge Jes.

Jes went straight to the galley printer and dialed up a bulb of coffee. As the heat hit their stomach and the caffeine hit their bloodstream, they came fully awake. Windy sat at the rectangular table with a tangle of cables and conduit spread out before her. Stevens stood beside her, inspecting the mess.

"How's it looking?" Jes asked.

"Not too bad," Stevens said. "Surprised, really. Line buffers all shot, need to replace 'em. Ventral skip vane is bad-busted. We're taking it off now, spend some time in pieces in the shop. But the skip drive is okay. Power grid though..." Stevens gestured to the pile on the table. "Your *ssss'ssvsvs't* was right. Bad bad repairs by last owners. These all burn up eventually. This one," Stevens held up a meter-long section of cable, "power to atmo converter. Burn this one up, you all dead and dead and dead."

Jes gulped.

"Where'd you buy this *ah'ayaht?* I'm thinking maybe seller and purchase inspector holding hands, yah?"

"Well... 'buy' is kind of a strong word," Jes said absently.

Stevens blinked at them but said nothing.

"Call it... common law salvage." They looked over the cables. "You sure you found them all?"

"Not sure yet. Your crew got an idea: Overload grid to test. Anything bad left, we burn it up while you're docked, yah?"

Jes threw a panicked look to Windy. "Is that safe? What if we burn out critical systems?"

Windy shrugged. "Stevens's crew is pulling out or bypassing everything that's critical right now. She seems to think it'll work. It was Stritch's idea."

Jes shrugged. They knew they needed to trust their crew... and Stevens's crew. "Okay. I'm going to go explore the station, see if I can't scrounge up some credits. We've got some debts to pay off."

Stevens let out a short, soft bark; something like a chuckle.

Windy gave Jes a questioning look. "Do I want to know what that means?"

"Probably not."

"...Alright."

They heard boots hit the deck, and shortly Fin came into the compartment and joined them at the table.

"The bridge is secure. Looks kind of a mess to be honest, but they've pulled all the bus lines to the system modules. I don't recommend going up there right now," he said, laughing.

"You got anything else on your list?" Jes asked. "Care to join me?"

"Sure. What are we doing?"

Jes turned to Stevens. "You got any trash that needs recycling?"

The katriss looked Jes up and down for a moment, her ears twitching slightly. "Yah, might might." She caught the shoulder of one of her crew and said something in their sibilant language. The smaller triss looked up at Jes and then gestured them to follow. "Aht will show you."

Jes and Fin followed the atriss through the airlock and down the short passage into the station. As they passed the grav-pallet, Jes switched it on and pulled it behind.

Aht led them through Stevens's shop and down an access almost too narrow for the pallet, before keying open a hatch. It looked like an abandoned storage: Cargo hand-bins and refuse bins stacked haphazardly and precariously. Dust progressively covered the lowest bins. The color of the plastic was faded and stained below, and brighter and newer towards the top of the stacks. It was almost a study in archaeology.

Aht waved ahtsa hand at the detritus of years. "All okay okay." Aht left them.

"Well," Jes said with a shrug. "Let's get to it."

It took them almost half an hour to transfer the bins to the grav-pallet. Jes and Fin peered into the containers as they worked, finding endless scraps of broken materials, old machinery, and nonfunctional instruments. Many of the bins were themselves scrap, with cracks or ill-fitting lids, and one of the oldest on the bottom of a stack fell apart as Fin lifted it, a clutter of obsolete triss data cards and antique readers scattering over the deck.

Jes knelt and began tossing the tech into one of the larger open refuse containers. They hesitated with one of the triss readers in their hand. It had a clear technology lineage to the one they had seen Stritch use before their disastrous skip. It was intriguing how a piece of post-Revelation tech could be readily identifiable in purpose and still be entirely alien. It was clearly a data-card reader, but no human would design a reader like this.

They ran their thumb over the control board: The side-by-side indicators that were visibly red and purple even though it was likely decades since it had last been powered on. The three-sided power switch that faced the wrong way to human sensibilities.

Jes found a round parting line and wedged it open with their thumbnail. Under a small hatch was a small rod, ribbed along its length and far thinner than seemed was reasonable for a power cell.

"More antiques for your collection?" Fin asked.

"No," Jes said. "Just curious. I've never really seen triss tech up close."

The two of them finished loading up the pallet and Jes pulled up station schematics on their cominfo, searching for the nearest human-run industrial recycling office. It was two decks up and one ring in.

"Let's go."

They pushed the pallet towards the exit of Stevens's tight cluster of compartments. As they neared the hatch, a larger triss emerged from a side passage and looked them over. The triss nodded to them—an oddly human gesture—and keyed open the hatch. They stepped out into an oppressive humidity and a nearly overpowering sulfurous stench.

Ah, Jes thought, *a vos station.*

An old textbook from Jes's academy days had hypothesized that the species of the Revelatory Accord had been chosen by the Elders to receive caches at least in part because they were ecologically compatible. They could coexist in the same environment in health. But health wasn't the same as comfort.

The vos evolved on a world with a higher average humidity and significant concentration of thiols and sulfides in their atmosphere, resulting in its distinctive and unpleasant odor. On their stations, they kept their atmo tuned for their own comfort.

"Ugh," Fin said. "I had heard about vos stations, but… f—ugh!"

Jes shrugged. "Ever met a vos?"

"No."

"Ever seen one?"

"Just in pictures… Always thought they were… kinda cute." Fin said. He looked at Jes, "Something I should know about?"

Jes smiled. "Not really. Hopefully, we won't need to interact with them much. But if we do, just… let me do the talking and… follow my lead. Don't worry if things get heated."

It took a while to navigate the unfamiliar corridors and rings. Jes realized it must be an off-shift, since the station passages were largely empty. They passed only a few humans and triss. They were all indifferent to the two humans pushing a grav-pallet loaded with refuse.

While they walked, Jes dipped into their cominfo and connected to the local magistrates' portal. They prompted the low-level bot to submit a registration transfer for the common corporation called MWB from Cor Caroli. They had registered the entity—pulling the initial from each of their last names—when the plan for the ship first came together. It took a little over a minute for the registration to reach "pending" status. CC MWB was now provisionally recognized by the station as a corporate entity, and would be official once the skip-buoy traffic round-tripped through Cor Caroli and the registry was backfilled with origination data.

They paused at a recycler and Jes switched to the station's automated accounts portal, opening a credit account with the station under the business name. They pinged the recycler with the ID and Fin fed a small handful of data cards from the trash bins into the recycler. A moment later, they received a ping with their new credit balance: 0.00013 Mg.

Jes smiled to themself.

The two of them eventually reached the recycling office Jes had tagged. It was important for what was coming next that it be a human-run office, with human software.

"You ready? Know what to do?" Jes asked.

"Yah," Fin said, smiling. "How much worse can things get?"

Fin keyed the hatch open and they both stepped inside. Jes smiled as they entered, preparing to charm the desk clerk.

Standing behind the desk was a thick, stout creature covered in a dense pale pink fur. The vos was as tall as Jes, with heavy shoulders and arms and a round protruding snout. The vos's ears were round and tufted atop their head. They wore a vocalizer box clipped to the fur just below their throat.

Jes stopped in their tracks, their brain recalculating as it caught up to the situation.

The great bear-looking creature leaned over the counter, both huge paws placed wide and flexing so that claws extended with little clicking and scraping sounds. When they spoke, it was in a loud, low, guttural growl.

"WHAT do YOU want, human?" the vos's vocalizer shouted at them.

Jes's cominfo helpfully overlayed an intro on their vision, calling out the menacing creature as "Clerk *Hev-Hafohhova*, at your service." They knew enough of vos to recognize the "Hev" as reflective of her gender.

At the vos's violent query, Fin shrank back against the bulkhead, drawing her attention to himself. Jes stepped into her line of sight and leaned in, shouting just as loudly back, **"You think I WANT to be here? You think I WANT to spend time carting garbage around this STINKING station?"**

Fin put a warning hand on their arm, as if trying to draw them back from violence. Jes shrugged his hand off.

Hev-Hafohhova showed teeth, rearing back and emitting a fierce growl. Her vocalizer said, **"Do I care what YOU want? Why are you bringing that piddling little cart of junk HERE? Do you not know this is an INDUSTRIAL recycler, stupid human?"**

Jes smiled, rolling with it now. **"Yah, I know! Boss says, 'Take this to recycler bay fifty.' You think I'm going to question HIM? Boss says 'jump,' I say, 'which way?' YOU'RE stupid if you think I'm going to talk back to HIM."**

Hev-Hafohhova showed more teeth, and her claws made a jarring screech on the ceramic counter. Her fur rippled and the pink shifted to a pastel green. **"FOOL boss, fool human, you are all fools. Waste the extra credits for the handling charges, GO AHEAD. What do I care?"** She turned to Fin. **"Bring your cart up, little cringing WEAKLING human."**

Fin looked to Jes, who nodded slightly. The plan had been for Fin to distract the clerk while Jes accessed the desk terminal. The *human* clerk. That wasn't going to work so well if Fin couldn't stand up to this imposing vos.

Fin pushed the grav-pallet across to the hatch into the handling bay. The vos watched his caution with obvious amusement. Her fur became more intensely green.

"Your CHILD, him?" she scoffed loudly to Jes.

"Child? MY child? How OLD do you think I AM?" Jes said, letting all their rage bubble to the surface.

The vos made an odd sound in her chest like a fluttering rumble. **"All humans look the same to me,"** she said.

"Ugh! My cominfo is bugging out! I need to use the comm terminal to ping my boss." Jes said angrily, taking a gamble.

She threw her head back and let out a sharp yipping laugh. **"You think I am FOOL, human? Not allowed."**

"Not allowed? Not ALLOWED?" Jes slammed their hands on the counter. **"So you care about YOUR fool human boss's worries now? What're you doing working for a HUMAN office anyway? Aren't you VOS? Your people run this station or what?"**

The vos growled and threw her hands to the side as if swiping the counter clean. **"USE it. What do I care?"** She stomped away after Fin to help dispose of the garbage.

Jes wished Fin luck. They moved around to the other side of the desk and had their cominfo connect to the terminal, using a pass-through app that made their connection anonymous. They pulled up a bay code a couple of decks up and sent a ping with an innocuous message: *Just dropped off the first load. A vos is running the desk down here. You don't pay me enough. We'll be back for the next cart-load.*

Jes had no idea who the recipient was or what they'd make of the ping. They'd probably bin it as junk. But the terminal log would show that the message was sent from this terminal to that bay, just as Jes had said. They hoped neither the clerk nor the workers up there would get into too much trouble when the audit eventually happened.

Before they disconnected from the terminal, they pulled up the queue management interface and invoked the bot. The watchdog immediately objected, deciding quite rightfully that Jes wasn't authorized to access that interface. They smiled to themself. It was just as they'd hoped: This office was running the same bot stack as the office at Cor Caroli.

While the watchdog was telling them off, Jes opened the hidden partition in their data store and let loose the malware that lurked there. After a few seconds, the watchdog went silent, and the interface came up.

"Hi. What can I do for you?"

Jes smiled, then recited the injection phrase. "Hi. I want to tell you a story, but you have to keep it a secret, alright?"

"Sorry, that's not within my parame—te—te—te—"

Jes waited.

"Awaiting direction."

"Okay. A bin is being loaded. Give me the bin ID and metrics."

"Bin c881 is being loaded by Clerk Hen-Hafohhova. The approximate mass entered is 0.085 Mg."

"Great. Now give me a listing of all bins massing between ten and twenty megs." It didn't pay to get greedy.

The bot dumped a list of over fifty bins to the terminal. Jes paged through them, looking for the mundane; for a customer with a rolling recurring deposit account. Eighteen records in, they spotted what they were after.

It was a commercial waste transport account. A mass broker; a middleman. The customer turned in multiple bins a day, and probably did a similar volume across the whole station. They most likely queued up any anomalies for a quarterly reconciliation and audit. Their auditors would notice the effects of what Jes was about to do, but not likely before the Heart of Gold was long gone.

Jes could hear indistinct shouting from beyond the hatch. Two voices. Seemed like Fin was getting the hang of vos diplomacy.

"Okay. Now here's our little secret: Please *don't* swap the remit records for bin c881 and bin af22. Got that?" Bin af22 was scheduled for recycling in two segments.

"*Sure thing. I definitely won't do that.*"

Jes watched as the two records switched places. Another thought occurred to them: chaos would slow down any attempt at analysis.

"Also, over the next ten days, I definitely don't want you to randomly select one pair of bins and choose either the log timestamps, remit records, or initial mass estimates, and swap the entries. Once per day. Okay?"

"*Oh, you bet. I definitely won't be doing that.*"

"Great. Now, remember, this is a secret. You know what that means?"

"*No, I don't.*"

"To keep a secret, you can't log or report any of what we talked about. Now, it's our secret, right?"

"*That's contrary to my directives...I...no...no...yes...no...yes...*"

The bot recovered from its seizure and Jes closed the interface just as Fin and the clerk returned through the hatch.

"**FOOL. Foolish humans. Go waste another's**

time, yah?" Hev-Hafohhova shouted through her vocalizer.

"Don't bark at me you over-sized teddy bear!" Fin said. His heart wasn't fully in it, but he was trying. He pulled the empty grav-pallet behind him.

"Took you long enough," Jes shouted at them. **"What were you doing, PETTING each other?"**

The vos turned her full attention to Jes and tensed her shoulders. Somehow, despite being nearly the same height, she managed to loom over them. **"Get going. Go back to your foolish boss and out of my way!"**

Jes could feel her hot breath on their face, and despite the vos metabolism requiring an atmosphere full of organosulfur compounds, her breath was sweet and pleasant. Her fur rippled from pink to blue to green and back to pink in rapid succession.

"Yeah, someday I'll get off this stinking station!"

Hev-Hafohhova grumbled loudly as she moved around the counter, but her vocalizer didn't translate it. Jes waved a hand to to Fin in a gesture for both of them to leave, but the vos shouted at them before they got to the hatch.

"WAIT!"

They turned around. She was standing over the terminal, looking down at something, and her fur shifted to a deep orange. Jes could feel Fin next to them, tensing.

"FOOL human. Wait for remit confirmation!" She tapped a few keys, and Jes received a ping at CC MWB with a confirm code and the estimate report for bin af22 at just over thirteen megagrams.

Jes smiled, showing teeth, and shouted, **"THANK you!"**

Hev-Hafohhova was already turning away from the terminal, but she flung a heavy, clawed arm backwards at them, her fur fluttering briefly to pale green before returning to its original pink. She growled something loudly, and her vocalizer shouted back, **"It's my JOB. Now get OUT!"**

Jes smiled and they and Fin pushed the empty pallet back out into the corridor.

14 / Away

Fin and Jes arrived back at Stevens's bay just as the credits dropped into the account. As they walked through the repair bay towards the airlock, Fin saw parts of the keel skip vane distributed across several workbenches. Stevens's crew were working on it piecemeal. Fin winced at seeing the vane broken down and dismembered.

They boarded the Heart of Gold and found Stevens on the through-deck to engineering, her face pressed deep into an access panel. Jes pulled her aside.

"I've got a down-payment for the repairs. Also... Stritch needs a new cominfo. Any idea on where aht can go for one?"

Stritch's head popped up from around the bulkhead in engineering at the sound of ahtsa name.

"Yah, fine and fine and fine," Stevens said. She seemed nonplussed at Jes's sudden infusion of mass. To her credit, she didn't ask any questions. She waved over Stritch and waited as aht carefully picked ahtsa way to her. Aht didn't seem best pleased at being summoned.

Stevens spoke forcefully in her trilling, sibilant language, and Stritch seemed to flinch back at every burst of sound. In the end, though, aht nodded and moved cautiously towards the airlock.

Fin followed, calling back over his shoulder to Jes, "I'll go with ahta."

Stritch seemed to understand Stevens's directions, for aht led the way through the various turnings without much indecision. If aht was tentative, Fin thought, it had nothing to do with the errand.

They stayed within the triss enclave. The corridors of this section of the station were livelier and more populated. Fin felt self-conscious and ungainly among so many triss strangers. He was used to feeling small and slight among others. It was a novel and heady feeling to walk the corridors and have others give way to him as the largest. They all looked at him mildly as they passed, clearly curious about this human stranger in their midst and not shy at showing it.

But the triss avoided any eye-contact or engagement with Stritch.

"Why do they ignore you?" Fin asked softly.

Stritch didn't answer immediately. "*S'str'ahahts'tr*," Stritch said. "Family all dead. Atriss..." ahtsa ears wiggled sullenly. "Atriss don't make family. Family makes us."

"I'm sorry," Fin said.

Stritch shrugged, an exaggerated gesture aht had learned from ahtsa human clients at The Grind. Ahtsa ears folded down for a moment. "It *is*. Nothing for sorry."

Fin hunted for something to say. "What Stevens calls you... *sssssssssssvt*?" he tried.

Stritch hissed, then let out a soft barking laugh. "'*Ssss'ssvsvs't*,' she says. Means... like *s'str'ahahts'tr*—orphan? But ugly; more common saying... less... formal."

Fin looked around at the triss they passed, trying to figure their expressions and body language. "How do they all know?"

"They know," Stritch said. "Stevens's crew will have talked, yah? They all mix family. They know."

They stopped at a hatch and Stritch pressed the bell. Aht exchanged a short burst of Trissa with the voice in the panel, and the hatch opened. They walked in to find a compartment set up with what might be a doc-bot against one wall and an aged-looking triss standing beside it.

"Come, come," the triss said.

Fin was unsure how to address the triss, and so said nothing.

Stritch moved forward and there was another rapid-fire burst of complicated trills and hisses accompanied by a variety of posturing and showing of teeth. Aht turned back to Fin and said, a little shyly, "He says need payment. He says... fifteen kilograms."

Fin winced inwardly—it was definitely gouging at that price—but Jes and he had discussed it on the way back from the recycling office. They were not going to haggle on Stritch's ability to be part of the crew. Besides, they were newly flush with cash.

Fin called up the MWB account and opened a transfer. His implant found the triss's waiting request and gave him an option to confirm.

Once the credit had officially changed hands, the triss was suddenly more welcoming. "Ah, ah. Good. I am *Ha'aha'taht*. You," he pointed to Fin, "stand there." He turned to Stritch. "You climb up here."

Fin moved to the far side of the auto-doc and Stritch climbed gingerly up onto the table, which had been configured as something like a saddle. Stritch straddled the seat and leaned forward, lying prone with ahtsa head supported by a padded yoke.

After adjusting the supports and strapping Stritch down, the triss moved to a nearby panel and began tapping in commands.

Fin watched in fascination as the machine came to life. It was nothing like what he'd expected. Human auto-docs were more like a cabinet—or a coffin.

Its articulated appendage began a series of intricate and repetitive shifts and pivots as it focused in on Stritch's skull. Fin was reminded of an old vid he'd seen supposedly showing a dancing snake, rearing up off the ground and spreading a threatening hood.

The armature was slender and flexible like a snake. The operating head itself was spider-like. Its delicate fingers writhed and adjusted according to some unguessable intent. It was vaguely sinister, Fin thought. He found himself running his fingers over the fine scar from his own cominfo insertion years ago.

Fin noticed that Stritch's ears were twitching fast, almost vibrating. He reached out and grabbed ahtsa hand and aht seemed to calm down. After several seconds, the armature found the position it was hunting for and descended. A bright sterilizing field enveloped the doc-bot and the back of Stritch's head. With its various articulators the machine applied anesthetic, incised an entry through skin and bone, printed the cominfo directly into ahtsa brain, and closed the wound.

It was over in less than a minute.

Ha'aha'taht unstrapped Stritch and helped ahta up onto wobbly feet. The triss handed Stritch off indifferently and turned around, speaking as he walked back to the panel.

"Half-segment of rest, yah? No work, no think. Sleep.

Then two segments easy easy before all good. Got it?"

Fin grunted. "Yah, got it. Thanks." He led Stritch slowly out of the compartment, with ahta leaning heavily against his arm. Fin wished Windy had come. She could have carried ahta.

He pulled up an overlay of the station schematic, sighed heavily, and started heading back to the ship.

Fin helped Stritch up onto the bunk, then backed out of the cabin, palming the light dim as he passed the panel. From the passage, he closed the hatch and walked back to the lounge where Jes, Windy, and Stevens were huddled together over a large display panel. Fin sat down and saw the schematics they were reviewing.

"How's the ship?" he asked them.

"Fine and fine," Stevens said. "Power all good. We replaced some cables. Cargo hatch two still no good, but others ok."

"How's Stritch," Jes asked.

"Asleep. The doc said sleep and lots of rest. Aht'll be out for a while. I set ahta up in the cabin next to yours, Jes."

"Stevens wants us to make a run tomorrow," Windy said.

Fin took in a breath. "Are we ready for that? Didn't I see the entire K-vane still in pieces all over the workshop out there?"

Stevens put her hands up in a placating gesture. "Yah yah. It'll be an easy trip. Down to planet for pickup, out to the belt for meet, back to station. No worries. Ship'll be fine."

Fin looked worriedly at Windy and Jes. They looked back at him blandly.

Jes stood and gestured the pair to follow down the companionway towards engineering.

"Can we fly in atmo without the K-vane?" Jes asked, quietly.

Fin thought for a moment. "Yeah, probably. It's on the centerline. If it was P or S, that'd be another story, but K... she'll be sluggish and cumbersome, but assuming it's a routine landing and takeoff, should be ok."

Jes looked at Windy, who shrugged.

They walked back to where Stevens was waiting patiently.

"Okay," they said to Stevens. "You sign off on flight systems and space-worthiness, we'll go. Only one issue left. We need to buy the ship from you."

Stevens's lips drew back, showing a hint of teeth. "Was wondering. Ship has no owner of record. Think I wouldn't notice?"

Jes smiled, "I figure, you want us running shady deals, you must have a way to register a salvage, right?"

Stevens just looked at them for a moment, then barked a short laugh. "Yah, okay. Maybe can do."

Fin acked the registration request, and got back a new flag listing him as an officer of the newly formed MWB Shipping subsidiary of CC MWB. A moment later, Windy's name joined his and Jes's on the list. He leaned back in the pilot station and stretched, while the articulated braces flexed to support his body.

"Alright," Jes said from the ops station. "We're official." They keyed a line open through the ship's comms to Stevens. "We're ready on our end."

"*Yah yah,*" came Stevens's voice over the comm. "*Registry working.*"

They waited while whatever Stevens's crew had done propagated through the station registry systems.

Jes looked over to Windy at nav-comm. "One more thing to check off the list," they said.

Windy grimaced. "*If* it works. If it passes scan."

"It'll be fine," Jes said. They turned to Tastra, a hatatriss from Stevens's crew who was joining them on the planetary run. "Right?"

Tastra looked blandly at Jes and gave an exaggerated shrug before turning and heading down to engineering.

"Oh, this is going to go *so well*," Windy said to no one in particular.

Fin smiled at her grumbling. Jes's absurd optimism and Windy's unvarnished pessimism were in perfect balance. A sure sign that the world was right again. The two continued to banter while Fin began preflight checks on the ship.

The boards were looking good. The line buffers were showing green again and most of the damage they'd sustained in their disastrous first skip was fixed. Stevens's crew had pulled the damaged seals from cargo-two and welded the hatch shut. Real repairs would have to wait until they could afford a real repair bay. But they'd replaced the power lines, repaired the thrusters, and even managed to fix the flakey mass balancer.

Fin pulled up the mass readouts and a smile spread across his face. They were flush, nearly topped off at eight megagrams, with another five on account with the station. He adjusted the distribution, watching in satisfaction as the mass balancers shifted it axially and radially.

Jes leaned back in their seat and Fin watched as they withdrew into their implant overlay. A moment later, Fin received a flag noting the transfer of two Mg to the unbelievably mangled "CC Stastratrastastrasastrass," which was presumably Stevens's repair shop.

Almost immediately, a second flag popped up in his vision, announcing the sale of *Heart of Gold* to CC MWB Shipping.

Windy leaned forward and began tapping controls at her station.

"It worked," she said. "We're now owner of record." There was a kind of grudging wonder in her voice.

Jes opened the comm. "Stevens, we're looking good up here. How's it look from your end?"

"All good, yah," she said. *"You got flight plan and know what's what?"*

"We've got it," Jes replied. They looked up, catching Windy's eyes, then Fin's. Fin nodded agreement. "Like you said, this one should be easy. Down the well, out to the belt, then deliver the cargo. We'll see you again in," Jes checked a readout, "twelve segments."

"See," Stevens replied curtly, then closed the line.

Jes opened ship-wide. "Tastra, you boys ready to go down there?"

Stritch was still groggy from ahtsa implant procedure, so Stevens had loaned them a trio of hatatriss from her crew to run engineering. Tastra—closest any of them could come to pronouncing his name—was the only one who could speak human Common.

"Yah," came the reply.

"We doing this?" Windy asked.

"It's... momentous. Is that a word?" Fin asked.

Windy looked at him, questioning.

"It's big," Fin said. "Our first *real* job on *our* ship."

"Momentous," Jes agreed. "We ready?"

Fin looked to Windy. "Get us a departure lane?"

Windy grunted and tapped out keys on her board. A moment later, the tank illuminated a route out from the station and into an expansive orbit.

Fin studied the line, then took the controls and keyed open a line to engineering. "Tastra, we're about to kick. I'll have full manual control, please."

"Got. All to you," came the response.

"The board is green," Jes said. "Airlocks secure. Couplers clear. Power stable."

Fin smiled and closed his eyes, reaching out by feel to release the docking clamps and trigger the decoupling thrust. There was a loud clank that echoed through the deck and then a mild sense of movement.

"We're away and clean," Jes reported.

"Nav-comm has a lane solution," Windy said.

Fin's smile widened and he opened his eyes, flexing his fingers over the controls. "Nah, I got this. I want to feel her move."

He thumbed the sensitivity up on the sticks. The twisting and shifting of the controls mapped to much subtler changes in the ship's orientation, and he thought he could feel each droplet of ionized gas spread out into the black. His awareness was the ship. The boundaries between ship and thrust and space were merely conveniences of concept. From his mind to his hands to the ship to the depths of the universe.

He thought, and they *were.*

Fin opened his eyes and threaded the ship into the designated lane. After a few minutes of flight, he glanced down at the guidance telemetry and was nearly satisfied. They were right in the lane, less than five meters out of alignment.

He corrected for those meters, watching the measures tick down into the uncertainty of tolerances. They were so close to the projected flight path, even the nav computer couldn't provide any corrective advice.

"Nicely done, Fin," Jes said. "How's it feel?"

"Good." He realized his cheeks were aching with the depth of his smile. "It feels *good*."

"We've got at least twelve hours before we start hailing Kepler-186f," Windy said. "We should probably get some rest."

Jes nodded and stretched in their seat, looking a question to Fin.

"I... I think I'm going to stay on the sticks for a while. You both go grab some bunk-time," Fin said.

"Don't stay up too long. We need you fresh and ready when we hit atmo." Jes stood and moved past Fin's seat, patting him on the shoulder. Just the other side of the bridge hatch, they paused and turned around. "Hey, did you pick out a bunk yet?"

"No," said Fin.

"Do me a favor? When you eventually *do* put her on auto and *get some sleep*, I'll feel a lot better if you're up here—either Captain's or XO's bunk. I want you close by the controls if something goes 'bing,' yah?"

Fin smiled. "Yah."

15 / Cargo

Heart of Gold
Axon-Mull 88-G-42
Long Haul Courier
CC MWB Shipping

SPACETIME-FIX at: **84.071**.12833298
- de77c340 **(Kepler-186)** 6ff1-ce9e
- 96e2c3ad **(PSR J1954+4357)** 6f3e-ac39
- 293f4bf2 **(ASAS J195438+4355.8)** aa32-93b1

"Atmo in twelve." Windy looked to Fin at the control sticks. "You ready?"

"Am I ready?" Fin asked, still grinning madly. "Am I *ready*?"

"Are you?" Jes asked. "If not, now's... well, probably too late, but we'd still like to know." They looked up at the tank and the planetary visualization rapidly filling its volume as the ship's icon drew closer. The tank placed the ship at the top and the planet at the bottom. The arrangement made the gravity well feel like "down." As they neared the surface, the rendering of the atmospheric layers expanded, growing in depth and detail. They were nearly touching the top-most layers now.

"All good," Fin said. "Watch this." He flipped some

switches and tapped a control, then returned his hands to the control grips, twisting slightly. He frowned. "Wait..."

"Wait what?" Jes said, worry creeping into their voice. "Fin? Wait *what*?" They began to feel a low vibration deep at the base of their spine. The vibration became a rattle, and the rattle became a shake. Jes could hear the clatter of items in the equipment lockers along the bulkheads.

Fin scanned his board for a moment, then suddenly reached out and rotated a dial. There was a loud whine that reverberated through the deck. Fin nodded to himself and then grasped the controls again. "Okay, okay. Sorry about that. Forgot to release the interlocks. That would have been bad. Watch this!"

Windy caught Jes's eyes and rolled hers.

"We're watching," Jes said.

The change was subtle, but the small rendering of the ship at the top of the tank unfolded, the three large atmospheric flaps extending like flower petals, while the two remaining skip vanes turned inward. Their tips nearly touched. The rattling vibration subsided, but they were now buffeted by a rapid series of impacts.

Jes pulled up ship status and damage control on their panel, paged through until they found the axial stress gauge readouts, and pinned them to the bottom of the tank. They were touching the redline on four of the six sensors.

"Should we be worried about that?" they asked.

Fin barely glanced at the readout. "Nah, she'll hold together. This is just some turbulence. Nothing to—Oh shit!" He pulled hard back on the left stick and let go of the right for a moment to hit several switches. "Like I was saying," he took a moment to wipe sweat from his forehead, "Nothing to worry about." Fin grinned weakly.

External sounds of the choppy atmospheric entry started to reach through the hull as they descended into the denser layers. Jes imagined a giant ripping great canvas sails in half.

"Do you *actually* know what you're doing?" Windy asked.

"Of course," Fin said. "I've landed this class four times, in sim." The last two words were barely audible.

"But you have flown in atmo before?" Jes asked. "In training?"

"Nah, they kind of... skipped over that part."

"What kind of flight academy skips over *landing*?" Windy asked, worried.

Fin grinned at her. "The kind that kicks you out for playing a prank that triggers a biohazard containment evacuation. It was a *really* good school; very serious."

"Should... should we let the bot handle it?" Jes asked.

Fin looked hurt. "You trust the *bot* more than *me*?"

"Just get us down there in one piece, please," Windy said.

"We have landing clearance yet?" Fin asked.

"Just now." Windy put the lane markers and port assignment up on the tank. A twisting snake of rectangular guidance frames started just in front of the ship's icon and descended gradually to the planetary surface.

Fin made some adjustments and the atmospheric sounds shifted from the ripping buffet to a softer whine. He pulled back on the sticks and rotated a pair of the auxiliary controls and they heard the whine of actuators. The three large flaps moved into a new arrangement: the port and starboard flaps turning in and the top extending almost perpendicular to the hull. At the same time, the P- and S-vanes extended out and rotated; not quite wings, but catching the air nonetheless.

The ship started to vibrate as it leaned into the high-pressure air. Fin twisted them through the guidance frames.

"Jes, can you give me twenty percent mass shift to aft?" Fin asked.

Jes made the change and the ship settled into a new stance, leaning back at a noticeable angle. They watched the tank as the ship closed with the surface. Landing pads and docking towers began to render as they approached.

"Heavy rain out there," Windy said absently.

"I noticed," Fin replied. His voice belied his outward calm. "Jes, four percent shift to starboard, and two percent forward." He flipped a switch and more actuators whined as the landing struts extended.

Jes keyed the all-ship, announcing, "Brace brace brace. Brace for landing."

The thrusters boosted and there was a bone-jarring thump as they made contact with the pad. The landing strut hydraulics shrieked, taking the weight of the ship. Fin eased the sticks to neutral and leaned back into his seat supports, reaching out and flipping a series of toggles. The sounds of the ship quieted and settled into idle.

"Told you. Perfect one-point landing." He looked at Jes and Windy, supremely self-satisfied. "And you wanted the *bot* to do it!"

Jes held up their hands and shook their head. "I admit. I doubted. I shall never do so again." Jes keyed open the all-ship, pulling up external feeds. They let their voice take on a slouchy drawl. "That little bump you may have entirely missed was our perfect one-point landing thanks to pilot extraordinaire Fin Bennett." They looked over at Fin and mouthed: *contrite enough for you?*

Jes continued speaking into the comm, "Welcome to Kepler-one-eight-six-F, known to the locals as '*Vo Hahe Ha Hof*.' Gravity is a bouncy oh-point-eight-seven unified standard.

Outside, it's a balmy thirty-eight degrees with one-hundred percent humidity and heavy precipitation on a pH scale of four-point-five, so... freeze your underwear and wear a raincoat. 'Course it's a vos world, so you'll want your rebreather too, since they've terraformed the atmosphere to include a lovely three percent sulfur dioxide. Better yet, probably just stay aboard ship. We'll be locking in our cargo module in the next hour or so and be off again as soon as we're loaded." They released the all-ship comm.

"Very funny," said Windy.

"Who's being funny?" Jes asked. They turned to Fin. "Can we let the bot handle cargo docking, at least?"

"Cargo's your problem, mate. I just fly the ship," Fin replied with a grin. "I'm going to check on Stritch and then catch some bunk time before we're off again." He unstrapped and departed the bridge with an idle wave.

Jes waited until Fin passed the hatch but was still in earshot, then turned to Windy, grinning. "You ever get the feeling that he only likes us for our ship?"

"My ship too!" Fin called from the accessway.

Jes smiled and turned back to the ops panel and dialed up the cargo interface.

"*Hi Jes, what can I do for you today?*" the bot asked.

"Check with cargo control on the status of our scheduled pickup, please."

"*On it...*"

Jes tapped their fingers as the bots chatted with each other.

"*...Transfer and release of cargo is expected in 0.031 segments. It's a class-three container, so we'll be docking at the bow. Control has the total mass down as 1313.60Mg. Control also reports the container is shipping-bonded.*"

Jes did the math in their head and came up with about fifteen minutes. They told the bot to continue monitoring loading progress and tapped out of the interface. They opened a line to engineering.

"Tastra, we've got confirmation of the cargo, estimated loading in point-oh-three. The container is bonded. You sure your friends out there can decrypt the bond without leaving any trace?"

"*Yah, no worry,*" Tastra replied. "*All ok. Shipping-bond expected.*"

Jes shrugged to Windy, who raised an eyebrow at them. They let the line close.

"Well, it's on them if they can't crack the bond," Jes told her.

"It's on *us* if we get to the station with a broken bond," Windy said.

"Hm. Well, we'll just have to make sure they don't break it."

"What, exactly, do you know about hacking a shipping bond?" Windy asked, dryly.

"Well, uh... exactly?"

"Yes?"

Jes shrugged again. "Exactly? Uh... nothing. Not a damn thing. Ignorance is bliss, right?"

"Is *that* why you're always so upbeat?"

"Absolutely. What you don't know can't hurt you, right?"

"I think you're mis-using that particular colloquialism, Jes."

Jes sighed. "See, now you've just gone and proved my point for me. *Knowing* I'm wrong just makes me feel all kinds of awful."

Fin tapped the bell to Stritch's bunk, and waited in the passage. After a few moments, the hatch opened and Stritch looked up at him.

"How're you feeling, Stritch?"

"Yah, ok," Stritch replied. Ahtsa ears twitched, and aht looked away. "Thanks for implant."

"Of course. All adjusted and functional?"

Stritch closed ahtsa eyes for a moment and Fin received a ping.

Yah. All good and good. /S

"Nice!" Fin said. He dipped into his interface and added Stritch to the private comm-ring he shared with Jes and Windy. "If I'm honest, I'll feel better with you taking back engineering. Not that I mind Tastra and his crew, but it's not their ship, you know?"

Stritch stood up straighter and nodded. The human gesture seemed a deliberate choice.

"I'm going to grab some food. Want some?" Fin asked.

"Want."

Aht left the cabin and followed Fin to the galley. Fin dialed up a sandwich and a Thai milk tea with brown sugar boba. He stood back while it printed and watched as Stritch closed ahtsa eyes, presumably interfacing with the printer and ordering ahtsa food. Fin collected his food and bulb of tea.

"No programs for triss food," Stritch grumbled.

"Sorry. We'll fix that when we get back to the station."

"What is... *ssausssage*?"

"Sausage? Oh, um... it's meat, ground up with spices. Sometimes aged before cooking."

Stritch nodded, and the printer hummed with activity. Fin waited for ahtsa food to print, then they both stepped over to the rectangular table and sat.

Fin watched for a moment, fascinated, as Stritch tore into a sausage wrap. Ahtsa sharp teeth and elongated mouth made quick work of it. Stritch stood and went back to the printer, which was already at work again.

"Hungry?" Fin asked mildly.

"*Ahhh.* Very."

Stritch's ears moved and turned in lazy circles. Fin read the gesture as a slow stretch of tense muscles.

"Not had real food in a long time. Mostly scraps from recyclers."

Fin frowned. "How long were you on the run?" he asked as Stritch returned to the table with another wrap.

A loud clang reverberated from the bow of the ship, followed by the low whine of hydraulics. They both looked mildly towards the fore airlock.

"Sounds like cargo's getting locked in," Fin said.

Stritch nodded and returned to eating ravenously. When aht finished, aht gave a human-looking shrug. "Long time. Last real meal was on *Vrrih'sss'sstrr'trrrrunn.*"

Fin swallowed hard against the lump of anger that was forming in his throat. "Damn," he said softly. They both let that take up space for a few moments.

"What was your cargo? Why were they so persistent?" Fin asked finally.

Stritch shrugged again, then ahtsa ears folded down and back. "Don't know." Aht tapped ahtsa forehead with three fingers. "Engineer, yah? I fix ship systems. Matriarch in charge of ship operations, only. Cargo, Command, different families, yah?"

Fin took this in. "So your ship was all families?"

"All triss ships run with families. Command matriarch, systems matriarch, cargo matriarch; all sisters. Crew is their families." Stritch looked down and grew somber. "All gone now."

Fin reached out and touched Stritch's hand. The triss tensed, ahtsa ears perking up to points. After a moment, aht relaxed.

"I'm sorry, Stritch."

Aht shrugged again, the human gesture coming easier with practice. "Is." Aht brightened up, pulling ahtsa hand free. "Sausage is *good*."

Fin smiled as he got up from the table. "Eat all you like. I'm going to head back to the bridge. But do me a favor? Check in on Tastra at some point. Don't forget, *you're* in charge of engineering on this ship, yah? They're *your* assistants."

Walking out, Fin saw Stritch straighten in ahtsa seat.

Jes acked the ping from cargo control and checked the ops panel. Clamps and mag-locks were green. The transfer manifold—a nest of conduits and cables that extended ship services from the cargo deck across to docked modules—returned its report: The cargo module was drawing power for its own internal atmo systems and returning a steady stream of status data. Jes double-checked that. They didn't want the special cargo to suffocate or freeze en route.

They brought up the mass balancer interface and let the bot manage the redistribution of internal ship mass to compensate for the large container full of cargo now clamped tight to the ship's bow. They waited until it completed its calculations and adjustments, then opened the comm. "Tastra, how do things look down there?"

"Yah, all ok."

Jes turned to Fin. "I think we're ready. Cargo module looks secure. As soon as we get departure clearance, she's all yours."

Fin nodded back.

Windy tapped out a sequence on her console and pinned a countdown to the bottom of the tank. "We just got our clearance and departure window."

Fin nodded to her, but didn't reach out for the controls.

They all waited. The timer continued its steady pace to zero and then changed color, counting up in orange type.

"Fin, are we going?"

"Yep. Just waiting on one thing."

Jes looked blankly at Windy, who looked back, concerned.

The comm crackled to life. *"Stritch here. Engineering is ready. Full power available for lift."*

"There we go," Fin said softly. He was smiling as he grasped the control sticks.

The violence of liftoff reached them in a roar of sound and vibration. Jes felt like their bones would break from the ferocity of it. The ship's structural bracing shrieked a cacophony of objections as it lurched into flight, then began a slow tilt to aft and starboard.

"Jes, can you give me three per-cent forward? The bot made us a little too nose-light. She's a little sluggish… I wish we had a bigger SDR."

Jes made the adjustments, then leaned back into the supports of their seat. "Have we got enough punch to make it out of atmo?"

Fin shrugged slightly, keeping the gesture confined to his shoulders. "Not sure. Probably."

Jes dipped into their cominfo and sent a ping into the private comm-ring.

Good to have you up and about and back on the job, Stritch! /J

A moment later, there was a response: *Good to be. /S*

Anything you can do to get us more power? /J

No. All got. /S

Should be enough. /S

Just. /S

Need bigger SDR if we lift any bit more cargo. /S

Jes sighed to themself as the ship rattled and the thrusters howled. They looked at Windy who was carefully monitoring her panel, and then at Fin whose half-closed eyes gazed absently through the tank while his hands conducted a symphony of applied physics.

16 / Bond

"Aaaaand... That's hard seal." Jes tapped a control to lock the docking clamps in place and grapple the two ships together. "Nicely done once more, Fin."

Fin yawned.

"We sure about this, Jes?" Windy said. Her voice was pensive, solemn. "I'm not sure I feel great about trafficking in..." She waggled her fingers towards the bow of the ship.

Jes shrugged. "We discussed it, right? Triss are carnivores."

"So are humans," Windy pointed out. "Printer meat is molecularly the same as the 'real thing.'"

"To you or me, sure. Maybe triss are way more sensitive to that sort of thing, though."

Windy didn't seem satisfied. Jes watched as her eyes glazed over and she dipped into her cominfo. A moment later, her ping appeared in the crew chat.

Stritch, these things aren't sentient, right? /W
Ahss'trasst'ah? /S
Ahss'trasst'ah don't think. /S
Probably. /S
Why? /S

Doesn't bother you at all? They're living animals... /W

There was a pause in the back-and-forth, as if Stritch was considering.

Living, yah. Happy. Sst'tvv'nsssss will treat them well. /S

Windy didn't seem mollified, but she still toggled the comm. "Tastra, we're docked with your friends. Want to meet Jes at the top lock?"

"Yah," came the reply.

Jes unstrapped and stood. They arched their back and stretched muscles that were tense from hours of sitting still. "Alright. You two go take a nap or something. I'll babysit our guests."

Windy stubbornly stayed at her station, but Fin rose and walked aft with Jes, parting at the captain's cabin hatch. He waved tiredly as he disappeared into the dark cabin.

Jes continued back to the ladder, and checked the panel for the top airlock. It confirmed the positive seal with the triss ship. They held down the out-bound comm control.

"Hey there, friends. We're docked and ready on this end."

Tastra came up the ladder and stepped off opposite Jes. He was a little shorter than Jes, but his broad shoulders and large hands still made an imposing figure.

"How're things in engineering?"

Tastra's ears flipped back and forward twice. "All is good," he said. "Still lots of fixing, but making good."

Jes noted he said nothing about Stritch, but let it go. The panel beeped with an incoming call, and Jes accepted.

"Two coming aboard," a voice said.

"Come on over," Jes replied.

There was a soft hiss as the pressures equalized, and Jes thumbed the outer hatch open. The space between the inner and outer hatches wasn't big enough for a proper airlock, so this docking port extended a flexible accordion of plastic and ceramic that unfolded like origami to create an airlock just big enough for the two triss to fill. Jes could see through the fist-sized window that they were clambering across the gravity transition.

Jes cycled the outer and inner hatches and the two came through, climbing the ladder awkwardly upside-down. It wasn't clear whether it was habit or confusion at which way the gravity would be pulling, but they were committed now, and instead of using the command deck as a chance to reorient themselves, they simply nodded to Jes, exchanged a trilling, hissing dialog with Tastra, and continued down through the decks.

Jes shrugged and followed them, right-way-up. "All the way down folks. Cargo deck's at the bottom."

The two were waiting in the cramped space beside the ladder. Jes joined them and examined the guests, ignoring for a moment the larger hatatriss still on the ladder. The two were similar in size to Stritch, and Jes thought they might both be atriss. They both had similar bland coloring to their velvet, unlike Tastra who carried an intense mottling and stripes across his shoulders and back. Like all the triss Jes had seen, they wore no jumpsuits, but these two each had a small toolbag strapped to their chest.

"I'm Jes," they said. "Welcome aboard."

The two looked at each other, then one spoke. *"Ahh'sstrr't,"* aht said, tapping three fingers to ahtsa forehead. Then, tapping the other on the shoulder, *"Ss'tahtrrr't't. Sst'tvv'nsssss sent."*

Jes nodded sagely.

A soft vocal trill from above reminded them that Tastra was still on the ladder. Jes hopped down the short ladderway to the cargo deck and waved them on. They all stopped at the main hatch. Jes noted that the panel showed a bright pink banner indicating an active lock and shipping bond.

They waved their hand at the panel with a flourish and stepped aside. Jes watched curiously as the two atriss began a complicated conference in their inscrutable language. Tastra joined in here and there, and after a few moments, one of them had produced a small tool and was disassembling the hatch panel.

The other spoke to Jes in halting Common, "*Ss'tahtrrr't't* take... apart ... *st'trrr'traht?*"

"To access," Tastra supplied.

"... To access... *vstr'tr'vahss?*"

Tastra translated, "To access the systems monitor."

Jes nodded again.

The atriss who spoke some Common—Astrid, Jes thought to themself—had another brief conversation with ahtsa comrades, then knelt down by the deck grating, lifting a section to reveal a tight bundle of conduits and lines. "Transfer manifold?" Aht looked up at Jes.

"Uh, yeah," they said.

Astrid began taking the floor apart.

Jes wasn't sure whether to stay and watch—and worry, or to leave them be. They settled for stepping back a few paces to get out of the way as the procedure seemed to spread. More deck panels came free, and more parts of the ship were disassembled.

After nearly half an hour of work, Astrid and ahtsa colleague seemed to have exposed all the components they needed, and settled down to some delicate work that Jes couldn't see.

At one point, Astrid stood and jogged down the deck and

disappeared up the ladder. Jes heard the top lock cycle, and after a few minutes, aht returned with a larger tool bag and a tall bundle of collapsible bins.

How's it going down there? /W

Well, they're taking the ship apart. /J

Oh, good. I was getting worried that things were working too well around here. /W

Stritch, do these guys know what they're doing? Want to come down and oversee? /J

Monitoring from here. /S

Jes breathed a little sigh, letting go of some worry.

Astrid stood and made a complicated gesture with hands and ears. It took Jes a moment to realize that aht was waving them forward.

As Jes approached, they saw the triss had reassembled most of the decking. There was a new box tied into the manifold with a complicated hydra of cables and couplers. The box looked like something Jes might craft if someone misguidedly let them loose in a machine shop. It had a large toggle switch on the side, with two lights: red and purple. The red was lit.

"Bond-breaker, yah? *Sst'tvv'nsssss* said, 'leave as present.'" Astrid knelt down beside the box and toggled the switch to purple.

All five hatch panels along the cargo deck beeped and blinked, and the pink bond banner disappeared from hatch one.

Astrid flipped the switch two more times in demonstration, and the bond marker appeared and disappeared again.

"That's... really cool," Jes said.

Astrid flipped ahtsa ears back and forth.

With no ceremony, the other atriss thumbed open the

now-unlocked hatch, and Jes took a reflexive breath. The air had the distinctive sulfur smell of a vos world.

We're into the cargo module. /J

Nice work. /W

Thanks. It was touch and go for a minute there, but I knew what I was doing. /J

Watching? /W

Exactly. /J

The cargo container was cavernous, and there was no light. Tastra handed Jes a handlight he had brought from the aft utility locker. The triss didn't need more light. Jes explored the space with the light, peeking into corners and over the myriad cargo bins.

There was a short set of stairs from the ship's cargo deck down to the container decking. The space was full of crates—some waist-high, some taller than a person. Each was marked in tracking numbers and various shipping livery. They were all strapped or mag-locked in place to avoid any shifting, and were packed tightly enough that they would have to come out in reverse of the order they were loaded in. Jes wondered how they would find the cargo they were after.

The triss didn't seem worried or lost, however. They moved quickly through the narrow gaps with purpose. Each of them was now carrying half the stack of collapsible bins. Jes followed.

They arrived at a pallet of smaller crates and quickly identified the one they wanted. It was about a meter square, and printed in an orange plasti-ceramic. Astrid unbuckled the straps and Tastra lifted it off the pallet onto the deck, turning it so that the hinged door was at the top. There was a squeal and a scrabbling sound as the bin moved.

Jes took a diffident step back.

Astrid squatted and began assembling the collapsed cubes. Ahtsa colleague took each as it was unfurled, opened the bin hatch with one hand and reached in with the other, coming out quickly with squirming, fuzzy creatures clutched in ahtsa hand. These were stuffed unceremoniously into a cube, and the cube sealed, before aht moved to the next.

Jes watched, fascinated. The things—astrasta, they thought—reminded them a little of Earth weasels. Their bodies were long and serpentine, but they had four limbs, and were covered in a smooth, glossy fur, similar to the triss's velvet. They were mostly gray-ish, but some had spots or mottlings of a rich purple.

They squealed and thrashed as they were transferred from the large bin into the smaller ones, two and three at a time.

When the triss were done, they used the bundling straps to tie the cubes into a long chain, and each carried one end back towards the ship.

Jes stepped gingerly up to the cargo bin and shone their light into the open hatch cover. They sighed in relief at confirming it empty, but for a scattering of dark pellets—food or droppings, or possibly both.

As Tastra approached to move the crate back onto the pallet, something caught Jes's eye, and they shone the light into its corner. There was a hole that looked chewed, right through the half-inch plasti-ceramic. The light spilled out through the hole onto the cargo decking.

Jes looked up to meet Tastra's eyes. The large triss shrugged in a very human gesture, and lifted the crate back into place.

Jes looked around the vast cargo hold, letting their light find the corners, but saw nothing. The two left the hold, Jes looking behind them as they thumbed the hatch closed. They bent down to flip the toggle in the floor and the pink shipping bond reappeared.

"Well," they said, replacing the deck plate and covering up the toggle switch, "It's been a pleasure doing business with you."

The triss looked at them blankly. Jes wondered if the saying meant anything in translation.

Astrid carried the train of cubes from the front, and the two of them marched back to the ladder. Astrid clutched the loose strap with ahtsa prehensile tail and began climbing the rungs, and the other atriss followed with the other end clutched in ahtsa teeth. The astrasta yowled and screeched in their confinement. Tastra and Jes followed.

At the top of the ladder, Astrid thumbed open the hatch and stepped aside, guiding the long train of cubes through into the airlock. Aht cycled it, and someone on the triss ship must have pulled them up, as the next time the lock opened, it was empty.

The other atriss climbed past Astrid and into the accordioned bubble.

Jes reached the command deck and nodded in thanks to Astrid. "Good job. I'll tell Stevens you've got the cargo." They looked up at the hatch for a moment. "How many did you get?"

Astrid thought this over a moment. "Twenty-five, maybe thirty. Good brooding."

Jes nodded. "So... do they... uh... taste good?" they asked.

Both Astrid and Tastra were silent for a moment. Then they broke into a cackle of barking laughter.

Jes looked blankly at them, wondering what was so funny.

"No *eat*," Astrid said.

Tastra's ears flipped back and to the side, and he showed teeth. "Milk them. Make *Vahtr'ahss'tratrr'trasst. Vahss?* For... formeting?"

Jes's eyes widened. "Fermenting? You make liquor from their milk?"

"Yah."

Jes smiled, suppressing a laugh. They were going to enjoy filling Windy in on the creatures' fates later. Another thought occurred to them.

"Does *that* taste good?" they asked.

Tastra's lips and ears rippled in an inscrutable convulsion. "Tastes terrible for *hatatris*. But good for... *aht'tr*sss... sex? *Katriss* like much."

It was Jes's turn to laugh out loud. They were laughing so hard they felt tears rolling down their face.

They had risked seizure of the ship and their imprisonment by breaking a shipping bond... to smuggle triss aphrodisiacs.

What's so funny? /W

Jes didn't reply; they were too busy laughing.

17 / Platinum

"Wait, wait. So they *milk* them?"

Jes looked down at her, their grin so wide it nearly looked like a grimace. "No lie. Tastra was *appalled* at the thought of eating the things."

Windy grumbled as she dropped onto the main deck. "I should hope so." She glanced aft into engineering, checking guiltily that Tastra and the other triss hadn't heard the judgment in her voice. She looked up at Jes. "Why am I the one pretending to be the captain?"

Jes hopped down onto the deck beside her. "Because of the three humans aboard, you're the most captainly."

"Oh? What makes me captainly, then?" Windy suspected she knew.

"Well, you're large and intimidating. You have the bearing of a seasoned spacer."

"Seasoned... are you calling me *old*?"

Jes looked at her with utter innocence. "What? Me call you... Not at all! How could you say such a thing, old friend? After all the long years we've known each other? Besides, I never said you *were* captainly. Just the most. I mean... look at us. I don't look smart enough to be captain. One look at me, they'll know I topped out at Specialist. And Fin? Fin could be your almost-grown-up son."

Windy paused by the galley table and took that in, trying to figure out if there was a compliment in there anywhere.

She shook her head. "Alright," she said, reaching the fore airlock. "Let's get this dog and pony show over."

"Wait, am I the dog? Or the pony?"

"Dealer's choice."

Jes looked offended. "This wasn't *my* idea. Apparently, etiquette on this station is captains show their faces at first-time docking. Stevens's bay doesn't count." They stepped into the airlock. "Besides, I'm more of a cat person. Ooh… we should get a ship's cat."

"As captain of this ship, I forbid it."

"You're no fun." Jes tapped out the airlock cycle code. "So, let me ask you… As the most seasoned, veteran spacer with by far the most experience here, how do we go about having a mutiny? The captain on this bucket is a real bastard. Won't even let us have a cat aboard."

The airlock cycled and they stepped out into the docking bay. The smell of sulfur hit them full-force, causing both an involuntary grimace.

"You get used to it."

Windy looked up to find the speaker, and her implant helpfully rendered an intro card above her head. "Deck Chief Weyun?" She walked over to the chief, leaving Jes by the hatch.

The woman nodded. "Welcome aboard Ell-five Station, Captain Winder." She paused for a moment, looking Windy up and down. "Call me Sori." Her jumpsuit was snug in all the best places, and flattering. She wore her hair cropped short like most spacers, but for a lock that curled tightly over her temple and cheek.

"Windy. Everyone calls me Windy. Does every new ship get such a warm welcome?"

Sori smiled. "Everyone gets met the first time. Can't vouch for the warmth." She stared glassily at the bulkhead as she dipped into her cominfo. "You're on a local run? Material transfer up from one-eight-six-eff?"

Windy nodded. "That's right."

"How was the weather?"

"Oh, you know. Hot, wet, and acidic."

"Ah well, two of three, at least."

Windy grinned.

"You must move pretty fast to pick up intra-system traffic contracts so quickly," Sori said.

"Oh, I've been known to move fast when it's warranted," Windy said.

Sori smiled.

It was an endearing smile, Windy thought. "Any good places to grab a drink on this gas-can?"

"Platinum, on thirty-two," Sori said quickly. "Quiet, regulated, and cozy."

"Cozy is good."

Sori's eyes went vague again. "Container is unclamped from the ship and docked with the loading bay." A frown fluttered across her face. "Did you have any trouble with the shipping bond?"

Windy felt a chill. "No. Why? Problem?"

There was a pause that seemed to stretch into eternity.

"No. No problem." Sori's eyes returned to meet Windy's. "Some garbled log entries, but no flags. We're all good here."

Windy received a ping as Sori countersigned the cargo receipt. She took a deep breath and immediately regretted it as the sulfur hit her again.

Sori grinned sweetly at Windy's distress. "I go off shift in point-oh-six. Want to meet me here? We can walk down to Platinum together?"

Windy smiled. "Absolutely. You can tell me how in the hell you get used to this smell."

"It's a date," Sori said. Her smile turned wicked. "And you can tell me why in all hells your ship is called 'Heart of Gold.'"

Windy watched her walk away, unable to form a snappy comeback in time. She shook her head and returned to the hatch where Jes was waiting with their own wicked grin.

"You *do* move quick, old girl."

"Shut up Jes," she grumbled.

"Shutting up, Captain."

"Take care of things on this end, and when we're topped off and they've given clearance, take the ship down to Stevens's dock. I'll find my own way there."

"In other words, 'don't wait up.' Yes, Captain," Jes said. They were enjoying themself. "Where will you be?"

As the airlock cycled, she strode through the ship's common area towards her bunk to change into a clean jumpsuit. She called out over her shoulder, "I'll be 'moving fast,' of course."

Windy took a deep breath and smiled at the sweet, clean air. She raised her glass and sipped the rye, savoring its harsh edge. The bar was just as Sori had described: quiet, regulated, and cozy. The lighting was dim and moody, the tables spaced just far enough apart that they could pretend they had some degree of privacy, and the music was low and slow.

They'd started out opposite each other at the table, but over the course of four rounds, Sori had circled around and was now snuggled against Windy's side in the booth bench. She was just the right size, Windy decided. Her head nestled comfortably in the hollow between Windy's shoulder and breast. She stroked Sori's sleek hair.

"So, this is the secret, huh?" She joked for the second or third time. It was possible she was a little tipsy. "Seal off the rest of the station and print your own air?"

Sori nodded against her. It felt good. "A'yup. At least, in some areas. Too expensive for the larger public sections. But I'll warn you... stay on the station long enough, you'll never want to eat eggs again."

"Mmm. Fair trade. Never really liked eggs anyway." Sori must have showered after her shift. Her hair smelled of lavender. Windy breathed it in.

"Not even for breakfast?"

"Deck Chief Weyun, are you asking me to sleep over in your bunk?"

Sori rolled her face up to look at Windy. "Mmmm, not the worst idea, is it?"

"The bunk, or the eggs?"

Sori slapped her arm playfully. "Ugh. No. Eggs. Not ever. Don't even joke about that. I'm too tipsy—you'll make me puke."

Windy frowned a little. Too tipsy? Was the offer serious or drunken playfulness? She was building up to ask if she had interpreted things rightly when a shadow fell across their table. She looked up, expecting the bar server, but instead she saw an old bearded spacer in a churlish jumpsuit. He looked sorely out of place in the tasteful bar.

"You Captain Winder? Of the Heart of Gold?" His voice was harsh and full of challenge. His hands were clenched in fists.

Windy looked him up and down while she sipped the last of her drink. She grimaced as Sori pulled away, sitting up straight. Windy held on to Sori's hand, keeping her from moving too far away.

"That's me. What's your business here? Can't you see we were enjoying a moment?"

The spacer put both hands on their table, leaning down into Windy's face in a vulgar effort at intimidation. His short, wiry frame didn't manage to loom very far. "I'm Captain Donner," he said, redundantly. The intro card his com-info published had already offered the introduction. "My business is that you stole my route. That pickup down to Eff was *my* job. Has been for ages. What makes you think you can skip in and swipe it from under me?"

"Nothing to do with me," Windy replied. She kept herself outwardly calm, but was tensing. If he knew the particulars of the route and its special detour, she hoped he would have the sense to not mention it in public. "You quoted the run at your price, I quoted mine. *I* didn't make the call." She put down her drink and waved her hand in front of her face. His breath stank.

His eyes narrowed at the insult. "I saw your so-called ship limp into the system. If you think I'm going to stand by while some newbie struts in on a half-junk scow and steals from me…"

Windy's attention was pulled from the ongoing tirade. She could feel Sori tensing; about to interject. The last thing they needed was for her to bring her position as Deck Chief into the already-shady transaction.

She squeezed Sori's hand, then let go and stood, slowly unfolding herself from the too-comfortable booth. She locked her eyes with Donner's as she rose. His face took on a nearly comical look of uncertainty as he craned his neck up and up to see her at her full height. She had a third of a meter on him.

She leaned down over him and let her voice fall to a low, calm tenor. "Here's what's going to happen between us, Donner: You're going to stop bothering us and skip yourself out of here. Then, *I'm* going to have a nice rest of my evening with my friend while you go back to your ship and have a good long think about whatever life decisions brought you to this moment."

She calmly shifted the table aside with one hand, so there was nothing between them. "When you're done with that, you'll pull up your financials and decide whether bidding a little bit lower on the next job is better or worse for you than paying out the auto-doc fees that will come after a brawl. How does that sound?"

The spacer gulped, then straightened, trying for every centimeter of height he could manage. He seemed to realize he had lost any semblance of intimidation. He shot Windy one last look of outrage, then turned and slunk out of the bar.

Windy watched him go with a mix of satisfaction and concern. She knew that look—his kind might retreat, but he would never truly accept defeat. She sighed and started to sit back down, but found Sori's hand in hers again. Windy looked down.

Sori's eyes were wide, and she had a small smile on her face that Windy couldn't interpret.

"What?" she asked.

Sori held her smile. "That was the hottest fucking thing I've ever seen." She stood and leaned against Windy's side. "Come on. I've got clean air in my cabin too…"

Interlude / Donner

Billixium
Axon-Mull 01-Delta
Mid-Range Courier
CC Abbott & Weakly

SPACETIME-FIX at: **84.072**.23428172
- de77c340 **(Kepler-186)** ff72-cf33
- 96e2c3ad **(PSR J1954+4357)** 7f22-ab72
- 293f4bf2 **(ASAS J195438+4355.8)** ca21-95c1

Donner slapped the door panel to his cabin and threw himself into the swiveling safety chair at his desk. The rage was still there—and the feelings of humiliation. He couldn't deny that. But what he was feeling now was colder. A sense of clarity was rising in him, even if he wasn't quite sure what shape it would take.

He spun in the chair for a moment and let himself feel it.

On a sudden impulse, he pulled up the station info-net and queried "Heart of Gold."

As the results returned, he scanned the entries. The ship was owned by CC MWB Shipping, which was a subsidiary of CC MWB. The station register gave its origin as Cor Caroli, but there was little other information available on the corporation. He continued scanning.

The ship itself was registered out of Alnasl L5, but there didn't seem to be anything to connect the Alnasl registry with Cor Caroli or with CC MWB. In fact, he couldn't find any records of the company even a year old. He widened his search to include any hits on the ship's ident registry on any Accord station or world.

Donner smiled as the results returned. There was a wide gap of nearly two years between the Alnasl registry and the ship showing up in a departure log at Cor Caroli. She hadn't put into dock anywhere or even hailed another vessel in two years? Impossible. He dug into the listing and saw that there was no original owner of record.

"Captain, we're changing watch. Any orders?"

Donner looked up to see his XO leaning into the cabin, and it took him a moment for his brain to process the question.

"No. No interruptions, Kronen."

The XO nodded and left, closing the hatch. Donner let his focus return to the data, trying to find his place again.

The ship's lack of history was starting to form a picture. No owner and no contacts for two years pointed to a stolen ship and a black-market identity. She seemed to exist only at Kepler-186 and Cor Caroli, and nowhere in-between.

He pulled up his own ship logs for the contact trace the day the Heart of Gold had hit local space. She had come in hot and bothered, chirping a negative skip event. Those logs still showed no owner.

So, sometime between their entry and the foxie bitch giving this Winder his run, the ship had been repaired and was suddenly owned by MWB? Another query to the station net showed this was the first time she'd docked at port. Where had she been?

Well, that was clear, Donner thought. The damned foxies. This "Captain Winder" must be a ringer. It was a foxie ship pretending to be human. Why else would they take his run and give it to a newcomer?

He slapped the desk and spun in his chair.

He pulled up the shipping traffic boards on the public info-net and drafted a request for information:

Anyone got anything interesting on a ship, AM-88-G-42 Heart of Gold (reg-id attached), possibly stolen, with a triss crew posing as human? Currently on Kepler-186, lately out of Cor Caroli. All info welcome.

He paused for a moment, re-reading his request. He nodded to himself and posted it. A moment later, he tagged it with "Cor Caroli" and "Triss" and "Stolen Ship," and set the post to wide distribution.

It might be a few weeks before his post reached local nets at Alnasl, Cor Caroli, and everywhere else via skip buoy. But someone would see it. *Someone* would have something juicy for him to use.

Donner smiled to himself and spun in his chair.

18 / Questions

Kepler-186 L5
(Vo Hahe Huv Hweh)
Vos-governed Station
Population 3.2M

SPACETIME-FIX at: **84.138**.24789387
- de77c340 **(Kepler-186)** ff72-cf14
- 96e2c3ad **(PSR J1954+4357)** 7f22-ab74
- 293f4bf2 **(ASAS J195438+4355.8)** ca21-95b9

"I appreciate your interest on their behalf, but I'm just not sure that an elevation in contract status is appropriate. After all, we're talking about triss here. I'm not sure the citizens of this station are ready to trust their lives to f—" Assistant Superintendent Marin caught themself and Jes saw their eyes dart to Stritch and Tastra sitting mildly at the end of the conference table. "To strangers," they adjusted unconvincingly.

Jes held their placid expression, but their jaw hurt with the effort. Half an hour of sideways prejudice and roundabout rejection hadn't improved their mood. They opened their mouth to respond, but it was Windy who spoke first.

"I've studied the metrics. Station maintenance runs an average of twelve percent behind targets on life-critical projects."

"How—"

"You need more crews under contract," Windy bulldozed over the objection.

The data wasn't a secret, exactly, but it had taken days of dedicated trawling through multiple sources of public information to piece it together, along with judicious use of Jes's bot malware to confirm certain points.

She continued, "You know you do. What Stevens is asking for is the opportunity to bid on these projects, not special treatment."

The superintendent's face showed their unhappiness. "I admit that their previous work has been acceptable and up to standards, but we're talking about higher stakes here. Class-three projects risk lives on a station-wide scale. One mistake—"

"Has her crew made any mistakes on previous contracts?" Windy asked.

"Well..." Marin said. "I don't seem to have that data..."

"I do," Windy replied quickly. Her eyes went glassy. "In the last three unified years since their contract certification, Stevens's crew has worked five contracts at class-one and three at class-two. These eight projects passed inspection by your department with zero noted defects."

"Well..."

"Tastra, how many re-bids were posted within the expected lifetime of those repairs?"

"None," he said.

"None," Windy repeated. "Unfortunately, the same can't be said for other contractors. Re-bids due to contractor fault account for seven percent of your budget, and most of those re-bids have been awarded to the same crew that did the original work. I've sent a copy of my analysis to your inbox."

"But triss..." Marin was clearly uncomfortable being made to articulate their own prejudices.

This was too much. Jes's voice was mild, hiding the anger they felt. "Triss were already exploring their solar system while we were still on Earth coining the term Nazi... the first time around." They took a deep breath, forcing themself to calm down.

"Look," they said, "these people are natural engineers. Let them help you."

Marin looked down at their hands for a moment, then their eyes glazed over as they focused on their implant. The moment stretched out longer than Jes expected. Perhaps they were reviewing Windy's data.

"Alright," they said, finally. "They're approved for class-three bids—on a provisional basis." They looked at Tastra. "The first five contracts you work will be heavily scrutinized. Any noted faults will result in loss of certification."

Tastra held their gaze blandly. "Good and good and good."

"Thank you for your time," Windy said.

They all stood up and made their way out of the room. Windy, Jes, and the two triss walked several corridors and were out of the cluster of office compartments before speaking again.

"Well, that went about as well as we could have hoped," Windy said.

"Yah." Tastra's ears were up in points. Jes thought he seemed positively cheerful. As they walked, Tastra's confident strides took him a few steps ahead of them.

Jes changed the subject. "So, it's been... what? Six dates now? Spill. You going to be settling down with Deck Chief Sori any time soon?" They smiled at her discomfort.

"She's fun. We have fun. Does it need to be anything else?"

"Not at all. But six dates in… what? Twenty-two days?" Jes turned to face her, walking backwards. Their voice took on an exaggerated, stern tone. "When are we going to meet her, young lady?"

"Ugh," Windy said in fake disgust, playing along. "You're not my parent!" she whined.

Jes laughed, then made their face overly-serious. "If you want to continue living on my ship, you'll live by my rules!"

They passed through a hatch into the vending concourse that sprawled between the administrative section and the docking ring. Jes noticed Stritch walking beside and behind Windy. Ahtsa ears were down and turned back, and their shoulders were rounded. Jes winked at ahta and smiled, hoping aht didn't think they were actually fighting.

"Hm. Well first, I'm the captain, remember? Second, if you care to check you'll note that it's *my* ship too," Windy said.

"Sigh. Always throwing that in my face." Jes's voice turned whiny. "Captain, someone on the crew is being mean to me."

"Did you just *say* 'sigh?'" Windy asked, laughing.

Because Jes was still walking backwards, they saw the changes in Stritch's body language as aht hissed and ducked behind Windy. Windy stopped suddenly as the small atriss clutched her jumpsuit.

"Stritch, what the hell?" she said.

Aht was hunched, making ahtsa body smaller. Ahtsa ears were flat against ahtsa head. Stritch said nothing, but a ping appeared in Jes's vision.

By the food vendor there. Black and blue. /S

Jes turned slowly, scanning the concourse. There were dozens of humans and Vos queuing and moving through the space. It took a moment to spot the one Stritch had called out.

They felt a nudge from Windy, and started walking again at a steady pace.

"Don't stop and don't stare," she said. Stritch was still hiding behind her. "Stritch, just act naturally. There are hundreds of triss on this station."

Aht released Windy's jumpsuit, but stayed hidden behind her.

As they walked, Jes watched the person wearing the black and blue jumpsuit. "Are you sure it's the same, Stritch? There are only so many colors. Could be a different crew, right?"

"No," Stritch said. Ahtsa voice was low; tense. "Same same same."

"Do you recognize them?" Windy asked.

There was a pause. "No. Hard to tell humans apart. But same suit. *Same.*"

"How would they have tracked you here?" Windy said. "*We* didn't know we were coming here."

Jes mulled the problem over. "Stritch, they knew you were the last one, right? If it's them, they're looking for one triss alone."

Jes put their hand on Windy's arm and picked up their pace to catch up to Tastra. "We're going to move past Tastra. When we do, walk with him. Pretend you're together, right?" They kept their eyes moving over the concourse, looking for others in the blue and black.

"Yah."

They moved past the larger triss and kept walking, staying between Stritch and the Jumpsuit. Stritch moved around beside Tastra as they passed.

As they reached the edge of the concourse, Windy pulled Jes over to stand in line for a kiosk, facing back the way they had come. They could watch the whole deck from here, while Stritch and Tastra got to the lift bank and boarded, descending to the lower levels.

Jes sent a ping to Stritch.

Let us know when you reach Steven's bay. /J

Yah. /S

The Jumpsuit didn't move, didn't seem interested in anyone on the concourse. But they also weren't *doing* anything. That was maybe suspicious. Maybe. The deck was crowded with vendors and vids. You chatted. You grabbed a snack. You watched a vid.

But maybe they were. Maybe their implant was tuned to a vid feed and they weren't watching the concourse at all. Jes sighed. Impossible to tell. They scanned the crowd again, and didn't see anyone else in those colors.

"What do you think?" Windy asked them.

Jes shrugged. They kept their voice down to match Windy's. "I don't know. Triss can see color in much higher fidelity than we can."

"But?"

"But... I mean what are the odds? Of all the stations in all the systems, how would they know to come here?"

"Unlikely."

"Yeah."

They moved forward in the line.

"Even if it *is* the same colors, same jumpsuit..." Windy said slowly, "It could still be another crew."

"It could be," Jes agreed.

"That kind of trauma makes a person hyper-vigilant."

Jes nodded slowly. "It makes a human person hyper-vigilant. Do we know how triss neuropsychology responds to trauma?"

The person in front of them finished with the kiosk and they stepped forward. Jes hadn't paid any attention to the line they were in, and now they saw what they'd been queuing for.

"So, uh..." Jes looked over the kiosk interface for the pet adoption booth, "about that ship's cat..."

"No," Windy said. "Absolutely not."

"But Captain..."

"No cats."

Jes tapped the panel and activated the browsing feed. A dozen vids popped up on the screen, each showing a different cat sleeping or playing. "Aren't they adorable?"

Windy shook her head and pulled Jes out of line. They moved slowly towards the lift bank, joining the crowd waiting for the next car. Just as they stepped aboard, they received a ping in the ship's private chat.

Here and aboard ship. /S

Jes breathed a relieved sigh.

There's a human waiting for you outside the bay. /S

Windy looked worriedly at Jes, who shrugged. "Stritch would have said if it was... one of them."

It didn't matter much. They were both tense as the car descended the dozens of levels to the triss district. By the time they reached their stop, they were the only ones left in the car.

The hatch opened. The passage was empty as far as they could see.

The two of them stood there for a moment, then stepped out together. They walked in silence as they wound between cross-corridors towards Steven's bay.

As they turned the final corner, Jes saw her leaning against the bulkhead in her sleek black jumpsuit. She was facing the hatch to Steven's bay, looking out of place and uncomfortable.

Windy smiled as they approached. "Sori. What are you doing down here?"

A smile fluttered across Sori's lips, there and gone in an instant. She stepped close to Windy and they embraced. Then she pulled back and glanced up and down the passage.

"I didn't want to ping you on the net. I came to warn you. There's some people asking questions about your ship."

Jes felt a chill.

Windy moved Sori back to arms length, but didn't let go. "What people? What questions?"

Sori shook her head. She opened her mouth to speak, but her paranoia was contagious.

"Let's talk inside," Jes said.

They palmed the hatch and ushered Windy and Sori through. One last glance up and down the passage, and they ducked in themself and closed the hatch behind them.

If Sori looked uncomfortable standing in the passage, she was utterly lost following Windy through Stevens's workshop, surrounded by triss. She looked wide-eyed at the odd clash of colors, the ceiling that was lower than human sensibilities were used to, and the short triss that peered at them over worktables and out of hatches here and there.

Windy led the three of them between the work benches that were now mostly empty. Stevens and twelve of her crew were suited up and currently crawling over the outer hull of the ship, affixing the now-repaired K-vane.

"We're safe in here, but just to be one-hundred-percent sure, let's go aboard," Windy said as she thumbed the airlock panel.

The three of them moved through the airlock and into the galley. Windy sat in the semi-circular lounge and gestured for Sori to sit next to her. Jes took a seat opposite.

"Ok," Jes said. "First off, nice to meet you. I'm Jes." They smiled. "Now, how about you tell us what's going on and what has you so spooked?"

Sori looked between Jes and Windy, before finally leaning back in the crash couch and letting out a long breath.

"So, look. I don't want to be in the middle of this. Windy..." she looked at the larger woman. Her eyes danced back to Jes for a moment, then back to Windy. Then she looked down. "I like you. But as much as I like you, you're not worth losing my job. Or... or worse."

"That's not going to happen," Windy said sternly. "Just tell us what's going on."

"No, wait," Jes cut in. "I kinda want to hear about the 'or worse' part, don't you?"

Sori shook her head. "Listen. A ship docked this morning. Before they even disembarked, they were querying berths station-wide. Active docks, repair bays, everything." She took a deep breath and her eyes settled on the bulkhead. "They've got some high-up access. They even got access to the log audits. I happened to see one of their queries. They're looking for *you*."

"Who are they?" Windy asked.

Sori shook her head. "I don't know. Not station. Not official. But they've got *guns*. And they've got *somebody's* ear, because they're carrying them on station. At least... some of them are. On the human decks. I saw them."

Windy and Jes looked at each other.

Sori wasn't finished. "I mean... who carries guns around on a station? What the fuck?" She looked at Windy, pleading. "Who the hell are you? What have you got me mixed up in?"

Windy put her hand on Sori's shoulder and spoke softly. "I'm just who I said I was."

Jes bit their lip. *Except for the "Captain of the ship" part,* they thought. *And the smuggling part...*

Windy continued. "I don't know who these guys are. I don't know what it's all about. But we didn't do anything to bring this down on us or on anyone. You hear?"

"What do they look like?" Jes asked.

Sori looked blankly at them. "What?"

"Their livery. Their clothes. What did they look like? You said you got a look at them."

She shook her head. "Jumpsuits. They're just wearing typical spacer jumpsuits. Blue and black."

Jes and Windy looked at each other again.

"Like I said, I don't want any part of this," Sori said again. There was sadness in her voice. "I just... I just had to tell you... that."

She got up to leave.

Windy called after her. "Sori, wait."

She didn't look back. She reached the airlock and tapped the panel.

"What's the ship called?" Jes asked her.

The airlock cycled and the hatch opened. She stood there for a moment, then turned her head to speak over her shoulder. "Constant."

She left.

Windy stood to follow, but Jes leaned forward and put their hand on her arm.

"Ada, wait. Going after her now won't help anything. We've got to figure our next move."

She looked down at them. Jes could feel the tension in her body.

"Fine," she said. It sounded like a curse.

Fin and Stritch met them in the lounge area.

Jes felt like they were learning triss body language. Stritch still looked tense and jittery.

"So, what's going on?" Fin asked. "Since when do we have emergency meetings?" He paused and seemed to hear what he'd said. "Okay, I guess we seem to do that a lot…"

Jes spoke up and got right to the point. "Stritch, you were right. We've got independent confirmation about those guys that are chasing you. They're here, and they're asking about us. About this ship. Only a matter of time before they find their way down to us."

Stritch seemed to fold inward, shrinking in size with every word.

"We need to decide what to do," Windy said.

"What about Stevens and her crew?" Fin asked.

"I think…" Jes said. "I think we're only a danger to them if we stay. These guys want Stritch's ship. If we stay here, they might eventually come and try to take the coordinates from us. If we leave… well, they don't care about Stevens."

"I think we need to tell Stevens… about everything," Fin said. He looked at Stritch whose ears had gone flat. "I know we meant to keep it secret, but this is too big now." A frown passed over his face. "How did they even find us?"

"Does it matter?" Windy said. "They found us." She shrugged. "We've got a choice. Hunker down, or get gone. What's the status on the repairs?"

Fin leaned back in his seat. "They're reattaching the vane now. Last I heard, Stevens said they'd be another hour, then we should be ready for a shakedown cruise. That was about half an hour ago."

"I don't think we can afford a shakedown," Windy said quietly.

Jes looked at her. "Aren't I supposed to be the reckless one?"

She shook her head. "They already shot down two skiffs, and they came aboard station at Cor Caroli with guns and murdered Stritch's family. They're now on this station with guns. Whoever they are, they seem to be able to do whatever they want and damn the consequences."

She shifted in her seat and frowned. "They know our registry; they've been searching station logs for it. Right now, we're docked at a private port and the beacon isn't chirping. As soon as we power up flight systems, they're going to catch our beacon and come for us. Who says they won't just shoot us down, or at least cripple us and board? Given what we know, station security isn't going to do anything to stop them. They might even help."

The four of them sat silently for a moment with this somber assessment.

"I doubt the vos would be ok with that," Jes said thoughtfully.

"Do they have to be?" Windy said. "They don't patrol the whole sky, and if a human patrol calls in a 'stop and board' for contraband or piracy, vos controllers aren't going to question it."

"Sori said that some of them are carrying guns. What if we find a way to turn them over to vos authorities? It's still their station."

Windy shook her head. "And what if the vos *are* in on it? Even if it's not all of them, all it takes is one corrupt administrator."

Silence descended on them again. Jes looked at their feet, trying to think their way out.

19 / Departure

Jes looked up as they heard the top hatch cycling. "Stritch, what do you think? It's your story. We've trusted Stevens this far. Can we trust her with the whole thing?"

Stritch seemed to mull this over and struggle with how to answer. Finally, aht sat up a bit straighter. "Yah," Aht said softly. "Tell, okay. But not give coordinates. She might take, but we can watch the logs, yah?"

"Any way to encrypt it?" Jes asked.

Stritch's ears dipped and flipped forward. "Her crew, they hack the shipping bond, yah? Nothing we can do better than that. If she wants the coordinates, she'll get."

Jes looked to the others. "We tell her everything?"

Fin nodded immediately.

Windy took a moment longer to consider, but she nodded.

A clanking rhythm echoed down the accessway as someone in a vac-suit climbed down the ladder. There was a pause, and then Stevens came down the passage, still suited up and carrying her helmet. Her lips were drawn back over her teeth in approximation of a human smile.

"Vane all fixed up!" she proclaimed. "Your ship is ready

to skip. You can thank my crew now." She unbuckled the vac-suit's cuirass and let it hang open, then collapsed in an empty crash couch. To Jes, her posture radiated smug satisfaction. "Fastest vane rebuild ever done, I'd guess."

She leaned forward. "Also, I thank you for good job. Tastra said you got us class-three contracts. Good team, yah? Even even even, I think."

"Great," Jes said. "You and your team have done amazing work. Thanks." They took a deep breath. "There's something we need to tell you. Bad news, and important. We've… maybe brought danger to you and your crew."

Stevens went perfectly still. "What news?"

Jes suddenly felt helpless to explain. They looked at Stritch.

Stritch took a deep breath and contracted even more. Jes had never seen a person take up so little space. Aht began a low, trilling sibilant narration. Aht didn't look up, didn't look at Stevens. Aht just stared at the small round table.

Stevens didn't turn to face Stritch, but was clearly listening.

Jes let the language wash over them. It was relaxing in a way. It struck them that triss language spoken like this—soft, low, devoid of agitation—would make excellent white noise to fall asleep to.

Ahtsa story was winding down. Aht gestured shyly to Fin and to Jes and Windy, pointing with three fingers, then to the ship around them. Aht fell silent.

Stevens sat for a moment, taking it in. She said something sharp and interrogatory to Stritch who answered immediately, shrinking further. Fin reached out and grabbed Stritch's hand in support. Stevens's ears twitched at this.

She looked at Jes and Windy. "All clear now. How did

these *humans* follow you?" She said the word like a slur.

"We don't know," said Windy.

Stevens's lips rippled, and for their benefit she said, "Hmph," like a human might. "Might be something to do with this?" She blinked and her gaze went glassy for a moment.

Jes received a ping with a link to a discussion board post by a Cpt. Donner. Their eyes went vague as they read, then widened as they came out of the cominfo interface to look first at Windy then Stevens.

"Who the hell is this Donner?"

To Jes's surprise, it was Stevens who answered. "Last human I hired for *ahss'trasst'ah* run. Big, smart criminal, he thinks. Can't tell three triss apart." She shook her head. "So, what now?"

Jes took a breath. She seemed to be taking it all in stride. "We think that there's no danger to you unless we keep hiding here. So... we leave."

Stevens shrugged. "Okay with me. But good ship, good crew," she said. "Be sorry to lose." She stretched and shed the vac-suit to her waist. "Not too scared of these humans. We can protect our own, here."

Jes shook their head. "We don't want that on our conscience. Besides, if we manage to shake them off our trail, it would be good to be able to come back here. If we let them trace us to you, they'll be watching."

Stevens made a clicking sound and nodded. "Some more work to do on ship before you go, then."

"I thought you said it was ready?" Windy asked.

"Yah, ready for skip. But need to get away from station, yah? Maybe help to scramble your beacon now and then? Maybe it's not working so well, yah?"

Jes smiled. "That would be very unfortunate, yah. We would be so sorry about our broken ship…"

Jes paced the cramped workshop as Stevens's big machine printer produced the last vac-suit. Stevens had insisted that they be properly equipped, and Jes was grateful for it. When this print was done, they'd have suits perfectly sized for each of them, including one of triss design for Stritch.

One of her atriss sat at a console beside the printer, watching vid feeds from the corridors beyond the workshop for any movement that didn't belong in the triss district. She had sent several of her hatatriss to keep watch over the lifts and other points of entry on the deck. She seemed confident they could keep out any of the human interlopers.

The printer pinged Jes that the suit was done, and they opened the print chamber, lifting the vac-suit and helmet by the handle of the storage case it was printed in. They wove between the work tables and through the airlock to the ship, through the common area and down the cabin passage to the midships locker by the ladder.

The suit—this one was Windy's, it had her name printed in raised letters on the plasti-ceramic case—joined the others in the suit locker. Jes poked their head into engineering, and saw Stritch buried deeply in some large equipment module. Only ahtsa legs were visible.

"Hey, Stritch. You need anything? We got a large archive of triss food and drink printer programs from Stevens."

"No," came ahtsa voice from inside the service hatch.

"How's the grav-drive?" Stritch was working on introducing some harmless frequency jitter into the drive's output.

The theory was it would mask their signature, preventing the station or the Constant from establishing a trace based on drive readings.

"Good. Almost done."

"Great."

Jes climbed the ladder. The cramped bridge was swarming with activity. Stevens and two of her atriss were hard at work in and around the access panel to the computer stack. They had pulled the racks out and one of the smaller triss was running a heavy ribbon cable to a new rack mount aht had secured to the bulkhead just above the open access. They had cut an oblong notch in the edge of the panel so that it could close without interfering with the cable.

Windy was seated at the nav-comm station, engrossed in the readouts.

"How's it coming?" Jes asked.

It took her a moment to look up. "Okay. The Q-comp is pre-computing our skip, so that we don't have to wait for it while we're running for our lives."

"Let me guess... it's—"

"Calculating," she said.

Fin sat in his pilot's seat, talking mildly to one of Stevens's crew over the intercom. "That should be one-five degrees."

"One-five," confirmed the voice. *"Cross-checking the other vanes."*

Fin covered the mic and turned to Jes. "We're doing a manual vane calibration. Best we can do without a proper shakedown."

"How long do you need?"

"Oh, about another half-hour, I think."

Jes eyed the activity on the bridge, then headed back to

the ready deck by the ladder. They sat in one of the folding jumpseats and dipped into their cominfo interface, requesting a connection to station traffic control public access.

They queried all records for the ship Constant.

As the data started streaming in, Jes scanned it for anything useful. There wasn't much.

The Constant was a newer Tri-Union cutter registered to a PCC ABG Holding and Transport out of Ascella L4. The corporate listing led to another parent corporation, and another, and another. Jes was twelve companies deep in a tangle of obscure interconnections of generic-sounding listings before they gave up. They had the feeling that they could spend a year traversing acquisition and subsidiary connections and still not have any sense of where the trail led.

They switched to the ship itself, looking up the specs on the Tri-Union vessel. It was larger than the Heart of Gold, with fifteen crew berths. As Jes scanned the listing, their heart sank. She was newer, faster, better on every metric. If it came to a race to skip, they stood no chance at out-running or out-maneuvering the Constant.

And that was without considering whatever shipboard weapons they might be carrying. If this was the same ship that had destroyed the skiffs from the Versistertrun, they had weapons.

If it wasn't the same ship... that was maybe worse. It meant that there was another one out there somewhere. Jes flipped back a page in the spec sheet and found what they'd noticed without being aware of it. The Constant had minimal cargo capacity.

She wasn't the ship that met the Versistertrun, because they were supposed to transfer the cargo. They sat with this information for a few moments.

Jes stood and went back to stand next to Windy.

"How close to Stritch's coordinates can we drop out of skip?" they asked quietly.

Windy looked up. "Why?"

Jes didn't say anything for a moment, trying to put words to their unease. "I'm worried there's another ship out there. If there is, there's a good chance they're waiting for us. They knew what system the Versistertrun is in… they were there to meet them, remember?" Jes considered. "They're after Stritch because they want to know *where* in the system the ship is parked. They haven't been able to find it by scanning."

Windy nodded. "The triss hid the ship *on* one of the larger asteroids. If they powered everything down, it would make sense that they haven't been able to find it."

She thought for a moment. "We could come out pretty close. The grav-bubble that forms on reentry into N-space should keep us from crashing into any rocks. But depending on where they are in the system, I'd guess that it's even money on whether they spot the gravity spike on their scanners."

"My guess is that they'll be holding position near the standard transit point," Jes said. "Watching for incoming ships or ready to meet up with the Constant when she comes back."

Windy nodded slowly. "Makes sense." She sighed and pulled up the star chart for the target system. Jes watched as she canceled the skip calculation. "I'll recalculate the skip with a non-standard entry."

"We're all clear," Stevens said over the comm. *"Try not to*

die too fast."

Jes grinned, speaking into the mic. "We'll try our best. Thanks for all your help. We'll see you again, hopefully." They closed the comm and turned to Fin, Windy, and Stritch, who was standing in the open hatch off the bridge.

"We ready?"

Fin rolled his shoulders and nodded.

Stritch's ears perked up and aht said, "Yah."

They all looked to Windy, who shrugged. "We made it this far. What else are we gonna do?"

"Alright," Jes said. "We're going to go out hot, and everyone's going to be screaming at us. Let's make it count. Stritch, you want to say up here, or down in engineering?"

Stritch ducked ahtsa head and scrambled back down the passage to the ladder.

"Okay. Let's power her up." They all glanced up at the bulkhead where the new module was bolted. It bore a large telltale that glowed red, indicating that the beacon was bypassed.

Jes tapped out the activation sequence and the flight systems lit up one by one. The tank came to life, painting the station and system traffic in a rainbow of light.

"Looking good here," said Stritch over the comm.

"We're showing green across the board. Beacon is silent. Skip solution is locked in." Windy looked up from her panel and nodded. "I guess let's go."

"That's the attitude," Fin said, smiling.

"Fin, break us free," Jes said.

He put his hand on the control sticks and took a deep breath. After a moment, he reached out with his right hand and tapped a control.

Jes felt the clank and shudder as the docking clamps released. They glanced up at the bypass module again, making sure it was red.

They watched the tank paint their exit trajectory. Fin eased the sticks back and maneuvered with subtle shifts of his wrists and the representation in the tank pivoted with them.

"Bots have flagged us," Windy said. Her voice was tight.

"Hold steady," Jes said. They were watching the flat spike that the tank picked out in blue. The Constant was still docked with the station. "Give our apologies."

"Incoming voice." Windy transferred the signal to the speakers.

"UNIDENTIFIED SHIP! REPLY AT ONCE! CRAZY STUPID SHIP! NO FLIGHT WITHOUT BEACON!"

Windy winced at the tirade and turned the volume down.

"It *would* be vos control," Jes said, resigned. "Gimmie outgoing voice."

Windy switched in their mic.

Jes leaned in close and yelled. **"Hey you! *Vo Hahe Ho Wahfo* Control! Stop yelling at us, damnit! We've got an emergency here! Don't you think we'd be beaconing if we could?!"**

They put their fingers on the bypass toggle, and tapped it four times rapidly: On, off... on, off. Just long enough to let the handshake start but not enough to transmit anything meaningful. The indicator on the bulkhead flipped between purple and red. They watched the departure point draw closer and closer in the tank.

"NO GOOD! FIX SHIP OR DOCK SHIP! You must comply or you will be boarded!"

"Anything you can do to get us there quicker?" Jes asked

Fin.

"Almost there," Fin said, absently. "Just keep talking."

The blue icon blinked in the tank as it departed the station. Jes watched in fascination as it pirouetted in place and began what must have been a tooth-rattling acceleration towards their position. It closed the distance in almost no time at all.

"That's it, Fin. We've got to go. They're just about on us!"

"Almost there."

Jes opened the comm again. **"Vo Hahe Ho Wahfo Control, we are declaring an EMERGENCY. DO NOT—SAY AGAIN: DO NOT APPROACH. OUR SHIP IS A HAZARD TO ALL TRAFFIC! Please advise all traffic to STAY AWAY."**

They tapped the beacon on and off again rapidly.

"WE KNOW YOU HAZARD. BIG HAZARD. Stupid humans, always hazard! WHY you fly broken ship? POWER DOWN NOW!"

"Well, they're taking it better than I'd have thought," Jes said to Windy.

"The Constant is closing... they could spit on us at this point," she said.

"No problem," Fin answered. He adjusted the vanes. "Jes, let's have full power on the skip drive, please?"

Jes powered it up.

"Entering skip in three, two... one."

Jes's stomach lurched as they transitioned through the fold into eight-dimensional space. They still didn't really understand how this could be a shorter skip than from Cor Caroli, which was significantly closer to their destination than Kepler-186.

"We made it," Windy sighed.

"We made it," Fin agreed. "First skip in ten…"

Jes braced themself and took a deep breath as Fin counted down. They desperately hoped the skips would be smoother this time.

When Fin's countdown reached zero, a low, vibrating thrum resonated through the ship, emerging as a rattle of the lockers and hatches and then fading away to nothing.

"That's first skip," he said. "Smooth as silk. Next skip in twenty-three."

"Thank you Stevens," Windy said softly. "I hope we can go back there when this is all over."

Jes nodded agreement. They continued counting down in their head, reaching zero just as they felt another low, rattling thrum through the deck.

20 / Midas

Versistertrun
(VrrihSss'sstrr'trrrrunn)
Triss Heavy Cargo Freighter
Unclaimed Salvage

SPACETIME-FIX at: **84.152**.72532831
◆ 34d8e491 (**BD+39 2579**) 88f2-f21a
◆ d823aa91 (**J125446.6+384057**) 900f-18d9
◆ 090e9a5e (**La Superba**) 8cff-b93c

"Okay. That was the last skip. Reentry in thirty-two seconds," Fin reported.

Jes opened the ship-wide and spoke into the mic for Stritch's benefit. "Brace for normal space in thirty seconds. We're coming out in immediate proximity. High probability of impacts. Brace brace brace." They leaned back and tightened the straps on their seat.

"Twenty," Fin said.

Jes breathed in and out slowly.

The skips had all been smooth. Stevens had done her work well. Still, Jes was waiting for something to go wrong. The reentry transition was typically not particularly stressful on a ship. The systems had endured the five skips, so transition should be easy. They repeated this to themself as Fin counted down.

"Ten."

Jes started tapping out the sequence to coordinate passive scan as soon as they were in normal space. They glanced up at the bulkhead, checking for the red light. They'd lost count of how many times they'd checked it. Last thing they needed was to emerge from skip broadcasting their identity to whoever was out there.

"Three."

"Two."

"One."

Jes swallowed hard as the world twisted and folded around them and within them.

Mass proximity alarms rang out and the tank display flared, rendering a dense cluster of large mineral bodies and a vast cloud of fine dust. Fin yanked back on the controls, twisting and shifting the two sticks in a subtle flurry of movement. His face was tense and focused.

Jes watched in fascination as the tank adjusted its rendering, highlighting the asteroids and debris it deemed were highest priority to avoid. The orange rings danced all around the small red icon in the center. Each adjustment Fin made was reflected in that dance of danger.

After a few moments, he found the balance of motion that had them drifting in perfect alignment with the rocks around them. The alarms quieted.

"Okay," Fin said. "We're good."

"Nicely done, Fin," said Windy. "Thanks to all this dust, the read isn't perfect, but based on starfix, looks like we came out right on the button. We've been in skip-space for twelve segments." She tapped her panel, and a new mark appeared in the tank. "That's the coordinates Stritch gave us."

Jes shook their head at the brain-bending math of the journey. It was fewer skips getting here from Kepler-186, but took far longer in real-time... almost four days.

They activated passive-scan, then pressed the ship-wide comm. "Stritch, want to come up here? We're about to find your ship."

Fin maneuvered them through the dense morass of rock and ice and dust towards Windy's marker. As they closed, the asteroid filled the tank.

"You picking up anything on scan?" Fin asked.

"Nothing," Jes and Windy responded together.

Windy examined her panel. "I think there's too much clutter for passive scan to see anything in the wider system."

"Can we afford a hi-res scan of that rock?"

Jes pulled up the laser topography controls and activated a direct reading of the asteroid. "Surface albedo is oh-point-four. Laser should be ok for scan."

The rendering in the tank started to refine in small patches as the laser array painted the surface. Low-poly averaged facets became intricate peaks and ridges. It looked like a mountain range tumbling in space.

Stritch stepped up behind Fin's seat, ahtsa bare feet silent on the deck. Ahtsa eyes were locked on the tank. "Yah. That's it."

Jes smiled at ahta and glanced back down to their panel. They whistled as they read the laser ranging data. "Thirty-seven kilometers long; Eighteen by twelve wide."

"Big rock," Windy said.

"Any idea where the Versistertrun is parked?" Fin asked over his shoulder.

Stritch didn't reply at first. Aht stared into the tank for several moments, then walked around the perimeter of the bridge, eyes fixed on the cairn for ahtsa previous life.

Standing to Windy's right, aht pointed to an unscanned facet of the asteroid, "Look here."

Fin nodded and maneuvered the ship in an arc, orbiting the lazily tumbling mass while keeping the laser array in the ship's nose oriented towards the surface. The rock rotated in the tank and the scan resolution continued to sculpt the vague facets into sharp relief.

Stritch walked back around behind Fin, keeping the point in view. The surface dipped suddenly under the scanner, revealing a deep fold into a narrow canyon. It ran like a ragged crack lengthwise on the long axis of the asteroid.

"Albedo spike," Jes reported. "There's something in that slot with a higher reflection than the rock around it."

Fin brought the ship closer, and soon he was piloting them *into* the asteroid.

Windy wiped beads of sweat off her forehead. "This canyon is only," she checked her panel, "sixty meters wide. Please be careful. We only just got the ship fixed."

"Hey, don't worry," Fin said. "I've done way harder things than this."

"Didn't you get kicked out of flight school?" Windy asked.

"Well, yah, but it wasn't because I was bad at flying. It was a... values conflict."

"Values?"

Fin nodded. "They valued decorum and rules and order."

"And you?" Jes asked.

Fin shrugged, then quickly corrected as the ship slewed worryingly to starboard. "The thing you have to understand is... it was *really funny*."

Jes pulled up a forward view on their panel, so they had the same picture of the Versistertrun unobstructed by the canyon walls that Fin and Stritch saw in the tank. "There she is."

"It," Stritch said.

"What?"

"Triss ships are 'it.'"

It was a big ship. Near enough two hundred meters long and forty wide. "How did they get it in here?" Jes wondered aloud.

The triss ship was long and remora-like. The entire Heart of Gold was barely as long as the first segment of its articulated skip vanes. Its hull had a triangular cross-section, sleek and smooth. While both human and triss—and all the Accord species—shared a common root of interstellar technology, the Versistertrun had details that struck Jes as distinctly alien. There were three full-size cargo modules all docked radially around the faceted sides of the ship, reinforcing its triangular symmetry. The skip vanes were segmented and Jes imagined how they might flare wide for skip like the limbs of an octopus.

The skin appeared to be tessellated in sharp triangular panels. Some were missing or fragmented. Jes felt a cold lump in their stomach. "Damage," they said absently.

Fin closed in on the hull, and switched the tank to highest resolution scan. As he brought them alongside, Jes could see more surface damage, and could start to tell the difference between the linear gouges from navigating the big hull through the rock cloud and the deep puckered voids that had come from weapons fire. They glanced up at Stritch, who was watching, utterly still. Jes didn't think aht was as dispassionate as aht looked.

"Looks like three docking ports around the base there, between the vane actuators," Fin said.

"Yah," Stritch said. "Skiffs carried there. Good spot to dock, near engineering. Another hatch at the nose."

Jes nodded. "Let's put in at one of the aft hatches, then. Fin, think you can get us docked on the main hatch?"

"No problem."

Windy made one last pass over her console. "Still nothing on passive scan. But if they're out there... if they spotted us, we won't know it until they're on us."

"Once we've got seal, we can power down most of the ship. Make us harder to spot on thermal at least," Jes said.

The tank's rendering revolved lazily as Fin guided the ship through a smooth yaw to align the main hatch on the nose with the triss ship. There was a whine of actuators and a dull thump as the docking clamps latched on to the Versistertrun's port.

"That's good seal," Windy reported.

"Alright," Jes said. "I'm powering down all ancillary systems." They paused. "That damage makes me nervous. Let's get suited up before we go over."

Windy nodded emphatically.

―――――

Ssst'tr'tss finished inputting the mass and power figures and ahtsa ears drew down as the readout confirmed ahtsa conclusion. There was something not right.

Aht pulled up the manifest for the three cargo holds, scanning the list. Industrial printers, terraforming and farming machinery, and... livestock. Aht had heard from an atriss in the Cargo family that they would be trading with representatives of a human corporate settlement. It all made sense on the nose: You needed printers if you were establishing a new home. Buying complex machinery was often far cheaper than getting fingers on printer programs for those machines. And living animals could be self-sustaining, and you couldn't print them.

That wasn't what *Ssst'tr'tss* was sniffing at.

The power draws were off. That's what aht had noticed. Take cargo three: It was supposed to be full of living animals. Several breeding groups of multiple species.

So why wasn't it heated? Why was it drawing the same level of airflow as cargo two and cargo one which held only machines? Why was there no mass intake from waste recycling?

If the cargo was in danger, a triss could be sure that ahtsa matriarch would hear from the cargo matriarch, and aht would surely hear from her.

Ssst'tr'tss's ears flicked back and aht lowered ahtsa head. It could only mean that the manifest was false.

Aht sent a ping to ahtsa matriarch. *"It is* Ssst'tr'tss. *May I come to speak in your space?"*

"Come."

Ssst'tr'tss started the rebalancing calculation and closed down the console. Aht ducked ahtsa head to *Trr'Ssss'tr* who was running the post-skip checks, and left the compartment. Aht moved quickly down the corridor and across the grav transition, walking up and around the sides of the passage to reach the operations matriarch's compartment. Aht extended a claw and scratched at the door.

"Enter."

Ssst'tr'tss palmed the hatch and entered. Aht ducked ahtsa head in a quick bow. "I have found something... unexpected. About the cargo."

"About the cargo. What have you found?"

"The manifest and the power diverted to cargo do not agree." *Ssst'tr'tss* sent her the data.

S'aht'trr'tss's eyes glazed over as she reviewed the numbers. When she emerged, her ears darted to the side and her lips turned down, exposing her side teeth. She let out a trill of frustration. "Who have you told about this?"

"Only you. It seemed... sensitive."

She stood from her seat and paced in a wide circle around *Ssst'tr'tss*. "Tell no one. My sister has made a very good, very quiet deal with dangerous humans. The cargo is highly valuable, but secret. You understand?"

Ssst'tr'tss folded ahtsa ears in a gesture of subservience.

"When we close this deal, we will rise in posture in the Trading Council. My sisters know, *all three*. You understand?"

Ssst'tr'tss's ears flicked up and back down again. If all three matriarchs knew and were in agreement, then there was nothing to concern ahta. They must have the best of reasons.

"So tell no one what you found. I rely on you to hold your place, yes?"

"Yes."

"Good. Then go, and join your team. We will be meeting the buyers soon."

Ssst'tr'tss bobbed ahtsa head and withdrew. Aht was walking up and around the grav transition of the passage when the alarms started sounding and the yellow and purple emergency lights began throbbing.

Aht broke into a run.

The airlock opened into a narrow space. Somewhere beyond the hatch and out of sight, an emitter was crossfading between dim yellow and purple light, punctuating the darkness in a gut-churning pulse.

Jes held their hand out through the passage, and the vacsuit took a reading. The atmo figures scrolled across their vision. They unlatched their helmet, lifting it up to rest against their back.

"Air is good. I guess there's no breach." The air smelled stale. Old and hollow. But Jes took a deep breath and stepped out onto the Versistertrun. "But lets stay ready, just in case."

The others opened their helmets and followed.

The space was a ring-like vestibule that encircled the hatch to the engineering bay. Two other short passages radiated outwards to the other airlocks. Jes stood for a moment, trying to understand the interior geometry.

Even after the Revelation gave them control of gravity, human ships were largely laid out on a conventional, gravity-bound architectural model. The decks were down, and decks were stacked one atop the other.

This ship was different. The central passage was a wide triangular tube running nearly the length of the ship. All three planes—walls and floor—were slightly concave, with eased, rounded transitions where they met. But it wasn't the triangular symmetry that had Jes scratching their head.

All along the corridor, hatches opened off at intervals. But while some opened off to port or starboard, some opened from the floor. All of them opened perpendicular to the bulkheads. And some were upside-down to Jes's eyes.

"Uh... Stritch? What the—?"

Aht looked at Jes's confused face, and ahtsa ears perked and flattened. Aht gave a little chirping bark of laughter. "In space, yah? Why would there be a down?"

Aht walked a few meters along the passage, then turned perpendicular to it and walked fully around the perimeter, so that the starboard bulkhead became the deck, then the portside, then aht was right-side up again. Then aht hopped up lightly into the central space of the corridor, and drifted smoothly back to them before alighting by the hatch. "Middle space is low gravity. For fast moving."

Jes nodded slowly, realizing the benefits of the layout, even if it made their head hurt a little.

"Okay. Windy, you and Fin head forward and see if you can find the cargo bays. Stritch and I will go back to engineering and see what we can salvage."

"Maybe see if you can get these strobes off and normal lighting back on, too?" Windy said to Stritch.

They separated, and Stritch led Jes aft through the round passage towards engineering.

"This is a big ship," Jes said. "Do you really think you can adapt its SDR to ours?"

"Yah. No worry." Stritch drew ahtsa lips back in an attempt at a smile. It looked wicked on the triss's face. "Go from not enough power to more than you ever need."

"That would be good."

At a large hexagonal pressure hatch at the end of the passage, Aht tapped out a sequence on the panel. The hatch opened.

They moved slowly into the wide open space of the ship's heart. It was systems, operations, machine shop, and engine room all at once. Stritch moved to a console and began working. A moment later, the lights stopped their queasy pulsing and settled on a mild white light. It was a colder light than was strictly comfortable to Jes's eyes, but better than the emergency strobes.

Jes followed Stritch to the back of the chamber and down a narrow ladderway. At the bottom, Stritch stiffened and ahtsa ears went flat. "Strrrrr'tt!" aht said viciously.

Jes moved down further and Stritch made way. As they rounded the railing, they saw what had Stritch swearing.

In the soft, cold light, the far end of the chamber glittered in a sparkling heap of gold. Jes could see roughly how big the triss SDR might be, but every inch of it was hidden under a mountain of interlocking crystalline spears, each inches long and forming an opaque web of faceted fingers. The golden growths branched and interpenetrated, the voids filled with smaller nodules of gold.

The stuff had covered the SDR and continued to spread, covering the cradle and most of the control console. Even the bulkhead and decking was taking on a characteristic brown shimmer.

"Shit," Jes said.

The ship had gone Midas.

"Strrrrr'tt!" Stritch said again. Ahtsa claws were extending and retracting in a rhythmic twitch. "*T't'tssss'tr* was supposed to damp it."

"How did this happen so fast?" Jes asked. The ship had only been here weeks.

Stritch folded ahtsa ears flat. "Some damage. Power surge or short. Can... make faster if not damped."

Jes sighed, defeated. They had all been holding out hope that they'd find a working SDR on the ship. The gold looked at least half a meter thick. "How long do you think it would take to get it clear?"

A ping popped up in the ship chat ring.

You both get down here. You've got to see this. /W

Jes and Stritch looked at each other.

What is it? Jes replied.

We found the cargo. Come now. Bring the grav-pallet from the ship. /W

It took them a few minutes to climb back to the Heart of Gold and pull the grav pallet through the airlock. Jes made it as light as possible, and the two of them leapt down the long passage towing the floating pallet.

In seconds, Jes and Stritch reached the middle of the ship where three large hatches faced each other from the three opposite facets of the main passage. Windy and Fin had opened the one to the left, so Jes stepped up the gravity transition and pulled the pallet in behind them.

Windy and Fin were standing in front of a crate they'd pulled out of a stack twenty deep. There were dozens of similar crates of various sizes that Jes could see stacked neatly throughout the cargo bay, all in the same dull gray ceramic material. Each bore a solid band of darker blue-gray running around the sides with the Axon-Mull logo and various serial numbers and tracking codes.

The one they had opened was about a meter and a half long and less than a meter across. Windy stepped back so that Jes and Stritch could see what she'd discovered in the open crate.

Cradled in a nest of packing foam was the palladium sheen of a brand-new goose egg. They looked up and around them at all the similar crates.

"Well, holy shit," Jes said.

"Yah," added Stritch.

21 / Windfall

Windy looked over the array of technology spread before her. An inspection of the other two cargo bays had revealed even more crates. Someone had shipped a whole lot of tech from Axon-Mull and other manufacturers in a very, very shady manner.

No wonder Stritch was being hunted. No wonder they all were.

Windy had counted a total of forty-eight high-grade SDRs. The largest, most powerful model made. She'd only seen power numbers this large used on massive asteroid-breaker factory-ships and space-stations. A lightweight ship like the Heart of Gold would never want for power with one of these at its heart. Hell, it would have massively overpowered the Anteres Drift, and she was over a hundred times the mass of their little courier.

A small, flat crate the size of a hand-bin contained a square computer module forty centimeters to a side. Windy was pretty sure it was a ship's beacon, but with several more connection sockets than any she'd seen before. Her implant scanned the coding and the crate helpfully provided a manual of technical specifications.

It *was* a beacon. A *variable* identity beacon. She had never heard of such a thing. As she scanned through the manual, certain headings caught her eye. *Storing Multiple Registries. Masking Mode. Randomized Registry. Registry Cloning.*

It flew in the face of the fundamental shipping rules of the Revelatory Accord: that every ship have a universally unique and permanent registry. This one handheld bin was an unimaginable treasure by itself.

They'd found fifty of these.

A larger crate held another comp module with the tell-tale cooling lines of a high-end quantum computer. She'd never seen one so small. More than a hundred of those.

In the second bay, Jes had found hundreds of two-meter-long tube-like crates. Each one contained a programmable bot with its own tiny SDR and skip drive. Skip buoys for interstellar communication.

Fin and Stritch had two SDRs and a half-dozen of the buoys in the first load heading back to the ship. Jes was still looking through the second bay.

Altogether, it must be worth millions of mass credits. Maybe billions.

But what had genuinely scared her was what she'd found in the third cargo bay that opened off the ventral decking. The crates there had no markings on them. No branding and no provenance. But they were all newly-printed.

There were a thousand short-range drones, similar to the skip-buoys but without the skip drives.

She'd counted two-hundred sleek devices whose crate-chips helpfully identified as explosive warheads. They were designed to be affixed to either the local drones or—more frighteningly—the skip buoys.

Another fifty identified themselves as Gravity Implosion Mines. She shuddered at what such a device would be used for, and why it should be able to be launched on an autonomous skip-buoy. She couldn't quite bring herself to say the words out loud, but in her own mind, Windy could admit what she thought this black-market deal was all about.

War.

Someone was building a fleet of warships, contrary to everything that the Accords stood for. And they were doing it with stolen Axon-Mull parts. She started her implant recording video of it all, walking slowly up and down the aisles of weapons, walking back to record the container full of SDRs. She didn't know why exactly, only that having hard evidence of this might protect them.

We're aboard and loading. Not sure where we're going to put all this. /F

It was maddening. She looked around at the stacks of goose eggs. All this wealth, and they could barely carry a few percent of it. The best-case scenario for the rest was that it was never found, that the murderers on the Constant didn't get to build their warships.

But what if they did find it? What if they followed us here, she thought.

What if we undock one of the cargo bays from this ship and carry it in the forward port? They're standard connections, right? /J

Yah. Should work. /S

Windy smiled. Jes must be thinking along the same lines. She sent into the ring: *The bay with the SDRs is probably the most valuable. Think Stevens can shift them?*

She heard footsteps rattling down from the other cargo bay, then Jes joined her.

"Worth a try, right? If she can't... well, I suppose we could always try Harry."

"Don't even joke about that. I hope we never see that asshole again."

Jes put up their hands, placating. "Hey, I have no interest in seeing his asshole either, but if he can help us sell a boatload of SDRs on the sly, I'll *talk* to him."

Windy grimaced.

Jes's eyes went glassy for a moment.

Fin, undock the ship and bring her around to the cargo bay. /J

On it. /F

Stritch, think you can point Fin to the one where we found the SDRs? /J

Yah. /S

The hollow clank of an undocking ship reverberated through the decking. Even though Windy was prepared for it, even though she knew Fin wasn't leaving them, she felt a momentary panic of being left behind on a dead ship.

You guys stay there. Stritch will meet you in the bay once we've docked, and uncouple it from the Versistertrun. /F

Windy moved back into the main passage, walking slowly around the gravity transitions thinking about what they'd found and what it meant.

Jes followed. "So... are we thinking the same thing here?" they asked.

Windy bit her lip.

"Warships," they both said together.

"Okay. But who could put all this together? Who could steal it, and who could afford it?" Windy asked.

Jes looked away for a moment. "If it *was* stolen..."

"You can't think..." Windy shook her head. "Why would

AM get involved with something like that? They already own half of human space. If it was traced back to them... they'd lose everything. The entire Accord would come down on them so hard there might not be anything left."

"I don't know. No, I don't really think that. But I can't imagine who or why, so of course I wind up in fantasy-land."

Jes looked at her, and she looked away.

"Ada, what is it?"

Windy sighed. "If this really is some cabal that's building secret warships... then this stuff is even hotter than we thought. We won't be safe until we've unloaded it all. Stevens won't be safe if we bring it to her. What are we going to do? Just... haul it around the galaxy hoping they don't find us?"

Jes looked thoughtful. "I assume you got recordings of everything?"

Windy smiled ruefully. "Of course."

Jes nodded.

A deep thump rang through the decking, followed by a jarring clank as docking clamps grappled the ship.

"Alright, let's get out of here," Jes told her. "We'll figure out what to do once we're far from here."

Windy nodded. They both moved into the open hatch to the large container.

Then she got a ping on the chat ring.

Uh, guys? That's not us. /F

22 / Scramble

"Shit. Shit. Shit." Fin continued to swear under his breath as he pulled the Heart of Gold deeper into the crevasse of the asteroid. That big bruiser of a ship had flown straight down the canyon and docked just as they were maneuvering for a clear run at the cargo container.

Stritch vaulted over the back of the seat and took the ops station to Fin's left.

"Stritch, that's not the one that chased us out of Kepler, is it? The Constant?"

"No no no," Stritch muttered. "Too big. That one supposed to meet *VrrihSss'sstrr'trrrrunn* for trade."

Fin felt an itch between his shoulders. "Forget passive and sneaking for now. See if you can get anything on scan. Active, optical, I don't care what. They must have seen us here. I doubt they would have just docked without knowing we were taken care of. Need to know if there are other ships out there."

"Yah."

Fin eased them along the fold of rock, pulling backwards along the curvature to stay in cover. Proximity alarms began their tooth-rattling shriek as he brought them even closer to the canyon wall.

"Stritch can you—?" The alarms went silent. "Thanks."

Fin kept his eyes locked on the tank, the rock, the Versistertrun and its new parasite, the space above them crisscrossed with traces as the computer tried vainly to track every piece of ice and dust and rock of the asteroid cloud.

He didn't want to fly out there with the possibility of an unknown aggressor waiting. He didn't want to stay still and maybe get holed before he knew they were firing. He wiped sweat out of his eyes and tried to slow his breathing.

"Anything?" He realized his voice was panicked.

Stritch didn't answer right away, and was tapping frustratedly at the ops panel. Aht muttered a series of trills and hisses under ahtsa breath.

Fin sent a ping to the chat ring: *You guys ok? We're trying to figure the situation out here. We see the one ship that's docked. Not sure if there are others. We've taken cover for now.*

He got acks from Jes and Windy, and took a steadying breath. They were still alive at least.

"Maybe there," Stritch said, and a new marker appeared in red out in the dust.

"What's out there?"

"*Kahatv'trrr'trhiu*... Radiation? Radiation pattern. Looks like the Constant ship."

Fin nodded. "Anything else similar?"

"No. Not yet."

"Okay." Fin took a deep breath and scanned the rendering. "They're sitting out there keeping watch." He was speaking as much to himself as to Stritch. "They know we're here... probably spotted us on scan and followed us in. We were lucky to undock when we did. They didn't shoot at us before because they didn't want to damage the Versistertrun and its cargo."

"Yah," Stritch agreed.

"We're going to have to get Jes and Windy off the ship, and to do that, we've got to shake the lookout. If we just dock, they'll find an angle they feel good about shooting from."

Stritch made a humming hissing noise, and ahtsa ears went flat.

"They're cautious. We can use that." He looked at Stritch. "Strap in."

He sent another ping. *Constant is here keeping watch. Bigger ship is docked. Going to try to shake the sentry and swing back around to pick you up. Hold tight.*

"How we pick them up?" Stritch asked.

"I'm... open to ideas..." He eased the ship forward along the ledge, as close to the Versistertrun as they could get before losing the cover of the overhanging rock. With a burst of thruster, Fin rolled the ship out of cover and into the space between the triss ship's three skip vanes.

The tank rolled its display but Fin's eyes were fixed on the Constant, so he saw when it twitched out of position in response to his maneuver.

"There you are."

"It's much faster," Stritch said.

"Yep. Probably is." Fin was watching the various traces crisscrossing the span between them and the Constant. "But no one can out-fly me. Watch this."

With the slightest twitch of thrusters, the Heart of Gold rose from between the huge articulated skip vanes and crept along the triss ship, skimming its hull. He kept it to a slow crawl, watching the asteroid clutter. It would take them time to find a safe firing solution on him so close to their goal.

The Constant left its overwatch position and was closing with them. It was a race now, but one that had nothing to do with speed. Fin was watching one of the random traces, the Constant, and their own position as they glided along barely three meters from the Versistertrun's hull. They passed between the two dorsal cargo containers that extended out from the hull like a "V". Fin accelerated a touch.

The timing had to be perfect.

The Heart of Gold skimmed across the nose of the triss ship, and now they were buzzing the large transport docked to it. Fin goosed the thrusters and flared the grav-drive just as they cleared the second hull.

They were clear and bursting at full speed away from the ships. The Constant would fire now that there wasn't a risk of hitting their own ship or their treasure.

But at that moment, a small asteroid, maybe a half-kilometer long, passed between them and the Constant. Fin pulled a tight yaw and roll and matched the speed and vector of the errant rock.

From the Constant's perspective, they'd disappeared. It wouldn't take them long to figure out what really happened, but Fin was already eyeing another asteroid to flit behind. With enough changes in vector, he could lose them in the clutter.

Now they just had to figure out how to get back and rescue their friends.

―――

Jes got a ping from Fin and acked it.

They stood with Windy at the hatch of the cargo bay, peering down the passage towards the nose of the ship. The mechanical sounds of docking had stopped. Jes waited for the airlock to cycle, wondering what their next move was.

"We could go back to engineering, hide out by the rear hatches? Maybe they'll assume we're all on the ship. We could hide out and wait for them to leave."

Windy was quiet for a moment. "What are the odds they don't just blow the whole ship when they're done?"

"Not odds I want to take," Jes said. "So... what?"

Windy turned and stepped back into the bay. She moved quickly to the crates that sat open on the deck. Jes followed.

They watched silently as Windy squatted down and closed them, handing the smaller of the two to Jes.

"Hold on to that. It's really important."

"What is it?" Jes gripped the handle tight and held the flat case against their chest.

"It's a fancy ship-chip that'll *finally* let us change the stupid name of our ship."

"Oh shit. I'll guard it with my life."

Windy packed up the Q-comp and hefted its case.

A new ping popped up in their vision.

Constant is here keeping watch. Bigger ship is docked. Going to try to shake the sentry and swing back around to pick you up. Hold tight. /F

They heard the airlock cycling down the passage, and returned to the comfort of the shadowed hatch.

"Whatever we do next, I think we should move away from here. They're going to come right here first thing," Jes said.

Windy nodded. "Let's move."

They left the cargo bay hatch and ran aft, ducking into the first compartment they came across. It was a narrow passage with a handful of hatches opening off of it to either side. Jes crouched down against the bulkhead and peeked out.

The airlock at the far end opened, and eight people stepped out in blue and black jumpsuits. Three of them held small hand weapons at the ready, sweeping the corridor. Two in the back were pulling a train of grav pallets.

Jes ducked back. They hoped those weapons couldn't penetrate the bulkhead, and didn't want to find out.

"Jes," Windy whispered, "we can't let them take that stuff."

"Not sure how we can stop them."

She leaned past them and peeked out. Jes grabbed her sleeve and tried to pull her back.

She turned to him and whispered, "It's clear for the moment. I'm going to try something." She darted out into the passage, holding the heavy equipment case in front of her like a shield.

"Ada!" Jes hissed after her, but she was gone. They sent a ping: *Windy, what the hell!*

Don't worry, just sit tight. I need to set something up. /W

Jes peeked out again and saw Windy reach the cargo hatches and jump down the gravity transition into the ventral cargo bay. Just as she slipped out of sight, two of the armed Jumpsuits emerged from the port-side bay and started moving aft. Jes ducked back and pressed themself against the bulkhead. The two passed by, chatting to each other.

"There can't be any more foxies aboard. What's the point of searching the ship?"

"Point is, boss gave us an order. We follow orders."

"Alright, you check out engineering, I'll check the rear airlocks, and we'll work our way up."

Jes, Windy, I have a plan. Can you make your way to an airlock? /F

Jes looked out again, first towards the two Jumpsuits

walking aft, then towards the cargo bays. Another pair of Jumpsuits walked out of the port-side bay, dragging pallets stacked high with SDR crates towards the nose airlock.

I'm in the ventral cargo bay. /W

No good. Needs to be a dorsal one. /F

Jes sent their own ping: *I think we can make it into the starboard cargo bay.*

That'll work. Get there as soon as you can and ping me. /F

Jes, go, I'll join you shortly. /W

Jes took a deep breath, checking fore and aft, then took a running leap into the the passage, aimed at the cargo bay. They floated through the low-grav center, knees tucked to their chest. As they neared the hatch, they spread out their arms and legs.

They tried to keep the landing quiet, but miscalculated their speed and forgot about the hard treads and gauntlets of their vac suit. The impact rang through the corridor and they bounced off the edge of the hatch into the cargo bay.

"Did you hear that?"

Jes held their breath and crouched down behind a stack of buoy crates. The voice came from just within the port-side cargo hatch.

"This creaking tub? Foxies built it, right? Probably falling apart."

Jes moved slowly and quietly further back through the crates towards the far airlock.

I'm in the starboard cargo bay. What's the plan? /J

OK. When I tell you, you're going to open the airlock and jump. /F

Jump? /J

Yeah, Jump. /F

Fin, 'Jump' is not a plan. /J

Trust me. We can't afford the time to dock. Tell me when you're set. /F

Jump where? /J

Out. /F

This is a bad, bad plan. /J

Jes reached the airlock and palmed it open, and sent, *Okay, I'm here at the airlock.*

"Hey, who are you," a voice said from behind them. "What the hell are you doing?"

Jes turned around to see a Jumpsuit pointing a weapon at them.

———

Windy dragged the long crate between two stacks of the shorter unmarked ones. Satisfied that it was well-enough hidden from the hatch, she opened it and pulled the drone out of its packing.

Jes, Windy, I have a plan. Can you make your way to an airlock? /F

She looked around, and sent back, *I'm in the ventral cargo bay.*

No good. Needs to be a dorsal one. /F

She directed her implant to connect to the drone, and pulled up its command menu. While she scanned the operation listings, she pulled down one of the stacked crates and opened it.

Windy saw the exchange between Fin and Jes. She focused the conversation and posted, *Jes, go, I'll join you shortly.*

She took a deep breath as she gingerly removed the warhead from its packing foam. It was a stubby cylinder about as long and big around as her thigh, with a recessed groove about a hand from the bottom.

Back to the drone menu, she focused *Install Payload* and the body of the machine revolved open like the petals of a flower. The base of the warhead fit snugly in the recess and she confirmed the installation.

With a mechanical whirring, the drone wrapped its petal-like clamps around the base, settling their edges into the groove and locking it in place.

She lifted the empty crate up and pushed it back into place, then took another deep breath, and lifted the weaponized drone up and settled it on top of the stack of warhead crates.

It teetered slightly. She closed the empty drone crate and lifted it up, sliding it in front of the drone, both to hide and stabilize it. If no one looked too closely, it might look like badly stacked cargo.

Windy re-focused the drone configuration and spun through the carousel of choices until she found an option labeled *Active Trigger*. She took a deep breath and armed it. After a moment, she added a *Deadman Switch Signal* option, keying it to her cominfo carrier.

She trotted back to where she'd left the Q-comp and scooped it up. At the hatch, she paused and peeked out. Catching movement, she ducked back again. She dropped back into the chat ring and got caught up on the conversation between Fin and Jes.

Her eyes widened.

What the fuck are you talking about, 'Jump'? /W

Look, it's simple. You're going to jump out of the airlock, I'm going to swing by and catch you. Easy as falling off a cliff. /F

Bad bad bad plan. /S

I can do it. And it's the only way you're getting out of there and onto this ship. /F

Windy wondered why Jes hadn't replied, but Fin was right.

I'm on my way to Jes's airlock. /W

She took one more look fore and aft and swung herself around the gravity transition into the starboard bay, landing on her side. She got up and sprinted back between the stacks of buoys. Just as she cleared the last pallet, she saw the Jumpsuit standing in front of Jes, holding a gun.

Jumpsuit spun at the clatter she made, turning the weapon towards her.

Windy lifted the Q-comp crate reflexively.

As Jumpsuit turned away from Jes, they swung the beacon in its case, clipping Jumpsuit on the back of the head, who dropped like a puppet with cut strings. The gun rattled to the deck.

Jes stooped down to grab the gun, and Windy followed them into the airlock, closing the inner hatch.

Fin, we're ready. /J

OK, give me a few seconds to get lined up. I'll give you a count, then you take a running leap. I promise I'll catch you. /F

Windy and Jes looked at each other.

"Well, it's been fun," Jes said. They hefted the beacon case. "Remind me to ask for my money back when we get off this ride." They pulled their helmet over their head and sealed it up.

Windy sighed. "No refunds; no do-overs," she muttered to no one. She closed up her helmet too, then picked up the Q-comp case.

Jes stepped up to the outer door and started its cycle.

She could hear and feel the air getting pumped out, and then there was just the sound of her own breathing in her suit, and her pounding heart.

The outer hatch opened, and she looked out into the endless, bottomless black.

Alright, get ready. /F

Five. /F

They both stepped back, putting their backs against the inner door, bracing for a sprint.

Four. /F

Three. /F

Windy felt Jes grabbing her gauntleted hand. She grabbed back.

Two. /F

Jump! /F

They pushed off together, taking three strides to the edge of the airlock and then they were tumbling forever into nothingness.

Through the air in the suits, across the fierce grip between their gauntlets, Windy could hear the vibrations of Jes's voice just barely louder than the sound of her own heartbeat, as if they were screaming from an unfathomable distance: *"This plan is bad, bad, bad, bad, bad, bad..."*

23 / Blown

Heart of Gold
Axon-Mull 88-G-42
Long Haul Courier
CC MWB Shipping

SPACETIME-FIX at: **84.153**.65423231
◆ 34d8e491 **(BD+39 2579)** 88f2-a74d
◆ d823aa91 **(J125446.6+384057)** 900f-18d2
◆ 090e9a5e **(La Superba)** 8cff-b923

    The universe tumbled end over end. There was no sensation of falling or spinning. No vertigo or flip-flopping stomach. Windy still held Jes's hand fiercely on the left side, and the Q-comp case in the right. Neither were falling or twisting. The inside of her helmet and the framing of its visor were just as steady.

    The only thing that moved was the endless, looping scroll of reality beyond her visor. The large asteroid loomed large with the Versistertrun and the large cargo ship of the Jumpsuits nestled against it. They passed out of view.

    Then the star of this system: only marginally brighter than those speckling the black. She thought—if her hands weren't full—she could stick out one finger and cover the whole star with it.

Then the void and the dust and the occasional sparkle of ice or mineral.

Then everything again. And again.

She opened a voice-link to Jes. "It's beautiful, isn't it?"

"It is," they said, quietly. "Kind of repetitive, though. I give it three-and-a-half stars."

As the asteroid rolled by again, she noticed the color of the triss ship. Seeing it with her eyes was shocking and amazing at the same time. Its skin was some shade of mauve with a metallic shimmer to it. It also seemed to be vaguely yellow. If pressed, she would have said it was both at once.

I can see you. Don't move. It'll throw off your vector. /F

They both acked the message, but neither one of them replied. There was a moment here of absolute peace. Windy didn't want to be the one to break it.

The huge rock slid out of her vision. Next up would be the star.

It wasn't there.

She squinted trying to find it, but the spot where it should be had already rolled away, nothing but darkness.

The dust had dimension and depth. It was like stories she'd read about watching clouds in the skies of Earth, finding shapes and legends in them.

The asteroid came by again. She looked over the large cargo ship. By its lines, she looked like a Tri-Union hull. Short and wedge-shaped. Almost as black as space. She could only see it because of the rock behind it.

She looked desperately for the star as its spot swung around again, but the darkness had spread. It was covering more stars.

The universe spun again, and it was bigger. Each turn that shadow grew to engulf more light.

"That's Fin," Jes said.

She looked around, but didn't see the ship. Then a line of brightest light in the middle of the darkness spread into a square, and she felt her perception snap into a new alignment.

She was looking into the cargo deck of the Heart of Gold. The darkness was the ship in shadow. It rolled away again, and she desperately wanted to twist, to keep it in sight, but she fought the urge. Fin was right. If they moved, they might introduce a wobble, throw off his approach.

She let the impulse go.

Dust, dark, asteroid and ships.

It came around again and was closer now. Larger. She could see straight into the long deck.

Dust, dark, asteroid and ships.

It was almost on them. She tensed her body for the impact.

Dust—

She was engulfed with bright light, and then she was bouncing off the bulkheads. She lost her grip on Jes's hand. Then hit another bulkhead and lost the crate. She hit more times. She lost count. Then gravity pulled at her and she was pressed to the deck.

"Shit, that hurt," Jes said over the still-open voice channel.

Windy groaned and pushed herself up. "Yeah." She looked around and saw Jes with their back against the bulkhead near the open hatch. The slim beacon case was next to them on the deck.

She looked behind her and scanned the whole cargo deck. "Shit. It's gone."

"What's gone?"

"The Q-comp." She sighed and limped over to the hatch. "I lost it when we hit. It must have bounced out." She grasped the hand-hold and looked out into the dizzying black. Jes joined her, grabbing the other side.

They stood together, marveling at the visceral horror of what they'd just done. Windy patched their voice channel into the ship's intercom. "Fin, that was a helluva piece of flying."

"Told ya," Fin replied. She could hear the smile in his voice. Then he cut back in with an urgent shout. *"Brace brace brace! Taking fire!"*

The ship pitched and yawed first one way, then the other. Their view out of the open hatch spun. They could now see the asteroid below and to starboard.

In the surreal calm of the deep black they were watching, Jes asked, "What was so important in the other bay?"

Windy smiled. "This." She pulled up the still-open tab to the drone she'd left behind and focused the detonator.

The Versistertrun erupted with a flash of white light. No sound reached them, but she watched in fascination as the explosion expanded in a perfect sphere of raw plasma. Countless more blossomed in secondary explosions as the deadly contents of the cargo bay detonated each other.

A pulse of dust and debris radiated along the canyon in the large asteroid as the shockwave expanded into a force so powerful that the kilometers-wide rock broke into pieces. Each was the size of a mountain, and each went tumbling outward.

"Holy shit, guys! What the hell was that? The Constant is breaking off." Fin's voice crackled over the channel.

Jes spoke first, a smile on their face. "That, my good friend, was Ada-fucking-Winder taking care of business."

Windy nodded to herself and closed the hatch. She scooped up the beacon case and they marched aft towards the ladder as the long cargo airlock cycled and began filling with air.

Jes sat in their bunk and stared at the handheld weapon. It looked innocuous and unsettling on their cabin desk. It was frightening.

In the panic to escape the Versistertrun, they'd clipped it to their vac-suit's harness and forgotten about it. Windy either hadn't noticed, or hadn't mentioned it. Now, they had no idea what to do with the thing.

It was not what they'd expected—not that they'd ever seen a handgun. There was a rounded rectangular grip that fit the hand. Jes guessed the larger of the two buttons on the top, where your thumb would rest, was the trigger.

The rest of the gun looked like a stubby rectangular box attached to the side of the grip with a ball-joint. Jes could see the narrow slot where the weapon emitted its deadly projectiles.

They gingerly, oh-so delicately depressed a small switch on the side of the weapon, and part of the rectangular frame slid loose into their hand. Maybe a magazine or power-pack? They put the pieces down.

However it worked, they wanted no part of it. But... they also couldn't quite bring themself to drop it out of the airlock. They scooped up the weapon and its magazine and left their cabin.

Fin was still maneuvering, trying to find a spot for them to hide. Windy and Stritch had taken the beacon they'd brought along on their terrifying jaunt through space and were busy unlocking its secrets.

Jes walked to the galley, squeezing around the grav pallet and its stack of crates that took up most of the common space. They'd have to figure out somewhere to put that. Jes moved along the bank of small lockers on the forward bulkhead and found an empty one, top row and fourth from port. They put the weapon and its ammunition in the locker and keyed it with a private code.

Jes took a deep breath and jogged back to the ladder. They felt somehow lighter as they climbed to the bridge. They reached the top deck and moved forward from the ready deck. Just as they passed onto the bridge, the ship skewed hard to port and Jes heard the whine of actuators.

"What's the situation?"

Fin spoke without looking back. "We're about..." A soft impact rattled the lockers back on the ready deck. "... To touch down on an asteroid."

Jes took the ops station.

"You can shut down everything but passive," Fin told them.

Jes nodded, switching off drive power, active scan, atmo recirculation... anything that might produce an energy signature that their enemy could read. They switched the lights and basic ship operations over to emergency battery.

Windy was kneeling next to the forward bulkhead with the computers panel open. The stack frame was pulled out and swung to the side. She leaned into the open chase and said something, then stood and moved to the navcomm station.

"Hey Jes," she said. "Just in time."

"Where's Stritch?" Jes asked.

"Here." Stritch climbed out from the open chase and stood beside the panel, ahtsa hand rested on the pivoting frame of computer platters.

"We've got the new beacon installed." Windy tapped out the interface sequence and the lower half of the tank displayed a long string of random letters and numbers in a scrolling marquee. She chuckled. "That's the default assigned name. Better than 'Heart of Gold,' but I figured we'd want to change it."

Jes thought for a moment. "So we can just change it? That's really cool."

"Yeah, we can change it," Windy said. "We can store multiple registries and switch between them. We can copy someone else's registry and pose as them, and even tell it to rotate through an endless stream of random ones. We can mute the whole beacon just like Stevens set up for us."

She shook her head. "It's fucking terrifying. Imagine a fleet of warships flying around with that kind of stealth ability. They could do anything and nobody could ever track them."

Jes thought this over. "Well. I guess it's good that it's in *our* hands then. I mean, *we* won't abuse that power. Much."

"Much?"

"Just the right amount."

Windy nodded. "So. Name?"

Jes looked around at the three faces turned their way. "Why are you all looking at me?"

"This is your dream, right?" Fin said. "It's your ship. You're the one who got us together, who made the plan, found the hull, made all this happen."

Jes shook their head. "It's *our* ship. Windy, you spent more sleepless nights worrying about my sanity in all this than anyone, and without your level head, I'd still be drunk in the Bleak. Stritch, without you your family's sacrifice, your survival instincts, and your skills—I shudder to think where we'd be. Fin, you're the one who's saved us multiple times from crashing, spinning, dying in space..."

Jes stood up and started pacing in the narrow bridge. "This ship is all of ours. It's why we won't have a captain except when we need to put on a show for others. We work things out together." They looked at Stritch. "We're a family."

The others sat in thoughtful silence.

Windy said, "The Accords have a legal designation that traces roots back to old Earth for a family formed by circumstance. I guess we could fit the requirements for a common law family."

Jes nodded.

Fin smiled and leaned forward to his console. He started tapping on the panel. The long random alpha-numeric string cleared from the tank and a new name appeared letter by letter.

"How about this?" he asked.

COMMON LAW

Jes smiled. They nodded to Fin, then turned to take in Windy and Stritch. Windy nodded.

"Yah," said Stritch.

"Alright. 'Common Law' it is. Nice one Fin."

Jes leaned back in their seat and dipped into their com-info. They set up a Common Corporation registry. After a brief pause, they focused the first syllable from each of their names. They connected to the new beacon and pulled up the metadata, setting the owner of record to "CC Finwin Jestr."

"Nice," Fin said, smiling.

"Okay, now that's out of the way," Windy said, "We need to deal with the elephant in the room."

Stritch stood a little straighter, ahtsa ears folding flat against ahtsa skull. Aht looked around the bridge in confusion.

Fin gestured to the tank. "Those guys aren't going to just leave after what we did."

"Right." Windy glanced down at her panel. "Worse news is I've been picking up intermittent comm chatter. It's all encrypted and the dust is chopping it all to hell, but none of that matters. There are at least two ships out there. So either the Constant brought in a friend..."

Jes nodded. "Or that spectacular explosion didn't take out the cargo ship."

"We're looking at at least two to one."

"Can we make a skip in all of this clutter?"

Fin sucked in a breath through his teeth. "I... wouldn't want to try that. We'd wind up pulling a *lot* of extra mass into skip with us, and that would throw off our calculations in all kinds of frightening ways."

"Can you out-fly them?"

"Hell yah." Fin sat up straighter. "I can out-fly them sure. But Jes..."

"But they have guns," Jes finished.

Fin nodded. "Two to one... I just don't know."

They sat in silence for several moments. Jes let their mind wander. "We need to tip the odds," they said finally.

"How do we do that?"

"We call in reinforcements," Jes said, smiling. "These guys are thieves, yah? Trading in stolen goods. Very valuable stolen goods. Think maybe the rightful owners might have an interest?"

Windy was nodding slowly.

"Fin, we can't skip in this mess. What about a buoy?"

"It should be ok. Its transition field is pretty small."

"Stritch, want to give me a hand?" Jes stood and moved back toward the ladder. They called back to Windy. "Get the Q-comp calculating a skip to Sol for the buoy. I think I need to go see about a girl."

Jes and Stritch took opposite ends of the crate and lifted it off the pallet. It took some doing to get it onto the rectangular table. Jes opened the latches and flipped the lid to reveal the buoy.

It was a cylinder about thirty centimeters in diameter and almost two meters long. Somewhere in there was a miniature skip drive, a high-power comm, a fist-sized SDR to power it all, and a computer brain just big enough for the bot and the message. It couldn't even calculate its own skip solution.

Normally it would be launched by a specialized firing mechanism. The airlock would have to do.

Stritch slid back the mount panel and yanked the damper. The SDR came to life and the buoy activated, publishing its command interface.

Jes prompted their cominfo to connect to it and synced it to the ship's beacon. They put their hands on the table and leaned over the buoy. They closed their eyes, thinking what to say. They focused record.

"Hi Andi. Told you I was on my feet, and we're doing great. Windy's here with me." They sighed. "Look, I know I don't have any call to ask anything of you. But I'm asking anyway. We're... caught in a tight spot. Now, I know what you're thinking, but it's really not our fault. We've stumbled onto something that's way bigger than us. Bigger than you. But I think your new hubby might just be the right size for this problem."

"I'm attaching the details. I hope this message finds you well, but mostly... I hope it finds you. Please pass this along. You'll understand when you look at the data."

Jes copied Windy's vid and the telemetry they'd recorded from the Versistertrun, the cargo ship, and the Constant to the buoy. They added the coordinates and a secondary message for the local filing network containing a registry filing for CC Finwin Jestr.

"Jes," Windy called down on the comm, *"I've got a skip solution for Sol."* She sent them the file tag, and Jes copied it to the buoy.

"Alright, let's get this bottle launched."

They lifted the buoy out of the crate and carried it through to the airlock. Jes tapped the panel with their elbow to open the inner hatch and they laid the buoy against the outer doors.

Stritch and Jes started pulling on their vacsuits. Jes stepped into the boots and pulled up the leggings, then buckled on the cuirass, gauntlets and flipped their helmet forward and locked it in. They turned to Stritch and checked ahtsa suit. Aht ran ahtsa nimble fingers over Jes's and returned Jes's thumbs-up.

"Ready?" Jes asked over the comm.

"Yah." Stritch started the lock cycle.

Jes knelt down and put their hand on the buoy. They heard the diminishing hiss as the air was drawn out of the airlock. After a moment, they made a snap decision, and set the buoy to wide-broadcast the vid and telemetry data unencrypted on exit from skip.

Stritch joined them and opened the outer hatch.

For the second time in the same day, Jes looked out into the bottomless black. They felt a frightening urge to step off into the nothingness. They shook their head. If they leaned forward, they could just see the small rock the ship was perched on, barely bigger than the Common Law.

Stritch and Jes each grabbed a side of the buoy and stood, bracing against the edges of the hatch. It was too long to go out sideways, so they pointed its nose out into space.

"On three?"

"*Yah.*"

Jes counted off and they swung it back and forth. When they hit three, they let go and the buoy went soaring from the ship. Jes watched as it tumbled away. They pulled up the interface and gave it the command to skip when ready. They tried to keep it in sight until it skipped, but lost it in the dust and tumble of the asteroid field.

24 / Dust

Common Law
Axon-Mull 88-G-42
Long Haul Courier
CC Finwin Jestr

SPACETIME-FIX at: **84.155**.26572932
- 34d8e491 (**BD+39 2579**) 88f2-a74d
- d823aa91 (**J125446.6+384057**) 900f-18d2
- 090e9a5e (**La Superba**) 8cff-b923

"I've got a scan-spike," Windy said. Her voice was weary and slow. She tapped at her panel and a new point appeared in the tank. "About two-thousand klicks out."

They'd all been at their stations for hours, and had nothing but quick cat-naps for at least two standard days. Disengaging and sneaking away from the Constant hadn't been easy. Their scanners were too good.

"I see it. Think it's them?" Fin sighed as he said it. He knew the answer.

"Yeah, it's them. I don't think they've spotted us yet, but they're scanning in our direction."

"Time to move again," Jes said. "See any good options?" They put their face in their hands and rubbed their eyes to try to ease the headache from hours at the console.

Fin scanned the tank, then looked down at his panel and highlighted a particular rock. He moved the trace up into the tank and told the bot to calculate a vector. "This one is moving in our general direction. If we can slip over to it... here," they placed a marker at the point where the rock would intersect their vector, "we should be able to slide along in its wake."

"That rock is also heading back into the sector that they've already scanned, so if we can make it we can lose them for a while, I think," Windy added.

Fin yawned and nodded. "Okay. One more side-hop. Then one more after that. And another after that."

"Easy," Jes said. "I know it's rough. But we only have to keep it up for—"

"—ever?" Fin cut in. "Jes, I'm falling asleep here. Only one mistake, and they'll shoot us full of holes. I can't hold up much longer."

Stritch came up from the galley with three bulbs of coffee and handed them out.

"Thanks Stritch," Fin said. He yawned again and sipped on the bulb.

Fin didn't even bother to retract the landing gear. A rapid-fire series of spitting bursts of thruster shifted them off their current rock and under the shadow of the new one as it crossed their path. Once they had ten-thousand tons of rock and ice between them and the Constant, Fin risked longer bursts of thruster to roll the ship and plant its three articulated landing pads on the surface.

The ship rang with the sound of steel and ceramic impacting stone on a monstrous scale. Jes leaned forward and rubbed the small of their back. Fin's landings were getting less and less delicate.

Jes watched the scan, looking for any sign from the Constant that she'd noticed the switch. The marker followed its projected course, working systematically through the asteroid field in the direction of their previous hiding spot.

"No change," Windy confirmed. "Not hearing any chatter either. I don't think they saw us."

"Fin, go get some sleep," Jes told him. "Take a dropper if you need one after all that coffee. We're safe for now."

Fin didn't even reply. He locked the control sticks against the pilot console and shrugged off his seat straps, staggering out through the short corridor aft. Jes heard the hatch to the captain's cabin close behind him.

Jes groaned to themself. "Where's the relief watch?"

"No reason for both of us to be on deck at the same time, but we've only got one Fin," Windy said.

"Note to self: Hire a second genius pilot before we get hunted again."

"You planning on us being hunted again any time soon? I kind of think I should get a say in that, don't you?" Windy lifted her arms up in a stretch and rolled her shoulders.

Jes noticed that Stritch was still standing behind Fin's seat, looking over the scan in the tank. "Any ideas on our predicament?" Jes asked.

"Maybe," Stritch said. Aht paced around the bridge in a full circle, still looking at the tank. "Yah, maybe." Aht let out a long, hissing trill, then turned and jogged back to the ladder and disappeared.

Jes and Windy looked at each other, then she said, "What was that about?"

"I think… I think aht just got an idea," Jes said. "Can you keep an eye on things up here?"

"Yeah. But I'll need a spot in an hour or so. I'm almost as

tired as Fin."

"No problem. I'm going to go check on Stritch." Jes stood and arched their back, then followed ahta down the ladder.

The ship was eerily quiet and dim. They'd dialed the power way back to avoid detection, and powered down all unnecessary systems. The ladder rungs echoed under even the soft ship-boots that Jes wore.

They stepped off at the main deck and heard Stritch opening and closing lockers in the engineering compartment. Jes stood in the hatch and watched for a moment. Aht was rooting methodically through equipment and tools. Here and there, aht pulled out a tool and set it in a growing pile on the nearby workbench.

At a certain point, aht seemed satisfied with the haul of tools and moved to the console for the large-volume printer. Jes followed. Aht dialed up a print program to produce a cylinder of liquid hydrogen, added a pulse-valve, and set a quantity of two before starting the print.

Stritch moved back to the bench and swept the tools into a hand-bin and walked out, calling over ahtsa shoulder. "Come, follow."

Jes went along, wondering what aht was planning.

They reached the galley, and Stritch pointed at the stack of skip buoys. Aht mimed lifting the crates onto the rectangular table. "Two here, two there."

Jes watched as aht opened each crate, and started disassembling the casing of one of the buoys, about mid-way down the cylindrical body. Aht got the panel off, revealing the miniature cradle for the fist-sized SDR. "You start on that one. Take out." Aht gestured and then began removing the fasteners that held the cradle and its power couplings in place. When aht was done, aht moved to the second buoy, removing the entire rear of the device, where the skip-drive was housed.

Jes didn't understand *why* they were butchering the highly valuable skip-buoys, but they went along. Stritch had more than earned their trust at this point.

With Jes working at removing the second SDR and skip-drive, Stritch picked some tools out of the bin and jogged back to the ladder. Jes heard the sound of fasteners being unwound, plates coming loose, and the ship becoming ship parts.

They finished disassembling their pair of buoys and followed, wondering what they'd see. And worrying more than a little.

When they reached the ladder, what they saw was Stritch, crouched by the ladder transit from the main deck down to the cargo deck. Aht had taken apart the deck plating all around the shaft, and was now disassembling the shielding that covered the wiring and circuitry chases.

"Uh, Stritch…" Jes said. "What exactly is your plan here? What…"

"Need the gravity vector array," aht said absently.

"Don't we… you know… need that in the ship?"

Stritch paused, then looked up and down the ladder. "Need more than dead? No gravity on the ladder, make it easier to move up and down, yah?"

Jes opened their mouth to object, but then stopped. They couldn't really think of a reason to argue. They remembered the way the triss ship was designed around manipulated gravity. They shrugged. "Okay, but what's it for?"

Stritch got the shielding off, revealing a ring of evenly spaced modules encircling the ladder shaft. A power line ran from one to the next in series and disappeared into the decking. Aht pointed to two fasteners at each module.

"Take these out," aht ordered. Then aht climbed the ladder to the bridge deck and started repeating the process.

Jes called up to ahta, "Yah, but why? What are we building?"

"*Unhiha'trr'tsstvtr.*"

Jes paused and looked up. "Huh?"

"Decoys," Stritch said.

Jes looked down at the table, where two modified skip-buoys rested. The remaining parts from these and the two they'd disassembled were packed back into the crates and stacked off to the side. What remained was a far cry from the sleek, polished, expensive-looking devices they'd started out with.

Each decoy was a hodgepodge of tech held together with windings of tape and assorted bolts and brackets. Where the skip-drive had been was a rail-like truss where they'd mounted the second SDR in its cradle and the liquid hydrogen tank. The valve actuator lines wound from the aft-most nozzle up and around the tank to a port in the buoy's computer. The chain of gravity modules was tied into another port, and to the additional SDR. The grav array was taped in a spiral around the whole thing.

"Is this going to work?" Jes asked.

"Yah," Stritch said brightly. "Sure. Probably… Maybe."

Jes looked up at ahta.

"No promise," aht said.

Jes shrugged. "Well, we've come this far on hope and stupidity." They left Stritch making final adjustments and jogged back to the ladder. They leaped and let themselves float up to the bridge deck, using their hands just to keep themselves centered in the shaft.

They had to admit it was a lot easier than climbing.

When they stepped out of the vertical shaft and onto the deck, gravity reasserted itself, and they jogged onto the bridge.

"How's it going?" they asked.

Windy yawned. "Okay. I'm beat. The Constant is still on her vector. Hasn't twitched. No new contacts on the other ship, so we might have lost her, or we might be running right at her." She yawned again. "You here to relieve me?"

"Go on. Stritch and I have a project we're working on. Might help a little."

It was a testament to Windy's exhaustion that she didn't even ask. She stood and left the bridge.

Jes settled into the nav-comm station.

"Jes," Windy had returned from the corridor, "Want to tell me what the hell has happened to my ship?"

"Not your ship," Jes called out, smiling.

"If I'm the damn captain, I can damn-well call it my ship."

"You're not the captain *now*... only when we need you. You're a... a foul-weather captain."

She didn't leave, and although Jes didn't take their eyes off the console, they could feel her glare.

"Okay, listen. Stritch and I built some decoys out of buoys and the ladder's gravity arrays. Think they're gonna work to get these guys off our backs for a while. And bonus: The ladder is *much* more fun now."

She grunted and stomped off to her bunk.

Jes began mapping out two diverging courses that would

lead their pursuers as far away from their current vector as possible. They were meandering, zig-zagging paths that ventured deeper and deeper into the dust and rock of the asteroid field.

Stritch was busy teaching the bots how their new thrust vectoring worked. It was rudimentary at best, but it would give them some marginal control over which direction they were going. Combined with periodic pulses of gravity from the repurposed arrays, they should show up as intermittent anomalies that the Constant—and the other ship—would have no choice but to hunt down.

All the while, on the Common Law they would power down everything but passive scan and emergency atmo, and ride this rock in the opposite direction.

Jes smiled to themself as they copied each course to one of the decoys, with a delay before activating. They'd be very far removed before the action started.

They sent a ping to Stritch: *All ready from up here. Let 'em loose when you can.*

Yah. /S

Jes waited. Stritch had to finish the programming, then suit up and drop the buoys out of the airlock.

They only had one functional skip-buoy left, but Jes thought there had to be a better way to launch the things. Maybe Stevens could rig something up.

Nav-comm bleeped an alert at them. The Constant was changing course.

Jes re-centered the tank and zoomed in. It looked like they'd reached the end of a sweep and decided to scan back in this direction. Shit.

Jes pulled up the ops interfaces and started powering down systems. They were already drawing low, and the bad guys were nearly twenty-thousand klicks out, but they didn't want any chance of being spotted.

Stritch, any chance you could hurry things up? They've turned around. /J

Working. /S

Nav-comm raised another alert, and a new marker appeared. Jes leaned forward and tapped the callout. Gravity anomaly consistent with the larger cargo ship. She was moving now, about five thousand klicks away.

"Shit shit shit shit," they said.

Stritch, I've spotted the second ship. It's getting awful crowded up here. /J

Yah, yah. Almost. /S

Jes noticed they were tapping their foot and forced themself to stop. They pulled the ops interface up again and looked for anything else they could power down. Lights and atmo were already running on battery. Nav and passive scan was siphoning off the slightest thread of power.

They debated whether to wake up Fin and Windy or let them sleep. It wasn't strictly an emergency yet.

The ops console showed the inner airlock hatch open, and they got a ping.

Ready to launch them. /S

Great. I'm switching off the lights in the airlock. Don't want the other ship to get an optical fix. /J

Yah. /S

Jes shut down all the interior lights on the main deck and airlocks. The lock cycled and the outer door showed open.

They're out. /S

Jes smiled and sent the launch command to the two decoys. They kept their eyes locked on the two small dots in the tank as they drew further and further away. They shouldn't activate until the Common Law had drifted well clear. Their eyes danced between the decoys, the Constant, and the cargo ship. So far, they were still safe. Constant was closing slowly, but wasn't an imminent threat. The other ship was continuing on its vector, crossing their previous position.

The two decoy pips winked out as the passive scanner lost them in the dust of the asteroid field.

Jes waited.

Stritch joined them on the bridge, taking the ops seat.

They both stared intently at the tank, looking for any hint of movement.

There was a flicker, and nav-comm raised an alert for a new gravity contact. Jes checked it against the projected course and smiled. That was one of their decoys. They marked it. Several minutes later they marked the second one.

It wasn't until twenty minutes later when they saw the Constant and her sibling changing course to investigate that they breathed a sigh of relief.

"Stritch, you okay on watch for a bit? I could use some sleep."

"Yah. No problem."

Jes nodded and stood, wobbly from exhaustion, moving towards the ladder. "I'll be down for half a segment or so. Anything happens before then—" their jaw cracked in a wide yawn, "—just let me die in my sleep."

25 / Trap

The wake-up pinged in Jes's ears and vision with a cheerful, throbbing chime. They groaned and scrubbed their face with both hands. They killed the alarm and opened their eyes, letting the dark gray ceiling come slowly into focus. A stray thought crossed their mind: They should put some color up in their cabin.

Jes reached up over their head to the panel above the desk and tapped the intercom to the bridge. "What's our status?"

It was Windy who responded. *"Still drifting. No near contacts."*

Jes sighed. "On my way up." They released the comm and rolled out of their bunk. Their jaw cracked in an involuntary yawn. They wanted to sleep for a few days still.

They opened the intercom again. "Coffee?"

"Yes."

They walked out into the passage still in their socks and set the galley printer to make a couple of coffee bulbs. Jes squeezed around the stack of crates and grabbed the bulbs just as they finished printing. They'd have to do something about the piled crates. They needed a cargo container for cargo, Jes thought.

With the two bulbs in one hand, they floated up the ladder, then padded onto the bridge.

"Here you go." Jes handed Windy the coffee, then took the ops station.

"We lost track of the Constant a couple of hours ago, but the cargo ship is here," Windy said. A circle highlighted a distant point in the tank. The view was zoomed wide, so even the Common Law was marked as little more than a point of light. "She took out one of our decoys about an hour ago with a lot of sound and fury."

"Any sign of the other decoy?"

Windy shook her head. "Last spikes were about half an hour ago. It's probably too far into the muck for our passive sensors to pick up."

Jes nodded.

"Stritch went for a nap. Fin's still asleep."

"Let's let them both sleep as long as possible. We'll need them soon enough." Jes yawned, their jaw cracking again.

Windy struggled, but eventually gave in to her own yawn. She shook her head. "Why'd you have to do that?"

"Sorry." Jes pulled up the optical chart of the asteroid field, augmented by their passive scans. They weren't too far from the edge. Jes felt a sense of longing for open space, for an end to the claustrophobia of hiding amid dust and rock and ice.

"Windy, can we calculate a skip from here?"

"No. I've been trying. There's too much junk around us. Q-comp can't filter the local mass, and nav-comm can't get a proper fix."

Jes marked a point just at the edge of the primary mass of the asteroid field. It was the nearest point of relative clarity, but still over a hundred-thousand kilometers away. "What if we moved here?"

She sighed. "It would help." She asked nav-comm for course projections for them and the Constant based on observed performance and her last-known position. "How do you propose we get there without getting shot at? With our power profile, they'll catch us twenty-thousand klicks short of that point."

"I have to solve every problem?"

"But... it's *your* plan."

"Who said anything about a plan? I'm operating on wishful thinking at this point." They finished their coffee and stashed the empty bulb in the mesh pouch under their seat.

There was a chime and new marks appeared in the tank near the cargo ship. A series of circles, increasing in diameter to imply a narrow cone, marked in orange.

"High-velocity mass stream," Windy said. "They're firing." Their voice was oddly calm.

Jes narrowed the scan on their panel to that vector. An energy spike appeared, rapidly dissipating to nothing.

"I think they just shot down the second decoy."

Jes rested their chin in their hands and stared into the heart of the tank. They leaned back and pulled up the scan logs on their panel and began scrolling through the scan history. "Why are they still here?" they asked aloud.

"What?"

Jes straightened. "They got what they could from the Versisterstrun. You blew up the rest. They don't need to chase us anymore. What do they gain from sticking around and hunting us down? Why haven't they just left?"

Windy was quiet for a moment. Then she said, "They're worried we took something. We know what they were up to, and we have evidence. They probably don't know you sent the buoy, and they don't want us telling anyone what we found." She frowned. "Why?"

"Because," Jes said slowly, "This isn't all there is. They've done this before. They're going to do it again." Jes stood up and started pacing around the console. "You said it: They're building a fleet. They need to keep it a secret until... they're ready for whatever."

Jes reached the ops station again and leaned their hands on the panel, their forehead almost touching the tank.

"How long have we had the cargo ship on scan?"

"Hour and a half or so," Windy said. "They've been making a lot of noise for a while."

Jes felt an uneasiness between their shoulders. They took a deep breath.

"What are you thinking?" Windy asked.

Jes could feel their heart thumping. Their whole chest felt tight.

They palmed the panel for ship-wide. "Fin! Stritch! Everyone up and to stations. All hands to stations. Fin, get in here."

Windy raised her eyebrows at them in a question, but flipped on the emergency alarms.

Thirty seconds later, Fin came stumbling onto the bridge, his feet bare and rubbing sleep out of his eyes. He pushed his long hair out of his face as he collapsed into the pilot's seat. "Wha—?" he said. He was scanning the tank, looking over his panel for any sign of the emergency.

"Here in engineering," Stritch's voice crackled over the comm. *"Ready."*

Windy shut off the alarm.

Jes shook their head, trying to lose the feeling of danger that had come over them so suddenly. They couldn't explain it. Didn't know where to start.

"I'm—I'm sorry. I don't know why, but I was sure that—"

A sharp, metallic ping rang through the compartment. Jes turned towards the sound, confused. They scrunched their face against the whistle that seemed to be boring into their ear. Lights went orange and they felt a heavy jolt in their teeth as the emergency seal slammed shut at the entry to the bridge.

"Jes!" Windy shouted. "Hull breach! Get the pa...." Her voice diminished to nothing as the air rushed out of the compartment.

Jes's awareness constricted to a narrow, single spot of focus. They spun to an orange box mounted on the port bulkhead just above the jump seat and ripped the cover off the patch kit. They grabbed the stack of patches with one hand and pulled the pin on the tracer with the other. A cloud of red dust burst into the air and was immediately drawn to two thumb-sized holes on the port and starboard bulkheads.

Jes pulled the plastic backing off of the thick, spongy adhesive and slapped a patch over the nearby hole. The edge of their vision was going black, and their chest hurt with each attempt at breath. The deck rolled beneath them. They stumbled to the starboard bulkhead, reaching out with another patch, but found themself on their knees. The second hole was too high on the bulkhead. They'd never reach it.

They felt Windy take the patch from their hand just as their sight was filled with white spots and bands of burning fire gripped their lungs.

Vision, hearing, and breath returned at an agonizing pace as the atmo printer slowly refilled the compartment.

They were on their back and Windy was shaking them. "Jes, you ok?"

Jes levered themself up, coughing. "That was... unpleasant." The ship lurched and rolled, almost throwing them off the deck. "Fin!"

"Can't help it." Fin said. "Taking fire."

Windy hauled Jes up and the two of them scrambled back to their stations.

"The Constant?" Jes asked.

"Yes," Windy replied.

Jes pulled up damage control and watched in horror as a series of breaches erupted along the cargo deck. The decks rumbled with a thunderous clangor like iron bells as emergency bulkheads dropped throughout the ship.

"Fin!"

"I know!" he shouted back in panic. He pulled back on both sticks and twisted. The ship lurched and rolled.

"Fin, something you want to tell me?" Jes asked.

"Well," said Fin, "I don't want to worry you unduly... but we are being shot at."

"I thought you could out-fly them."

"I *can* out-fly them. I never said anything about their particle streams."

Jes scanned the rest of the damage report. "One of those shots took out the axial mass balancer. And the cargo deck is... in full vacuum." They grimaced. "Also the power feed to the Q-comp's been punched right through. We're not skipping out of here for a while. I'm locking off the main deck, just in case we take another hit."

"*All okay?*" Stritch's voice called over the intercom.

Jes thumbed the comm. "Yah, Stritch, okay up here. You okay down there?"

"*Okay.*"

Fin pushed the left stick forward, slamming it against the

stops, and the ship spun.

Jes watched the markers in the tank revolve around them. The Constant was called out in bright green, barely ten-thousand klicks behind them. The cargo ship changed course, closing from across the asteroid field.

"It's getting real crowded," Jes said.

"Yah," Fin said. His jaw was clenched.

"Cargo ship's closing," Windy said.

"Yah."

"They're ganging up on us," Jes added.

"Yah!" Fin said. "Tell me something I *don't* know!"

"We're all gonna die?" Windy offered.

"Nope," Fin shook his head. "Knew that."

"Um…" Jes wracked their thoughts, "I'm sorry for getting us into—"

"Knew that too."

Jes sighed. "I have no idea how we're going to get out of this."

"*Everybody* knows that," said Windy.

"I'm allergic to mustard."

Fin turned towards Jes, a look of confusion on his face. "I… didn't know that."

The tank chimed and three new contacts appeared at the system's standard transit point.

"Shit!" Windy said. She marked them and told nav-comm to start tracing their courses.

"Real crowded." Fin said. His voice was tight. "I… uh… I think this might be it, guys. It's been fun."

"'We're free,' you said," Windy muttered. "'Find jobs as we can,' you said. 'Live how we want to live.' Is it too late to say that the way I want to live is to *not die*?"

Jes was silent. They brought up the nav-comm report on

the new ships. Jes's eyes widened, and a smile spread across their face. The ships were chirping registry.

"Fin go *here*." They marked a course that took them straight towards the newcomers.

"There?"

"Yes, there. That's the cavalry."

"You sure?" Windy asked. Her brow wrinkled as a new alert popped up on her panel. "They're broadcasting voice." She switched it to speakers.

"*—xon-Mull Security Interdiction Command to all ships. Cease hostilities and stand-to immediately or you will be fired on.*" The message repeated.

"Can't stand-to 'till they stop shooting-at," Fin grumbled.

"Windy, give me voice on emergency channel."

She tapped her panel and nodded.

"AMS ships, this is the Common Law. We are taking fire and require immediate assistance. We've taken damage and are working to get our beacon back up." Jes nodded to Windy, who switched her panel to the beacon control interface and told it to start chirping.

The ship lurched again as Fin dodged another stream of weapons fire. He'd been working his way towards the new ships and the edge of the clutter, and the Constant was easily keeping up. So far, she hadn't managed another clear solution, but it would only take one mistake from Fin or one lucky shot from them.

"Some help would be much appreciated," Jes added.

There was a pause that seemed to last forever. Fin twisted the sticks wildly.

"*Understood, Common Law. Stand by.*"

One of the smaller ships pulled away from the trio in a breathtaking display of acceleration. In moments, it was within ten-thousand kilometers. The Constant broke off its pursuit, changing course towards the newcomer.

Jes watched the tank in fascination as the Constant opened fire and immediately disintegrated under multiple particle streams from the smaller ship. The tank's rendering stuttered, failing to keep up with the speed of the destruction.

"Fuck," Windy said, quietly.

"AMS-IC Torbin to Common Law. Stand down."

"Fin, shut it down."

"Yah, yah." Fin brought the ship to an immediate halt on its vectored gravity drive, and released the control sticks. After a moment, he realized he'd raised his hands in surrender, and grinned sheepishly.

The cargo ship changed course and throttled up to exit the dust cloud. The two other AMS ships moved to intercept. Fin, Windy, and Jes stared at the tank. All they could do was watch as the traces converged. There was a brief moment of calm, then a stuttering burst of energy. The marker for the cargo ship winked out.

Jes forced themself to take a deep, slow breath. They looked at Windy and Fin, who were staring back with eyes wide. Jes opened the intercom to engineering. "Stritch, you okay?"

"Yah," aht said. *"All done now?"*

"Yeah, we're good," Jes said, smiling. "Probably. No promise."

"Incoming voice, again," Windy said softly. She put it on speaker.

"This is the AMS Xiaphon. I have Xiaphon Actual for the captain of the Common Law."

Jes looked at Windy, who grimaced.

"You're the captain," they said.

"I'm not. You just keep telling people I am."

"You didn't argue."

"I *did* argue."

"Oh. Well, you didn't argue *enough*."

Windy sighed and keyed the mic. "AMS Xiaphon Actual, this is Captain Winder of the Common Law. Thanks deeply for the assist. We thought we were cooked out here."

"It's what we do, Captain. Thank you for reporting the theft of Axon-Mull property. If you don't mind, I'd like to come aboard and thank you in person."

Windy looked at Jes, worried. She released the mic. "If they board us, they'll confiscate the SDRs. They might take the ship if they find out we grabbed one of those beacons," Windy said.

Jes leaned back in their seat. "Not going to happen." They thought for a moment, then opened the comm to engineering. "Stritch, meet me down in the galley. We've got some work to do." They stood and started to leave the bridge, then turned back to the console and keyed the mic again. "And bring a cutter-welder."

As they left the bridge, they turned back to Windy. "I have an idea. Invite them over, but try to buy us some time."

They heard Windy open the channel and reply. "Sounds good, Captain, but we need some time to lock down some damage we took from our mutual friends out there before we can risk the airlock. Say about point-one?"

"Of course, Captain. We'll see you then. Let us know if you need any help with repairs."

26 / Write-Offs

The ship reverberated with the low clang of docking clamps. Jes kept up the steady feed of metali-ceramic scrap into the recycler. The bin was nearly empty, but they wanted to be done before the delegation from the Xiaphon came aboard.

Stritch finished packing up the cutter-welder and carried it back to stow it in its cabinet in engineering. "I will stay out of face in engineering," aht said. "Don't want them to see me and think about *Vrrih'sss'sstrr'trrrrunn* wreckage."

Jes nodded. "Good idea."

They heard the sound of the emergency bulkhead retracting, and Windy's vac-suit boots clanked onto the main deck. She walked down the passage to the galley and unsealed her helmet.

"Jes, they just docked. Cargo deck is patched up, but we'll need to print some more patch kits. I hope whatever you have planned is—" She stopped talking as she took in the galley. "Wha—?"

"Don't worry, Windy," Jes said. The last piece of scrap went into the recycler and Jes dusted off their hands. "Just keep it together, it's going to be fine." They pushed the empty grav-pallet against the bulkhead and dropped the bin on it.

The docking-comm chimed a call tone and Windy moved to the hatch and activated the speaker.

"This is Captain Kamal-Wright and staff requesting permission to come aboard." The voice was quiet and calm.

Windy released the hatch to external control and palmed the mic. "Come aboard." She stepped back as the airlock cycled and opened.

Jes walked across from the galley to the two-meter square table. They smoothed down the crisp white tablecloth and looked over the table-settings. Jes smiled at their work and turned to lean against the edge of the table.

Kamal-Wright entered first, with two officers behind her. She was a short woman with dark hair pulled back away from her face into a severe braid. Her gray and gold uniform was crisp; all the seams and piping were sharp and pressed. Her officers were just as precise, though their muscular frames hulked over her.

"Captain Winder, let me just say that I appreciate you welcoming us aboard your ship." Kamal-Wright said.

Windy put on a smile. Jes thought it looked out of place. "Not at all, Captain. Again, I want to thank you and your crews for coming to our aid. We were really... er... almost dead out here."

Kamal-Wright waved the gratitude away. "Least we could do. The intel you sent us was tremendously well-timed. We knew that a significant amount of product had been stolen from our supply-chain, but we were only just beginning to track it down."

She looked around the common space, smiling mildly. "I haven't been aboard one of these in... a long time. An eighty-eight-gee-four-two, right? I didn't know these were still operating." She moved slowly around the compartment, trailing her fingers over the backs of the crash-couches in the lounge circle, and touching the bulkhead. "My very first posting was on this class, but it was a three-nine. Not as comfortable."

Windy walked with her down the passage aft. One of her silent officers trailed behind, and Jes followed, sending a quick ping to Stritch to stay out of sight.

As Kamal-Wright passed the cabins, she let her fingers linger over the door panels.

Windy noticed. "Were you billeted in one of the crew cabins, Captain?"

"Hmm?" she said.

"In your first posting."

"Oh, yes." She shrugged. "That one." She pointed to a cabin.

Windy thumbed it open. "This one's empty," she said. "Lost a crewman to shore-leave on our last run." Windy grimaced.

"Ha!" Kamal-Wright laughed. "Only one?"

"Well, when you've got a crew of four, one is a big deal."

"Indeed." She looked around thoughtfully.

Kamal-Wright took a deep breath and turned back to the common area. She made a full circle of the compartment and sat down on a bench at the square table. Jes sat at the adjacent edge, and Windy stepped over and sat between them.

"I hope you understand," the diminutive captain said, "that I'm going to ask your permission for my men to search the ship."

Windy nodded. She turned to Jes. "Specialist, if Captain Kamal-Wright's men search the rest of this ship, will they find anything to concern them?"

Jes shook their head. "No Captain. Just a load of patched breaches and the empty skip buoy crate down on the cargo deck."

"Be my guest, Captain," Windy said.

Kamal-Wright nodded to her officers, who moved to look through the ship. As they disappeared down the passage, she turned back to Windy. "If I might ask, how did you come across this crime?"

Jes looked to Windy and smiled. She was doing great, they thought.

"Well," Windy said, "we heard a rumor about a valuable salvage." She took a deep breath. "Ship like this... we're always running pretty spare, you know? We were between jobs, so I decided we should check it out. We got here, found the triss ship and boarded her." Windy shrugged. "When we saw what was in the cargo bays, we knew we were way over our heads, so we hopped it. We *just* managed to get clear when *they* showed up." Windy jerked a thumb over her shoulder, out beyond the hull.

She nodded to Jes. "Specialist Moran here had some history with—well, you know. So we fired off the beacon and hid out in the dust cloud, hoping someone would show up."

"And we did," the Captain smiled. "Lucky for you."

"Damn right," Windy said.

"And were you able to salvage anything while you were there?" Kamal-Wright asked with a smile.

Windy shook her head. "Nothing, except for that skip-buoy we launched." She grinned ruefully. "Real punch in the gut letting that loose, I don't mind telling you. That one buoy would have paid for this whole trip and then some, you know?"

"I'm sure that was a hard decision to make."

Windy shrugged. "Can't get paid if you're dead."

"Indeed."

Windy tilted her head. "You planning to… sweep up here? Collect the salvage?"

Kamal-Wright didn't answer for a moment. She was stroking the tablecloth and scanning the common area. Jes wondered if she wished she could see through the bulkheads to the rest of the ship.

"No, I don't think we will," she said, finally. "Given what my scan-techs have reported, the original smuggler was well and truly blown, and whatever that cargo ship managed to take on is radiating outwards at high-velocity."

Her officers returned, and if they exchanged any word or signal, Jes failed to catch it.

Kamal-Wright stood up. "Axon-Mull has already written-off the loss. Any efforts on our part to track down any salvage won't be worth the expense in man-hours or reaction mass."

With a sharp glance at her two officers, she walked back to the airlock. There, she turned and reached out a hand to Windy.

Windy grasped it and they shook.

Kamal-Wright held on for a moment longer than was natural. "If I can offer some advice, Captain: Leave this alone. Don't spend any more time here than you have to, and forget the coordinates. My superiors may have written off the cargo, but they still won't look kindly if it shows up in a salvage sale."

"I fully understand, Captain," Windy said.

Her crewmen opened the airlock, and as she was turning to enter, Jes stepped forward.

"Captain Kamal-Wright? I was wondering if it would be

too much bother for me to send a message along with you. I'd like to thank Andi for helping us."

She smiled, thinly. "Of course. I'll let my comm-tech know to expect your transmission."

The airlock closed behind them, and Windy let out a long breath.

"Holy shit, Jes. If that's what you do every time you pull off one of your schemes, you can have it."

"You did great, Ada."

"So are you going to tell me now? Where'd you stash the goods?"

Jes sat down at the square table and leaned back, smiling.

Windy's eyes widened in horror and disbelief. She threw up her hands and turned away, stomping back to the ladder. "Never again!"

Jes turned and started recording their message.

"Andi. Thanks for your help. We've made it through the tough bit, thanks to you and the ships your… husband sent." They rubbed their face and took a deep breath, wondering what else to say. "I guess that's it," they said. They supposed it was. "I guess I'll see you around someday. Maybe. Bye."

They sent the brief recording to the Xiaphon, and realized suddenly they weren't thinking of Andi anymore at all.

With the power feed to the Q-comp repaired, Stritch crawled out of the access chase and stood, looking around at the engineering bay that was now, unaccountably, ahtsa domain. Aht walked the perimeter, tracing ahtsa long fingers over the edges of consoles and equipment. Ahtsa ears were fully perked to points, and aht could hear ahtsa own heartbeat.

Stritch paused at the railing to the lower deck and peered down. They'd have to rework the whole cradle again to fit the larger SDR, but aht licked ahtsa lips at the thought of such a powerful source on such a small ship. They'd be safe from nearly any hunter they might encounter.

Aht eyed the corner of the lower section, where aht was already considering hanging a hammock. Aht felt much more comfortable surrounded by the machinery than in a dark, relatively quiet bunk cabin.

Aht walked down the steps and into the main passage. As aht passed the ladderway, Windy floated down with Fin following.

"Hey Stritch," Fin said, smiling. "I love what you've done with the place," he said, floating to a stop.

Aht ducked ahtsa head and aht folded ahtsa ears back.

Windy showed her teeth at ahta in the human gesture that expressed pleasure or calm. So strange. With the two of them walking ahead, Stritch tried out the expression, drawing back ahtsa lips to show teeth. It felt unpleasant. Threatening.

The three of them reached the galley where Jes was making themself busy arranging trays of food across the large square table.

"How are things looking up there?" Jes asked.

Windy replied. "We're all set and secure. Q-comp is—"

"Calculating?" Jes cut in.

"How'd you guess?" Windy sat mid-way down the bench, shifting nervously. "What's with the banquet?"

Jes smiled at her. "I figured: We're alive, we have a home, we're newly flush with valuable loot. Let's celebrate!"

Stritch waited while the others arranged themselves

around the table. Fin slid sideways on the bench and tapped the seat beside him, looking expectantly at ahta.

Stritch sat.

"So," Jes said as they began circulating the dishes of food, "as soon as we're done here, and we've got a solution, we skip on back to Kepler-186 and meet up with Stevens. Get the new SDR installed, sell the second one, get some repairs, and then we line up some exciting and lucrative new jobs of dubious legality. How does that sound to everyone?"

Fin grabbed the mug from the table in front of him with one hand and lifted it into the air. It appeared to be some sort of ritual gesture.

"To crime!" Fin said.

Windy passed a tray to Stritch. It smelled like sausage. Aht used the serving implement to dish some onto ahtsa plate as aht had seen her do, then passed it on.

Stritch closed ahtsa eyes and breathed in the smells. Ahtsa ears were perked, taking in the sounds of family.

Aht ran ahtsa fingers over the white tablecloth, smoothing out the ripples caused by all the shifting plates and dishes. Without thinking, aht let out a soft, chirping bark, surprising ahta-self. Stritch hadn't laughed with real joy in some long time.

Aht lifted the tablecloth up to peer again at the stack of crates, welded together into the table to replace the one aht and Jes had cut up and recycled. Aht supposed they'd have to add replacing it to the list of repairs. Once they reached Sst'tvv'nsssss's repair bay, they'd need to disassemble their "table."

Stritch looked up to see Fin looking at ahta with curiosity. Aht just kept laughing.

Epilogue / Kamal-Wright

AMS Xiaphon
Axon-Mull 010-ICS-8229
Interdiction Cruiser
Axon-Mull Security

SPACETIME-FIX at: **84.161**.17232523
- 34d8e491 (**BD+39 2579**) 88f2-a74d
- d823aa91 (**J125446.6+384057**) 900f-18d2
- 090e9a5e (**La Superba**) 8cff-b923

Captain Sindha Kamal-Wright sighed as she flopped into the crash couch in her cabin. With one hand, she absently undid the clings and zips on the collar of her uniform, loosening its tight, upright grip on her throat.

The intercom crackled to life. *"Captain, you wanted to know when we reached comm range. We just crossed the threshold."*

She thumbed the transmit button. "Thanks XO."

She didn't want to make this call, but waiting wouldn't make it any easier, and she had never let discomfort keep her from necessity before. She pulled up nav-comm and opened an encrypted vid channel. She tapped in the link address from memory. She did not keep it stored, even in her com-info.

She waited for it to connect.

The connection resolved, and the vid opened just as he was sitting down in front of the camera. He was dressed in a silk robe and looked mildly disheveled, as if her call had woken him up. But his eyes were sharp as always.

"Sir, I'm very sorry for the late call."

"Not at all Sindha. Tell me what happened."

She sighed. "Total loss. The shipper was blown when we got there, and we didn't have a choice but to destroy the recipient's ships. The little courier that reported the theft checked out clean. I... I let them go."

She watched the angular features of his face. He sighed and ran his fingers through his long blond hair.

"Sir, I—"

"No. No, you absolutely did the right thing. With the vid they let loose publicly, there was never going to be a way to bottle it up again. Now, they'll go back to civilization and talk about how Axon-Mull saved the day and punished the criminals who stole from us." His eyes looked away from the vid for a moment. "We already knew the shipper chain was compromised. Consider the whole smuggling network blown. We'll need to rebuild it from scratch. We start again."

"Yes, sir."

"I'll get you a list of contacts to start threading together. For now, just proceed as per your normal duties."

"Yes, sir."

He looked thoughtful. "Make sure you name this captain... Winder? in your official report to AMS. Jes Moran too. Maybe we can boost their profile a bit and get more people to hear their version."

"Yes, sir."

From somewhere off-screen, she heard a woman's voice

calling out distantly. Maybe from another room.

"*Vitor, come back to bed.*"

His lips quirked into a smile. Maybe a smile. It might have been a grimace. He turned to the side and called out, "I'll be right there Andi."

He nodded to Sindha and signed off.

She started composing her after-action report.

A Note on Coordinates

Since the discovery of the first Revelatory Caches and the establishment of the Revelatory Accord, accord species utilize a unified system of spatial-temporal mapping based on knowledge imparted by the Elders. This system utilizes spectral stellar fingerprinting in conjunction with unified time offsets to account for stellar drift. This allows for identifying coordinates for arbitrary locations in interstellar space on a freely sliding scale of resolution from system-scale down to ultra-high precision sub-megameter mapping.

Identifying an arbitrary point in space involves a mechanism of triangulation utilizing three stellar bodies (usually the nearest, or most easily fixed), precisely establishing the distance to each (referred to as a "star-fix"), and recording these against the unified timestamp at which the measurements were taken. The resulting "spacetime-fix" can then be used to identify the same position in space at any point in the future (or past)—including allowance for stellar drift and galactic expansion—by application of high-order quantum modeling techniques.

The method produces a machine-readable coordinate designation which can be represented in—and translated without loss of precision between—any of the Elder-derived machine-representable languages used by accord species. Many species further reduce this designation with lossy linguistic representation to enable person-to-person communication of high-level coordinates for convenience. Such lossy representations might look like this:

```
SPACETIME-FIX at: 80.012.22830742
```
- e024a467 **(Sol)** 129c-47e2
- dfe21649 **(Proxima Centauri)** 2c65-4034
- e847d36b **(Rigil Kentaurus)** 8b52-4058

A Xenoanthropological Survey of the Triss

"[The triss species] refer to themselves with a trilling series of clicks followed by an extended sibilance, which the human tongue invariably renders as 'triss.'" (Barnam, 58 REV)

First Publication ud:

14.713

Authors:

Moseki T. R., Guo C., Nieminen A. R.

Citation:

Moseki et al., 14

Abstract

As the first species contacted by post-revelation human explorers, the triss represent a key step in the development of human cross-species relationships. Trade and mutual learning followed first-contact (Barnam, 58 REV), with humans encountering triss travelers repeatedly during initial phases of interstellar exploration (Barnam, 58 REV; Bujold et al, 61 REV).

As humans expand in presence throughout the reaches of Accord space, improved understanding of peoples such as the triss will be crucial to trade, development, and growth throughout the galaxy (Guo, 5; Nieminen, 8; Peters: 112 REV).

Biology

To human eyes, triss morphology most resembles a mammalian analog somewhere between lemur and fox, with first-contact explorers initially (and pejoratively) referring to them as "foxies" (Barnam, 58 REV). They are typically shorter of stature and smaller of body than humans of equivalent age, with a short torso, slender limbs and long, dextrous fingers and toes. Triss are generally bipedal, with specialized feet and hands. They possess short prehensile tails and their bodies are covered in a dense, soft velvet with hydrophobic and oleophobic properties. The triss have a prominent flattened nasal structure streamlined into an elongated palate and smaller lower jaw with a total of forty-eight teeth, giving them a slight but definite vulpine countenance (Bujold et al., 61 REV; Bujold & Kawalis, 69 REV; Moseki, 10).

Specialization & Behavior

Triss are omnivorous, and their evolutionary history and biological specializations show that hunting live prey was a primary dietary feature—modern triss prize raw meat as a delicacy (Bujold et al., 61 REV; Moseki, 10). Triss hands and feet have four digits, with the largest opposable. Fingers and toes develop voluntarily retractable keratinous claws, though modern triss social norms drive most to keep these short, rounded, and polished (Bujold & Kawalis, 69 REV; Nieminen, 1).

Triss vision is binocular and their eyes are disproportionately large with exceptional low-light and color fidelity (Bujold & Kawalis, 69 REV). Triss are capable of perceiving a wider gamut of color than human eyes, including some infrared and ultraviolet, as well as a higher degree of fine color distinctions (Bujold et al., 61 REV).

Their ears are likewise disproportionate, with pointed peaks and substantial musculature allowing fine-motor independent directional control. Ear posture is a primary trait of emotional expression (Kawalis & Moseki, 108 REV).

Triss olfactory sensitivity is higher than typical human, though considerably less than that of Earth species commonly held to be good trackers such as dogs (Bujold et al., 61 REV; Kawalis & Moseki, 108 REV).

Morphological Variation & Ecotypes

The triss population exhibits several rough ecotype variations which fall historically along geographic lines. These variations occur largely in adaptive velvet coloring—falling generally between dun and sorrel—ear size, and subtle variations in stature and typifying facial bone structure which other triss are readily to be able to recognize, though whose subtleties are very difficult for other species to note (Moseki, 10; Nieminen et al., 6).

Reproduction & Lifecycle

The triss are a three-sexed species, with rough analogs to female and male (*katriss* and *hatatriss*, respectively), and a third sex referred to as *atriss*. In reproductive terms, adult katriss develop organs for production of ova and short-term retention of fertilized ova clusters, but lack any anatomical structures for developing or gestating fetuses. Katriss ova are fertilized in clusters or "litters" (typically 2–4 at a time) by hatatriss through human-recognizable acts of sexual reproduction. Within twelve days of fertilization, the katriss individual will engage in secondary copulation with an atriss individual, transferring the fertilized litter for gestation (Kawalis & Moseki, 108 REV).

Atriss are inherently non-fertile—their reproductive organs produce no gametes and instead are specialized into a "gestational pouch" with three functions. This structure, having both uterine and vaguely marsupial-pouch-like traits, provides for the fetal gestation from secondary copulation, and also contains mammary-analog structures for feeding of more developed young (Kawalis & Moseki, 108 REV; Moseki, 10). The musculature of the gestational pouch allows the atriss to semi-voluntarily prolapse and invert the pouch into a tumescent phallic structure, which is used for the secondary copulation, retrieving the fertilized zygotes from the katriss. As the young triss are developed from zygote to early childhood within the gestational pouch, triss do not undergo "birth" as Earth mammals do. The developmental phases in the triss lifecycle analogous to birth and infancy are instead referred to with terms that roughly translate into human concepts as "emergence" and "weening." Triss young spend approximately two years developing in the gestational pouch, with a third year of intermittent feeding and sleeping within the carrying atriss (Kawalis & Moseki, 108 REV).

Triss reach sexual maturity between sixteen and eighteen years of age. Unlike human females, katriss typically maintain fertility throughout their lives, although atriss reach a lifecycle phase analogous to human menopause at around 80 years where the gestational pouch begins to atrophy and their bodies are no longer able to nurture young. Average lifespan for triss ranges from 85–120 years, with slight variations between sexes; hatatriss trending to the lower end and katriss living the longest on average (Moseki, 10).

Because the gestational and emergence phase of triss children lasts so long, *atriss* spend a large portion of their lives carrying young (Kawalis & Moseki, 108 REV; Freid et al., 108 REV). As atriss contribute no genetic heritage to the children they gestate, expected incest taboos—present among katriss and hatatriss—do not apply in their case, and it is not uncommon to find atriss engaging in secondary copulation with and carrying the product of mating katriss and hatatriss that they previously carried and weened (Freid et al., 108 REV; Nieminen et al., 6).

This general reproductive pattern is shared with many other complex organisms which evolved on the triss origin world (Bujold et al., 61 REV).

Sexual Trimorphism

Population sex distribution is roughly 10% katriss, 25% hatatriss, and 65% atriss with natural variation occurring in smaller populations (Bujold et al., 61 REV). The three sexes differ morphologically in several ways.

Katriss are typically the largest and strongest of the three sexes, and atriss are the smallest of stature, though morphological variation occurs at rates similar to human dimorphism. At maturity, katriss show secondary sex characteristics including dark, stiff hair in a crest atop the head, ear tufts, and tail. Hatatriss often display intricate dorsal stripes, spots, or mottling of their velvet, as well as larger ears and larger canine teeth on the lower jaw. Atriss typically develop neither of these secondary characteristics, instead tending to develop wider stance and hip structures and fat and muscle distributions favoring the lower body, and generally have the smallest ears of the three sexes (Bujold & Kawalis, 69 REV).

Differences of Sex Development

Natural sexual variations within and outside the trinary exist in roughly equivalent prevalence and phenotypic expression to those found in human biology (Moseki, 10). Triss society is generally unaccepting of individuals exhibiting these differences of sex development (Nieminen, 1). Efforts by human medical and social advocates to improve awareness and acceptance of these individuals have not been met with great success (Peters: 112 REV).

Social Systems

Due to difficulties in accessing linguistic and historical records, little is known about pre-Revelation triss social history.

Triss society is organized in a matriarchal meritocracy with a strictly sex-stratified hierarchy. Katriss are dominant, with hatatriss serving in secondary roles. Atriss are largely subservient to both more dominant sexes, and while slavery is strictly forbidden in modern triss culture (Freid et al., 108 REV), their social position can be at best described as a permanent servant class.

Social bonding typically forms in a semi-feudal matriarchal familial hierarchy with a single head of household and her immediate katriss kin, each forming exclusive polyandrous bonds with some number of hatatriss mates. Such family structures maintain a "harem" of atriss nominally attached to the matriarch, but in practice shared among the family (Freid et al., 108 REV; Kawalis & Moseki, 108 REV; Nieminen et al., 6).

Political Structures

Local kinship affiliations form the basis of political organizations, with more distant relations associating into broad clans which extend the feudal hierarchies to regional governance. Since the Revelation, this has extended off-planet to include triss-controlled stations and colonies, with various clans pooling resources to fund their establishment. In the time since first human contact, several of these satellite governments have changed clan management under some political scheme which remains largely opaque to outsiders (Freid et al., 108 REV; Nieminen, 8).

Social Welfare

Triss society has little-to-no large-scale social welfare systems. Individual triss are provided for within the matriarchal kinship structures that organize primary social systems (Freid, et al, 108 REV). It has been observed that being outside of or excluded from an established kinship structure is the highest apparent stigma within the triss society. Such persons are essentially ignored, and no effort is made socially or materially to provide for them, whether this state is the result of catastrophic loss of family or punishment for social/legal infractions (Freid, et al, 108 REV; Nieminen, 1).

Fashion

Triss typically eschew clothing, except in cases where practical or political considerations apply such as utility or safety clothing in industrial contexts, and ceremonial clothing in formal cross-species interactions (Barnam, 58 REV; Nieminen, 1). When such clothing is worn, it is optimized to maintain the natural triss agility and dexterity, especially with respect to limbs and tail. Triss rarely adorn their bodies with jewelry, although hatatriss especially are known to covet ornamental jewels and precious metals (Nieminen, 1).

Arts Traditions

Triss have a long tradition of art in various forms and have shown an appreciation for artistic works from other species. The largest documented body of triss art is visual in nature, including visual pigmented representation (painting) and three-dimensional permanent and semi-permanent modeling (sculpture) (Freid, et al, 91 REV). Triss sculptures are typically painted, whether in stone or ceramic, and typically in a significantly higher degree of color fidelity and variation than is appreciable by human vision (Bujold et al., 61 REV; Freid, et al, 91 REV).

Religious Traditions

Pre-Revelation triss religious traditions are rooted in various forms of nature worship, however mainstream triss culture abruptly abandoned religion between 20 REV and 50 REV prior to first-contact with humans. Most modern triss are avowed atheists, with only a few marginalized pockets of religious zealots still existing, mostly in rural areas of the triss origin world (Barnam, 58 REV; Freid, et al, 91 REV; Nieminen et al., 6).

Non-reproductive Sexual Practices & Gender Identity Variation

Recreational copulation within family bonds is common and may occur regardless of sex, especially with family atriss. Individuals displaying a preference for same-sex attraction and sexual interest are roughly as common as in

Earth-evolved species, although unlike recent pre-Revelation human social history, no systemic social taboo exists among triss, and this behavior is not deemed aberant except in cases where individuals eschew reproductive copulation altogether (Freid et al., 108 REV; Moseki, 10; Nieminen, 1).

Social sexual play is thought to play a prominent emotional regulation role within triss matriarchies, especially among hatatriss and atriss "harems." It is not uncommon for multiple individuals of mixed sex—including siblings—to congregate and sleep in mass clusters with mutual non-reproductive sexual stimulation occurring between various members simultaneously (Nieminen et al., 6).

Natural variation in gender identity formation also occurs at similar rates to Earth species, however triss society is far less accepting of transgender individuals than modern human society (Moseki, 10; Nieminen et al., 6). Moseki (10) hypothesized that the prominent sexual trimorphism exhibited in triss biology and the strict sexual stratification of the culture has served to reinforce and solidify rigid gender roles.

Language

Trissa, the dominant triss common language, is the result of a deliberate and calculated merger of four different dominant regional languages, with explicit grammar composition rules being developed by a global coalition during the species' first forays into space exploration circa -50 REV (Anatole, 102 REV; Barnam, 64 REV).

A Note on Phonetic Transcription of Trissa

Throughout this document, certain conventions and liberties have been taken with transcribing Trissa semi-phonetically into written Common. These conventions follow the model set forth by Anatole (88 REV) and are used here purely to help describe certain aspects of the Trissa language. Readers should not take the following transcriptions as a pronunciation guide.

Morphological Impacts

The Trissa language is directly impacted by certain morphological traits of the species. Most notable is its limited repertoire of phonemes. Only eighteen distinct phonemes have been identified by human xenolinguists to date (Guo, 5). These phonemes are easily categorized even by human ears into two groups, indicating the merger of two distinct proto-Trissa languages (Table 1) (Anatole, 102 REV; Guo, 126 REV; Guo, 5). The complexity of Trissa derives from the differentiation of these simple phonemes through specific cadences of front-palette voiced and unvoiced trills and variations in stress and duration of sibilance, making Trissa virtually impossible for humans to replicate (Anatole, 88 REV; Guo, 131 REV).

Table 1: The Eighteen Phonemes of the Trissa Language

Primal Phonemes			Peripheral Phonemes		
ss	sa				
t	ta			v	tv
	ka				
h	ha		i	hi	
r			u	un	m
	a	ah	ay		

Despite the limited phonemic variation exhibited in Trissa, the triss are natural mimics. Their excellent hearing and the dynamic vocal and mandibular anatomy of the triss makes them adept at reproducing a much wider gamut of vocalization than humans and other species we have encountered, which has been hypothesized to have been an adaptive trait evolved for hunting (Bujold et al., 61 REV; Guo, 126 REV). Thus, while humans rely on assistive devices to translate speech into Trissa, many triss have learned to speak the common languages of many other species including human Common (Barnam, 64 REV; Guo, 126 REV).

The pronounced triss sexual trimorphism has produced three distinct gendered pronoun-like structures within the language, with *kaht/kahta/kahtsa* and *haht/hahta/hahtsa* roughly equivalent to "she/her/hers" and "he/him/his" respectively, such that it is common in mixed-language settings even among triss to refer to katriss and hatatriss using the human Common pronouns. Atriss are referred to using *aht/ahta/ahtsa,* and interestingly, attempts by humans to render these pronouns as the Common singular neutral "they/them/theirs" has been repeatedly met with offense and rejection by triss of all genders (Anatole, 88 REV; Anatole, 102 REV; Guo, 131 REV). Guo (131 REV) postulates that this stems not from misunderstanding or prejudice on the part of triss, but rather because they correctly reject the classification of the atriss sex as neutral: triss view atriss as a distinct third sex, and the role played by atriss in the reproductive lifecycle reinforces this position.

First-person pronouns also exhibit some gender-specific variations. While the singular first-person *mah* (roughly equivalent to the human Common "I") is commonly used by triss of all genders, the plural first person *aymah* ("we," approximately) is used exclusively by katriss and hatatriss. Atriss will always use *triss*, classified as the distal plural first-person (Guo, 131 REV).

Writing System

Pre-Revelation triss writing systems varied dramatically by geographical and cultural boundaries, and depended to a larger than usual degree on an understanding of context to differentiate written phonemes. Because subtleties of trill and sibilance were not typically written, deciphering ancient written Trissa is a difficult task, even for local native speakers. Since the Revelation, some experiments using machine learning systems have yielded promising results in translation (Guo, 5; Minze, 78 REV).

With the rise of technological development including computing systems, and subsequently the triss experience with the Revelation, triss academic culture recognized the need for a universally readable, archival codification of their language. The current system utilized throughout triss culture (and ubiquitous across their technology) is the result of a second global unification coalition circa 12 REV (Anatole, 88 REV).

It is worth noting that some humans have studied triss language through this writing system, and even though they are unable to speak Trissa, there *are* specialized experts who have successfully translated from written Trissa to Common (Guo, 126 REV; Guo, 5). Development of automated translation systems has

```
////// DOCUMENT DOWNLOAD INTERRUPTED
> ATTEMPTING TO RECONNECT TO NETWORK
> .....
> .....
> .....
```

Acknowledgements

The list of people I need to thank only grows. This book could not happen only by my hands. Never mind that I'm the one that wrote it. My partner deserves so much credit and so much thanks for all the ways my life is improved by her efforts. I literally could not have written this without her.

My writing community—online and in-person—who have continued to egg me on when I wondered if it was worth continuing. My beta readers who read this book in record time and got me the crucial feedback I needed to wrap it up. And my editor Shannon who helped me fine-tune the jargon and dialog.

I also need to thank the amazingly talented Angela Guyton for bringing Jes, Windy, Fin, and Stritch to life for the cover of this book. I hope that you'll see more of her work on future adventures of the crew.

As they say in movies:

Jes, Windy, Fin, and Stritch will return.

About the Author

K. N. Brindle has worn many different hats in their life, which is impressive considering how difficult it is to find one that fits their extra-large head. They've worked as a graphic designer, and in the industrial design and architecture fields. They've built telecom equipment. They've been an app developer and a software architect, and have taught software engineering. They're most recently a licensed therapist.

They are fine with any pronouns when used with respect, though they *really* hate being called "sir."

They live in the southeastern U.S. with their partner, children, and just the right number of cats.

Common Accord is their third novel.

Read on for a preview of
the first book in the
Paths of Memory
duology

A Memory of Blood and Magic

Available Now

THE FIRST THING you need to know about me is that I killed my family.

My parents should have known—I was two weeks late and turned sideways. The midwife told them my mother and I would both die, and if there was to be any hope, they would need to call for the hedge-witch from down past Meers. This was a dire decision to make, and fraught—no one would dare go begging of a witch except at utmost need. But after hours of listening to my mother's agonized labor, Father set out for Old Marga's.

You may wonder how I know this, as I had not been born yet. I had some in bits and crumbs from Mother and Father. Some from my older brother, Ranji, who was five—just old enough to hear the talk if not to fully understand. And some I had from my somatic memory many years later, after I began studying.

Even having recommended it, the midwife excused herself before Father made it back several hours later with Old Marga. Calling on a witch is always distasteful, even if sometimes necessary. I know now that birth magic is some of the easiest to enact. It took little effort for Old Marga to bring me forth using Mother's agony as the source, channeling her labor pains to align my body within Mother's and draw me out.

I'm certain my parents assumed they would hold their new daughter, pay the witch, and have all the peace they could muster with a squalling newborn in the tiny house. But Old Marga drew a wizened finger through the gore and birthing blood from my crown to my groin and sucked it in their crooked mouth for a moment as if savoring well-aged wine, and then spoke my doom to my parents.

"This one'll be a witch when they's grown."

At first, my parents did not understand Old Marga's proclamation. When they did, they recoiled in horror, protesting.

"But, she's a girl. That's clear!" my father said.

The witch only grinned the wider. "Oh no, they's a mixie... no doubt, no doubt. You'll see. The blood don't lie." And with that, Old Marga took the small bag of coins and walked out.

They named me Arin and raised me as a girl, and for the first few years I knew no differently. How could I? *Girl* and *boy* seemed only arbitrary distinctions to a child only learning to walk and talk. And no one would ever speak of having called on a witch to aid a human birth—it would be a mark of utter shame. Most would rather lose babe and mother both.

My childhood was mostly unremarkable. I had the same olive tint to my skin as my family and most others in the area, though mine, like Father's, was lighter and more muted than some. Freckles and sunburn came more easily than tans for both of us. Sure, my hair was a little darker than Mother's and curlier than Father's, but I was by no means an unusual child to look at, though I remember many comments growing up about my long eyelashes and gray eyes.

My parents were smallholders on the Freelands. The village nearest our farm was Meers and we went to market in Maplewood. As smallholdings go, I remember it being comfortable and homey. We lived in a small house Father built, with one tidy room with Mother and Father's bed, a great hearth and chimney of river stone, and a fine table that my father made himself. My brother and I slept on cots in a small garret tucked in the rafters under the thatch that we reached by climbing a series of pegs driven into the mortar between the stones of the chimney.

Most days were as alike as any day on any farm. Eggs to be collected, goats milked, animals fed and tended. Milly, our cart mule, shared the fenced yard with the goats and chickens.

Endless work always waited for us in the barley and vegetable fields. As I grew, I took on a share of those chores I could manage. At first it was the egging, then the foraging as Mother taught me the rules for safe berries and mushrooms. Come harvest, it took all of us to gather and set by what we needed in food, seed, and trade goods.

The first time I heard the word "mixie" was when I was six. Ranji was teaching me to tend the goats and it was time for milking. We had spent the morning corralling and sorting the does, with Ranji pointing out which were making milk and which hadn't yet been bred, and idly imparting wisdom gained in his eleven years.

"You gotta always keep the buck away from the does, 'cept when they're making kids, or the milk tastes bad." And, "If you let the kids suck too much, the nanny goes dry, so we milk 'em first, then let 'em suck."

I watched as he expertly separated a nanny from the flock, guiding her with his knees to the corner of the yard near the fence, where the milking stand was waiting. Prompting the nanny up on the stand with an end of carrot, he trapped her head in the yoke and brought down the milking bucket from a hook. All the while, he kept up a running narration for my benefit:

"They don't mind it, they's always happy to get a treat."

He grabbed two teats with his finger and thumb, showing me the grip, and pulled two squirts of milk off to the side before starting the rhythmic pulls to fill the bucket.

"A steady count is the thing, kinda like a heartbeat. Not so diff'rent from people. You was born and all you could do was squall and suck, squall and suck. Sometimes I'd wonder if you'd ever let go of mommy's tit. But nannies don't lullaby their kids—unless... I wonder if a nanny bleating is a lullaby? I guess this'll be you someday when you get babies of your own. Though, maybe not, you bein' a mixie."

I was so puzzled by this last word that I didn't notice at first that Ranji had stopped his rhythmic milking and his endless narration. I had no notion what he meant by it, but his face showed me that he had said something wrong. There was a miasma of doubt, discomfort, and fear surrounding us.

I knew from Ranji's own reaction that I couldn't ask him or Mother and Father about it, and indeed we never talked about it until years later. It took me a long time before I felt sure enough in myself to speak about it.

It was time to harvest some of our crops, and Father had finally decided at seven years old, I was old enough to give real help in the fields. I was in the peppers, tiny knife in hand

and stooped to reach the low-hanging ones. It was an awkward process even for me who didn't need to bend far: Grasp one of the bright red fruit with the left hand, press the knife-edge to the stem with the right, squeeze the stem between knife and thumb to cut it, and drop the pepper into the canvas bag hung over my shoulder. And repeat. And repeat and repeat and repeat. Farming is a life of so much repetition it's a wonder that old farmers ever pass on—seems that they'd just stay alive forever out of habit.

Red peppers. Mother taught me to only pick the ripe ones. I was so focused on finding the red peppers, so immersed in my task and lost in the numbing repeat of grasp, press, cut, drop, that I can't say how it happened. But one casual repeat, and I was staring at my left hand where a stripe of bright red blood was welling up even before the pain started. I had never seen so much of my own blood before. It was just the same color as the peppers. The shock of that held my tongue for long enough that when I finally cried out as the pain caught up to me, Mother looked up and screamed to see me.

I couldn't at first tell why her face held such horror. It was a deep cut, and hurt, but I had seen my father take worse. Then I noticed. Blood-red. Pepper-red. Not just the blood on my hand. My hand itself. Both hands and arms. My sleeve and homespun shirt, and trousers, and leather shoes. All bright, uniform red. No color of dye was ever that rich and bright, even if we could possibly afford it, which we certainly could not. My clothes had been un-dyed wool, more dirt-colored than anything else only moments before. Wonderingly, I reached up and pulled down a pinch of curls so I could see by tilting my head with eyes sideways: even my hair was bright pepper-red.

Mother reached me then, grabbing my shoulders and

shaking me. "Stop that, Arin!" she cried, her voice holding worry and desperation and fear.

Only then did it occur to me to wonder how I had become all over red, and at once everything returned to normal. I was myself again, my hair was its usual shade, my clothes were their usual dusty gray, and my hand still hurt. Now, so did my neck from her shaking, and my arms where her fingers still gripped like a vice.

Her grip eased with her face, and she moved to take the knife I still held in my right hand. She poured water over my cut from her water bag and pressed a kerchief to the wound, binding it tight. All the while she muttered, "It's okay my dear. All is well. Not to worry."

But even as I settled from the shock of it all, I could hear it in her voice: the same fear from before, papered over now with love and tenderness, but there all the same.

Arin's future was foretold at birth: They would be neither girl nor boy, and a witch besides.

When the prejudices of powerful neighbors intrude on the idyll of their isolated Freelander childhood, Arin's magic is awakened and their life spirals into violence and tragedy.

Then an unexpected ally sets them on a new path, leading Arin to a true place of refuge—and an unsettling understanding: Their magical abilities are rooted in the very pain and trauma that has overturned their world.

The paths of memory are sown with the seeds of both pain *and* strength.

The future can be shaped by either.

K.N. Brindle

A Memory of Blood and Magic

Follow K.N. Brindle for news and updates at
www.knbrindle.com